ENGINEERED UNDERGROUND

METAMORPHOSIS BOOK 1

By Melissa Donovan

Swan Hatch Press | San Francisco

Engineered Underground
Metamorphosis Book 1

Melissa Donovan

First Edition, 2015
Published by Swan Hatch Press • Melissa Donovan

ISBN 10: 0692384197
ISBN 13: 9780692384190

Library of Congress Control Number: 2015904104

ENGINEERED UNDERGROUND

METAMORPHOSIS BOOK 1

Contents

For
Grandpa Bob
and
Poppy
in loving memory

- 1 -

The Pilot

Carter Air Force Base
Swenson, Colorado

Captain Dessa Rae Andrews was light on her feet. Today was the big day. Everything she'd ever worked for was about to come to fruition. She was going to pilot the most advanced aircraft in the world.

She hopped on the tram, punched up the menu, and tapped her destination: "HANGAR 4." The tram was ancient, but it still worked, and with all the budget cuts, the air force wasn't about to replace functional equipment, even if it was several decades old. She was settling into her seat when First Lieutenant Connor Hamilton, her weapons systems officer, strode toward the tram. He tossed a knapsack onto an empty seat and then slid in beside it. He tipped his hat to her, and she gave him a giddy grin as the tram took off, its old engine rumbling as it bounced across the airfield.

Dessa Rae stretched her legs and rolled her head around to loosen her muscles. It helped her relax and eased the excitement that was coursing through her body. Hamilton was

1

busy watching a video on his e-glasses, probably a message from his fiancée. A devilish smile spread across his face, and Dessa Rae rolled her eyes. Hamilton and his woman were worse than rabbits.

Dessa Rae had more important things to focus on. As one of the most promising young pilots in the air force, she had been selected to pilot the WASP. The Wingless Air-Space Plane was a top-secret military project—and it was a gorgeous machine. Triangular in shape, its angles were curved, with a black body that shone like obsidian. It was downright sexy. The WASP's functionality was even more impressive. It hovered and soared through Earth's atmosphere and into space, and it was the first military vehicle equipped with a fully functional laser weapon and force-field defense system. Just thinking about flying it made Dessa Rae feel superhuman.

As they pulled up to the hangar, Dessa Rae gripped the edge of her seat and prepared to jump out of the tram. Her feet hit the pavement before Hamilton had a chance to gather his things. He hopped out a couple of seconds later, laughing.

"I get it. You're excited. I am too, but don't let the big dogs see how eager you are. Play it cool."

Dessa Rae grinned and gave him a sarcastic two-finger salute. "Don't I always?" she asked.

He laughed and nudged her shoulder, and they entered the hangar together.

Inside, mechanics were scurrying around, quadruple-checking everything. The $40 billion WASP stood proud at the center of the hangar. Dessa Rae's heart leapt when she saw it. She'd spent countless hours in the virtual simulator, which was built to scale with a full hydraulics system, but nothing compared to the real thing. Thinking about what she was about to do took her breath away.

"We'd better not mess this up," Hamilton whispered.

Colonel Kell and his right-hand man, Major Nichols, were

milling around near the hangar's office. Lieutenant Smith was never far from those two during operations like this. Dessa Rae looked around and spotted him leaning against a doorframe, tinkering with an electronic tablet. He looked up, and when Dessa Rae caught his eye, he smiled his crooked grin at her and tipped his hat like an old-fashioned cowboy. She nodded and then bowed her head to hide her blushing cheeks.

"Come on, let's check in with the boss," Hamilton said, oblivious to Dessa Rae's flirtations.

She took a deep breath as they approached Colonel Kell, their commanding officer. Dessa Rae was still surprised he'd approved this assignment, although Hamilton had suggested Kell might not have had a choice.

"Everybody has a boss," Hamilton had said, "and everybody knows you're the best pilot in the air force, even if Kell refuses to admit it." It was an exaggeration, but Dessa Rae accepted the compliment and the implication about Colonel Kell.

She had suspected Colonel Kell didn't like her from the moment they met. Dessa Rae and a dozen other airmen recently assigned to Kell's unit at Carter Air Force Base had been lined up on the field, standing at attention as the colonel inspected each of them, eyeing them from head to toe and demanding their attention and their respect. Dessa Rae had gotten the distinct feeling that he didn't think she deserved to be there; she'd been certain he had a problem with her. In the years since, as Dessa Rae rose through the ranks, she had learned that Colonel Kell had disdain for almost everybody.

She examined the colonel's face as she walked toward him. It was hard and weathered. His icy blue eyes gleamed with arrogance, and his paper-thin lips rarely smiled. She couldn't imagine any woman marrying him, but she'd heard he was widowed.

"Reporting for duty, sir," she announced, clicking her heels together and giving him a proper salute. Hamilton mirrored her greeting.

"At ease, Captain," he said. "You too, First Lieutenant. Just relax. I want you to enjoy this flight."

Dessa Rae blinked her eyes. Had she heard correctly? He wanted her to enjoy this flight?

"The team's waiting for you," Kell said, and then he dismissed them, saying, "Good luck."

"That was weird," Dessa Rae whispered as they walked toward the bird.

"Maybe he finally got laid," Hamilton quipped, and then he gave her a high five.

Dessa Rae didn't know what she'd do without Hamilton. He was older and had been in the service three years longer than she had, but she outranked him and was a better pilot. Hamilton put that on his own shoulders instead of blaming Dessa Rae. He wasn't the jealous type.

They got prepped and went through several last-minute checks before climbing into the cockpit. Dessa Rae let herself take a moment to revel in its glory.

As long as the WASP stood on the ground, it was physically impossible to tell the difference between the interior of the simulator and the real thing, but knowing she was about to fly this futuristic marvel made Dessa Rae's heart race. She eyed the controls and felt like she was in a science-fiction movie. But this wasn't a movie. She was sitting in the cockpit of an actual spaceship.

Directly in front of her was a primary touchscreen that she would tap, swipe, and pinch to control the WASP. Panels lined with buttons and switches were positioned on either side of it. The system allowed her to take off, fly, and land on autopilot. She didn't intend to use that feature unless she was ordered to do so, although Hamilton had bet her that once she got into space, she'd want to turn on autopilot so she could enjoy the view.

She settled back in her seat and tugged on the shoulder harness to make sure it was secure. After checking in with the control tower over the com system, Dessa Rae fired the starter, checked all the systems, and then gently swiped the ascension slider.

The WASP lifted off the ground and hovered in the air. Hamilton hooted, "Woo-hoo!"

Dessa Rae gave him a sideways glance. "So much for keeping it cool," she muttered with a grin, restraining herself from hollering. The excitement was almost unbearable. She lifted the WASP higher and brought the bird half a dozen feet off the ground. Then she eased it forward, and they floated out of the hangar.

Past the hangar door, she took them on a slow trajectory straight up, up, and up until they were two hundred feet in the air, and then, following the test-flight protocol, Dessa Rae guided the WASP on a slow, ascending tour around the perimeter of the base. When they came full circle and were once again directly above the hanger, she hovered the WASP for two minutes.

"Damn," Hamilton whispered.

Damn was right. The view was spectacular. The sun's rays reached out from the horizon, casting a dim orange glow that reflected against the sparse clouds in pink and purple hues.

She brought the WASP straight down until all the officers, mechanics, and airmen huddled outside the hangar door were visible. Then she ascended again, until the people on the ground were specks of dust and the hanger a small dot below.

Dessa turned her head and looked at Hamilton. "You ready, Ham?"

"I've been ready for this my whole life," he said.

She kicked the engine into full gear and braced herself for the pitch of the flight. Within seconds the WASP was hurtling toward the edge of the sky.

"Check out the rear view." Hamilton's voice was quiet with awe and wonder.

Dessa Rae toggled the monitors and watched, mesmerized, as the Earth's surface shrank behind them. It was an image she'd seen many times before, but witnessing it in person was something else.

She checked the tiny clock at the corner of the screen. "Entering space in eight minutes, fifteen seconds."

The WASP's engines were nearly silent, but as the craft adjusted its speed to prepare for exiting the atmosphere, there was a rumble she'd never heard in the simulator. The plane stalled, hovered for an instant, and then jerked from side to side and up and down before it dipped and then glided into a slow and wide downward spiral.

"That's not right," Hamilton said as Dessa Rae flicked the controls.

"WASP, this is control tower…" The voice cut in and out. "Altitude dropping…emergency protocol…respond."

Hamilton's voice was shaking. "Control tower, this is WASP, please acknowledge."

Dessa Rae furiously went through the emergency protocol while Hamilton continued trying to contact the tower, but there was no response. The WASP quietly descended in wide arcs. They had lost control of the aircraft.

"I got nothing," he said, and Dessa Rae could hear the terror in his voice. Her heart raced as she flicked the manual switches, but the WASP didn't respond. It started twirling and picking up speed. Within seconds the descent became dizzying. She could barely make out the scene beyond the windshield, everything was turning and moving so fast, but one thing was clear: the ground below was getting closer and closer.

"Eject!" Dessa Rae screamed.

Even as the word came out of her mouth, she knew it was

too late. The WASP had entered a deadly spin.

Her heart lurched into her throat, and she broke out in a sweat as she simultaneously pressed the ejection button and braced herself for impact. She gripped the armrest as Colonel Kell's words echoed through her mind: "I want you to enjoy this flight."

And that was the last thing Captain Dessa Rae Andrews remembered before she became somebody else.

- 2 -

The Engineer

BIM Lab, MIT Campus
Cambridge, Massachusetts

Eli Levine was perched on the edge of his desk, throwing a yo-yo, when a loud *bang* reverberated through the laboratory. He caught the yo-yo in midair and turned toward the BIM.

"Need some help in there?" he called.

"Nope, I'm good. I just dropped a panel door." Wendy's voice was tinny, coming from deep within the belly of the massive machine she'd built.

Eli resumed tossing his yo-yo. There was some more banging and clanking, and then Wendy Watson emerged from the hatch door, crawling on her hands and knees.

She was wearing blue coveralls, and her wavy, red hair was tied back in a ponytail. Her blue eyes were sharp and bright, and her lightly freckled face was pale, but her lips and cheeks were rosy—probably a reaction to the heat emanating from the machine's innards.

"All set?" Eli asked, letting his yo-yo spin on the end of its string.

Wendy got to her feet and pushed a stray strand of hair out of her face.

"All set," she said.

Eli snapped up his yo-yo and tucked it into his pocket before sliding into the workstation chair. He tapped a command on the keyboard as Wendy secured the hatch and closed up the BIM.

"Run diagnostics," she said.

Eli tapped the keyboard. "Diagnostics initiated."

"How long?" she asked.

Eli glanced at the screen. "Two hours."

"All right, in the meantime, we can—"

She was interrupted by chimes emitting from her wristcom. Wendy glared at her wrist and then looked up at Eli, her eyes wide.

"That's them," she said. "The grant committee."

Eli nodded. "What does it say?"

"Come on," Wendy said. "Let's read it together."

He followed her the length of the laboratory, to the office area. Wendy walked with grace and confidence toward her desk. She was certain she would get a renewal of the grant that had been funding her project for the past eight years. She pulled up a chair for Eli and slid into her seat as she tapped her wristcom, sending the message to the smartscreen that dangled above her desk.

"Dear Dr. Watson," Wendy began. She turned to Eli. "I hate when people call me doctor. It's really a title that should be reserved for medical doctors, don't you think?"

Eli shrugged. His stomach was in knots. He'd had a bad feeling about this grant for weeks.

"The Federal Grant Committee for Scientific Development has recently and unexpectedly undergone significant changes. More than half of our committee members have stepped down, and we have been under tremendous pressure to fill

9

their seats and issue this year's grants by today's deadline. While we have successfully filled all seats and allocated most of the grants, we are still in the process of making a decision on the grant for which you applied. In the meantime we are forced to extend the deadline by one week. We apologize for any inconvenience this may cause. Please be assured that grant funds will be dispersed on time, and this delay will not affect your receipt of the funds if your project is approved."

The letter closed with a list of the new committee members.

Wendy leaned back in her chair and silently read the message again. Eli looked away. The grant was Wendy's whole life, and he couldn't imagine what she'd do if she had to shut down her project. His nerves were acting up, so he resumed tossing his yo-yo.

Wendy frowned. "That committee has had almost the same membership since I started applying for federal grants more than eight years ago."

Eli caught his yo-yo in midair. "You think this could affect the outcome of their decision?"

Wendy nodded. "Yeah, it looks like some kind of power play. Why else would they replace so many members at once?"

"Sounds political," Eli said. He threw a flying saucer to tighten the string on his yo-yo.

"I don't like it." Wendy leaned back in her chair and glanced down the length of the lab, to where her machine resided. The BIM, or Biological Imaging Machine, had been the center of Wendy's life for the better part of a decade. Eli had come to the project three years ago as the lead programmer, writing the software and building the BIM's user interface.

The BIM was the size of a small bedroom, with the bulk of its innards hidden behind a facade, a wall with a hatch on either side. There was a corridor running through the BIM from hatch to hatch that allowed Wendy to access its innards. In the center of the facade, between the hatches, there was a hole from which protruded a patient table that glided on tracks and took subjects in and out. It looked like an MRI machine on steroids.

In fact the BIM performed the functions of an MRI machine and a CT scan and took a full-body X-ray while putting out half the radiation that either a CT scan or X-ray machine exposed patients and lab technicians to. It also monitored the patient's vital signs: blood pressure, heart rate, respiration rate, and temperature. It even measured the subject's height and weight. Altogether the BIM performed more than half the diagnostics that were typically performed during a routine physical checkup.

Wendy was excited to get the next round of grants and begin working on a pair of goggles that would interface with the BIM and perform full eye exams, diagnosing a host of ophthalmic diseases. But the machine wouldn't be completed for at least another ten years, at which time it would scan the human body down to the cellular level, providing a full health diagnostic.

Eli nodded at the machine. "So what's the backup plan?"

Wendy stared at him for a long moment.

"If we don't get the grant," he said, "what's the backup plan?"

"There is no backup plan," she said. She suddenly pushed her chair back and stepped over to the kitchenette. She filled the teapot with water and clicked the power button.

Eli's jaw was hanging open. Wendy Watson didn't have a backup plan? That was hard to believe. She was the most meticulous person he knew, and she didn't like to take risks. How could she not have a backup plan when the project she had dedicated her life to required tens of millions of dollars in funding?

He watched as she pulled the band from her hair and then twisted her long, auburn locks into a bun at the nape of her neck and wrapped the band around it. She was chewing on her bottom lip, gazing at the floor.

"Can I ask why?" he said.

Wendy snapped out of her daze. "Why what?"

"Why there's no backup plan?"

She stared at him for a moment, as if she were searching for the answer. "I used to have a backup plan," she said.

"What happened?"

"I built relationships with the people on the grant committee. They kept investing in the BIM. Several of them practically guaranteed that they would fund the project through its completion."

"Would any of them happen to be members of the committee who were recently replaced?"

Wendy bit her bottom lip and nodded. "A few, yes."

Eli sighed. "So reactivate one of your old backup plans."

She shook her head. "I can't. Most of them were for private grants. I'm pretty sure the window for applications is closed for the year."

"How much money is left?" Eli asked.

Wendy sighed. "We have enough to get through the end of summer. If we tighten operations, maybe we could make it to the end of the year."

"So four to seven months?" Eli said.

Wendy nodded as the teapot whistled. She turned around and dropped a teabag into her favorite mug, and then she poured hot water over it and set it on her desk to steep before sinking into her chair.

"So, worst-case scenario, we apply for more grants for next year and maybe have to put the project on hold through winter and spring?"

Wendy stared into her mug with a dazed look on her face.

"There's a huge waiting list of engineers and scientists vying for an MIT lab. Once we lose this space, it's gone for good. It would cost several million just to relocate, and the costs of operation could skyrocket, depending on where we end up."

"Are you saying that plan is not feasible?"

"I'm saying it would be costly and labor intensive. We'd lose months of development plus weeks, if not months, relocating. We'd fall behind."

Eli nodded. They weren't the only ones building a medical diagnostic machine. At least eight other teams around the globe were working on similar projects, all competing to produce the first machine that could diagnose at least 90 percent of all known human diseases and illnesses.

His mind was racing. "We could find investors," he said.

Wendy shook her head. "I don't want to run a business. If we get private financing from investors, it becomes about profit, not helping people. That's why I've always applied for grants."

Eli stared at the floor. He was business minded, but he understood where Wendy was coming from. "We could raise the money ourselves," he said. "Crowdsource it."

Wendy laughed. "Sure, we'll just raise fifty million dollars to get us through the next two years. No big deal."

He contemplated their options as he studied her face. She looked dejected. "Well, we're not out of the running yet, right?"

Wendy picked up her cup. "Right," she said, taking a sip of tea. She didn't sound convinced.

They sat there, wordless, for what felt like several moments, until an alert emitted from Wendy's wristcom.

"Shoot," she said, scrambling out of her chair. "I've got to go."

Eli glanced at the time as Wendy gathered her things. "What do you mean? It's not even six o'clock yet. It's Friday night. Aren't we going to order pizza and work until after midnight like we always do?"

"I'm supposed to meet my friend, Jane, for dinner." She paused and caught the disappointed look on his face. "Sorry, Eli. I'll make it up to you. Pizza next Friday, my treat." She shuffled toward the door. "Are you going to stick around here?"

Eli looked around the lab. "Nah. I guess I'll head home."

"Practice your yo-yo? Read a comic book? Play a video game?"

"Something like that."

"Have fun," Wendy said. "You and your all-nighters." Her voice faded away as the door closed behind her.

"Only on the weekends!" Eli called after her. He frowned and scanned the lab. Wendy had left it in disarray. Mechanical parts littered the worktable, tools strewn about nearby. Her smartscreen was still on, and the cup of tea she'd been nursing was still steaming on the edge of her desk.

He sighed and went about the task of cleaning up. When he was done, he washed his hands with soap and warm water, counting to thirty as he did so. Then he gathered his things, turned off the lights, and set the alarm before heading home for the weekend.

- 3 -

The Lawyer

Fuego Cantina
Boston, Massachusetts

The Fuego Cantina was the best Mexican restaurant in Boston. It was homey and old-fashioned, with wood-plank floors, piñatas hanging in the corners, and sprawling windows draped with colorful curtains. The food was authentic, and the place was always packed thanks to its full bar, the dance floor in back, and the mouthwatering food they served right up until last call.

Jane Sanchez sat at a table near the patio doors, scanning the crowd, sipping whisky, and munching on homemade tortilla chips. She checked the time on her wristcom. Wendy was ten minutes late. For anyone else that would have been normal, but Wendy was never late. Jane thought about calling her but decided to wait five more minutes. In the meantime, she entered an order for another drink on the e-menu that was affixed to the table.

Jane and Wendy had enjoyed many lunches and late-night cramming sessions at Fuego during their undergrad days at

Boston University. Wendy had been a bioengineering major, and Jane was a political science major with a minor in sociology. In those days Jane had spent most of her free time frequenting Boston's bustling downtown night scene while Wendy was usually at the library, studying. Jane had earned a reputation for being a party girl, but her grades had never suffered, and she had managed to hold memberships in almost all the political clubs on campus by the time she'd graduated—including the ones she'd opposed. Hey, someone had to keep an eye on the enemy.

During law school Jane had found it necessary to crack down and spend more time with her textbooks. Still, she had never let her social life suffer.

She was about to bite into a crunchy chip laden with Fuego's homemade ceviche salsa when someone tapped her on the shoulder. She turned and broke into a huge smile when she saw Wendy standing there, grinning and looking tired.

"Girl, you're late," Jane said, getting up and giving Wendy a great bear hug. She held Wendy out at arm's length. "I haven't seen you in forever. How long has it been?"

"Oh, about six months," Wendy said.

"That's ridiculous. We live ten minutes away from each other." Jane settled back into her chair.

Wendy hung her light jacket over the back of a chair and sat down. "Sorry I'm late. I lost track of time at the lab."

"Don't sweat it. So what's new? Are you seeing anyone?"

Wendy smiled as she shook her head. "You never did beat around the bush. The only guy I ever see is my programmer, Eli."

"Is he hot?" Jane asked with a sly smile.

Wendy grinned. "No, it's not like that." She glared up at the ceiling trying to find the right way to describe Eli. "He's more like a brother. Maybe a cousin."

"A cousin to you, maybe." Jane was a notorious flirt. She

knocked back a sip of whisky.

"He's not your type," Wendy said. "I don't think there's a political bone in his body."

"Everybody has a political bone in their body. Some people just don't know it yet."

"Speaking of politics, are you working on any interesting cases these days?" Wendy asked.

"Yes, I just landed a VIP client." Jane swooshed the last sip of whisky around in the bottom of her glass. "He's a whistleblower."

"You always had a soft spot for whistleblowers," Wendy said.

Jane leaned forward and lowered her voice. "It's a government thing," she said. "I can't talk about it."

"It sounds exciting," Wendy said.

Jane leaned back in her chair. "Exciting, controversial, messy. It should be fun. And when this case is closed, I'm taking a sabbatical, heading to Mexico to train some young upstarts."

By *upstarts* she meant activists. Jane had a side job training activists around the world, teaching them to engage in civic debate and civil disobedience. Every year she took a few weeks off from her job at the law firm to work for some cause she believed in, anything from solving world hunger or saving the planet to the latest greatest feminist cause. She'd been involved in activism since the first day she had set foot on the BU campus.

The server appeared and set a whisky down in front of Jane. "Can I get you anything to drink?" she asked Wendy.

"I'll have a lemonade," Wendy said.

"Got it," the waitress said. "I'll be back in a few minutes with your order."

"Lemonade?" Jane asked when the waitress was gone. "What are you, twelve?" She laughed heartily while Wendy

17

smirked and rolled her eyes. Wendy had never been able to hold her alcohol. Jane, on the other hand, could outdrink an entire frat house.

"I have to drive home later," Wendy said.

Jane's grin widened, and Wendy protested. "It's illegal to operate a driverless car while under the influence. You're a lawyer. You should know that."

Jane swallowed a sip of whisky. "It's a traffic ticket," she said. Then she cocked her head and studied Wendy's face. "I never could follow the rules like you did. Did you ever miss curfew when we lived in the dorms?"

Wendy shook her head. "Never."

"I don't think I ever made curfew."

"I had to study night and day," Wendy said. "You used to cram for your tests for a couple of hours, and you still got straight As."

"That was a long time ago." Jane waved hand in the air like she was swatting away an insect. "Can you believe the two of us? An engineer and a lawyer?" Jane reached her arm around Wendy's shoulders and gave her a squeeze. "I'm so proud of us."

"I know," Wendy said. "Me too."

"I don't know how you remember all that scientific mumbo jumbo."

"Says the woman who remembers all that legal mumbo jumbo."

Jane laughed and raised her glass. "Touché. But you're going to heal the sick with that awesome machine of yours."

"And you're going to save the planet with all your civil lawsuits and activism."

"No wonder we're best friends." Jane smiled and pushed the chips and salsa toward Wendy.

"Thanks, I'm starving," Wendy said, digging in.

The server came by and dropped off Wendy's lemonade.

Jane lifted her glass of whisky and said "A toast. Wendy Bird and Calamity Jane—best friends forever." They clinked their glasses together and then Wendy took a delicate sip and watched Jane gulp her drink.

"I still can't get used to you wearing a suit," Wendy said, eying her friend's attire.

Jane laughed. "Remember when we met in the dorms, I had a purple Mohawk and a big ring dangling from my septum?" Jane shook her head.

"And by the time we graduated, you were wearing tie-dye, and you hadn't shaved your legs in months," Wendy added.

Jane sighed, a wistful look in her eyes. "*Those* were the days."

Wendy shook her head. "I don't know how you managed to get a date back then."

"It turns a lot of guys on," Jane said, a nostalgic smile spreading across her face. "A few girls, too."

Wendy laughed and shook her head.

"Anyway, enough about me," Jane said. "What about you? How's that machine coming along? How are your parents? I'd love to see your mom."

"She retired, you know," Wendy said, wrapping her hands around the icy glass.

"No way!" Jane said. Wendy's mom, Claudia, was a journalist who had a lot in common with Jane. On the rare occasions when they got together, Jane and Claudia would find some corner where they could sit and talk about current events and social issues of the day.

"Well, she retired from freelancing. She's working on a book."

"Right on," Jane said, dipping a chip into the salsa. "About what?"

"You'll love it," Wendy said. "It's about the history of women in the US military."

"Nice," Jane said, nodding her approval. "What about your dad? Has he retired yet?"

"No," Wendy said. "He'll never retire. The air force will have to kick him out of their lab if they ever want to get rid of him."

"You never knew exactly what he did for them," Jane said. "Did you ever find out?"

Wendy shook her head no. "All I know is he's a civilian scientist, and whatever he does for them, it's top secret." She frowned and gazed at the table.

"It bothers you?" Jane said, raising one eyebrow.

Wendy sighed. "He's an engineer. I'm an engineer." She shrugged. "But we can't discuss his work because it's secret. When I went home for the holidays last year, I was telling him about these goggles I'm going to be developing—they're complicated and require..." Wendy stared at Jane for a beat before she continued. "Well, I won't get into the scientific mumbo jumbo, but the parts have to be so small, the human eye can't even see some of them."

"Sounds pretty cool."

"Yeah, it's just that when I was talking to him about it, he got all excited, and I got the feeling he wanted to say more, like maybe he could offer some guidance."

"Except he can't because what he knows is top secret."

"Right," Wendy said.

"I think it's bullshit," Jane said. "We pay for the military. Technology like that should be public domain. I get that they need to keep some stuff secret, but there can be some transparency, too. Ever since the government started downsizing the military all those years ago, they've gotten more secretive." She shook her head and reached for the e-menu. "Are you ready to order?"

Wendy opened her mouth to answer, but before she could get a word out, a boisterous voice boomed across the restaurant: *"Las dos amigas!"*

A plump Mexican woman with long, graying braids and sporting a beat-up old cowboy hat approached. She carried a little albino dog in the crook of her arm.

"Abella!" Wendy and Jane stood and took turns hugging her. Abella Cortez had opened Fuego Cantina two decades earlier. She ran the place with a stern hand and a smile on her face and now, apparently, with a little white dog tucked under her arm.

"¿Quién es este?" Jane asked, reaching out so the dog could smell her fingers.

"This is Conejo," Abella said with her thick Mexican accent. "Runt. Albino. Nobody wants him, so I said give him to me, and we'll make a home for him here." She pointed her finger upward, indicating her apartment above the restaurant.

Conejo sniffed Jane's fingers but wasn't interested in her. He reached his snout toward Wendy.

"It's been too long, Abella," Jane said, resting a hand on the woman's shoulder.

"Yes, you ladies graduate, move on, and I never see you again." Abella shook her head and pouted. Conejo made a whining sound, still arching his head toward Wendy.

"I think he likes you," Abella said, stepping closer to Wendy. "He won't bite. Just let him smell your hand. That's how he says hello."

Wendy smiled and reached out to the dog. He sniffed her palm and gave it a couple of licks just as her com rang.

She recognized the ringtone. It was her aunt Louise, who rarely called. "I have to take this," Wendy said. "I'll just be a minute."

She stepped away from the table, moving toward the back of the restaurant, where it was quieter. She snapped the wristcom off her arm and held it up to her ear.

"Hi, Aunt Louise." She squeezed the com against one ear

and pressed her palm against her other ear.

"Wendy." Aunt Louise's voice was shaky. "Oh, Wendy." She cried softly.

"What is it, Aunt Louise? What's wrong?"

"It's your parents. Something terrible has happened. You have to come home. Now."

- 4 -

The Funeral

Wendy returned to the table where Jane and Abella were merrily catching up. Their chatter trailed off when they saw Wendy's face. The color had drained out of her cheeks, and her eyes had glazed over.

"What is it?" Jane asked.

Conejo wiggled in Abella's arms.

"My parents are dead," Wendy said. Her face was expressionless. Her arms were hanging limp at her sides. Her heart was sinking into her stomach, and her entire body was going numb.

Jane's jaw dropped, and Abella's eyes went wide, but within seconds they leaped into action. Jane guided Wendy out of the cantina and across the street to Wendy's car. She pressed Wendy's hand against the lockpad, and the locks popped. Then she tucked Wendy into the passenger seat and activated her seatbelt.

"It was a car accident," Wendy said, still dazed.

Jane stared at Wendy. A car accident? She was certain Wendy's parents owned modern, automated cars, which rarely crashed, unless they had been driving in manual mode.

Jane wrapped her arms around Wendy and held her for a moment, and then she scurried around to the other side and let herself in just as Abella came running out of the restaurant. She pushed a bag filled with containers of food through the window and into Jane's arms. Jane thanked her and set the bag on the backseat.

"Take care of our girl," Abella said. Jane nodded and punched the car's control panel to activate the engine.

Abella rushed around to the other side of the car, leaned in, and gave Wendy a kiss on the forehead. "I will pray for you. Be strong, *mi amiga*."

Wendy nodded as Abella backed up and stood on the sidewalk with one hand over her mouth and her eyes filling with tears.

"Home," Jane said to Wendy's car. "Maximum speed."

As they drove off, Conejo's beady little red eyes locked with Wendy's distant gaze.

* * *

At Wendy's apartment Jane hurriedly packed Wendy's things as Wendy sat on the bed, staring off into space.

"I'll need my e-tablet," Wendy said.

"Already got it," Jane said.

Wendy tried to stand up. "I should help."

Jane took her by the shoulders and sat her back down on the bed. "You just rest. I'll take care of everything. We'll have you on a flight to Colorado in no time."

She flipped through the hangers in Wendy's closet and chose three outfits that would be suitable for a funeral. Jane blinked away the tears that welled up in her eyes as she thought about Wendy dressing for her parents' funeral. She rummaged through the bathroom, stuffing the few cosmetics Wendy used into a smaller travel bag, which she tucked into the larger suitcase.

"I need to call Eli," Wendy said.

"I'll take care of it. I'll call him after I take you to the airport." Jane gently took Wendy's wrist in her hands and removed the wristcom, and then she sent all of Wendy's contacts to her own comunit. "I've got a key to your apartment. I'll be here every day, checking the mail and watering your plants. I don't want you to worry about anything."

Jane rolled the luggage out to the car and got Wendy settled in the passenger seat again. Within two hours of learning the news, they were in the departure terminal at Logan airport.

Wendy vaguely noticed Jane talking to a flight attendant, pointing at Wendy as the flight attendant nodded.

She didn't eat, drink, or use the bathroom the whole time she was on the plane. She sat there, staring out the tiny porthole into the black night sky for the entire four-hour flight.

Images flashed through her mind—memories of her childhood. Her mother reading to her, patiently teaching her to trace letters. Her father, always tinkering with gadgets and showing her how they worked. The memories were interrupted when she recalled Aunt Louise's words: "a terrible car accident." But that was impossible. You were more likely to win the lottery than die in a car accident—unless you drove one of those old manual vehicles. But according to Aunt Louise, no other vehicles had been involved. Had her dad been driving manually? That wasn't like him at all.

In her mind's eye, Wendy saw her mom and dad cruising along a country road. The radio would be playing softly, and they'd be talking quietly. Then a flash of terror, a tree slamming into the car. Wendy shuddered and sank back into her memories. Her father taking her to her first judo lesson when she was six years old. Her mother trying to make Thanksgiving dinner and burning everything and her father laughing about it. Aunt Louise's words interrupted her memories again. "They died instantly." Wendy saw the car slamming into the tree, her parents' bodies flung about like rag dolls. She swallowed hard and pushed the vision out of her mind. The memories were safer. They were real. Her father's promotion—he called it *high-security clearance*. He had started his new job the same day Wendy had started junior high. That was the year she'd finally quit judo, and her mother had become a freelance journalist. Wendy could still hear Aunt Louise sobbing. She saw the car's metal twisted into the tree. A fire and then an explosion. Tears streamed down her face, and she pushed her forehead against the tiny window. There were no stars out tonight.

She was going home to bury her parents, and she hadn't said good-bye. Nothing seemed real anymore.

The world came back into focus once the plane landed, and Wendy exited the terminal. Aunt Louise was waiting for her with a tearstained face. The days that followed were pure chaos.

Aunt Louise took charge and escorted Wendy to the funeral home and cemetery. They saw her parents' lawyer about the estate, which included two life insurance policies and the family home that sat on twenty acres with a small wood and a stream. Wendy had to speak to the police, the coroner, and security forces from Carter Air Force Base. She thought it was odd that the air force had gotten involved, but the accident had happened near the base. Apparently her father had been swinging by the base to pick something up before heading out of town for the weekend with his wife when the vehicle had spun out of control and ran into a tree at high speed.

But driverless cars didn't run into trees. The officials insisted he must have been driving manually. There was no other explanation. Wendy couldn't make sense of it, and the car was burned beyond examination.

Aunt Louise brought her things to the house and set herself up in the guest room. She filled the refrigerator even though Wendy refused to eat. She kept a kettle on the stove and made sure Wendy's favorite mug was always filled with freshly brewed tea.

And then Wendy found herself sitting in a neat white folding chair beside her parents' graves with Aunt Louise by her side and Jane sitting behind her, resting a hand on Wendy's shoulder as a chaplain performed the service.

There was a mix of family, friends, and strangers in attendance. Most of the strangers were military, a bunch of men and women in dress uniform. The commander of the base, Colonel Michael Kell, was there and gave a eulogy extolling the virtues of her father's work. He talked about Tom Watson's early service as a young man, barely out of his teens, the injury that had forced him to resign from the Air Force, and his return as a civilian engineer, years later, after he had earned his PhD. But it didn't move Wendy or touch her heart. She found Colonel Kell to be stiff and cold.

Wendy breathed her way through nausea and anxiety when they performed a three-volley salute and folded the flag as a trumpeter played "Taps." She stared into the eyes of the solider who handed her the flag, neatly folded into a perfect triangle, but she didn't see his face. She blinked away hot tears and squinted her eyes against the sun during the missing-man flyby.

The world went upside down, and she felt like her heart was being ripped out as the caskets were lowered into the ground.

When it was over, and the guests had left the cemetery, Wendy sank into one of the chairs beside the open graves and sobbed quietly into the handkerchief that Aunt Louise had tucked into her pocket.

"Now what?" Wendy said when Aunt Louise sat beside her and took her hand.

"Now everybody gathers to celebrate their lives."

"Gathers where?"

Aunt Louise's eyes filled with concern. Wendy tried to remember if she was supposed to know where this gathering was taking place.

"At your house, dear."

Wendy sighed and closed her eyes. She just wanted to be alone, but as it turned out, the gathering wasn't as bad as she anticipated. It was good to see how many people cared about her parents. Even though they were gone, they'd left memories behind with all these people, Wendy most of all.

Jane was the last guest to leave. She squeezed Wendy, kissed both of her cheeks, and made her promise to call if she needed anything—even if it was just to talk. Then she climbed into her rental car and headed for the airport, muttering something about grabbing a drink at the airport bar before her flight.

Aunt Louise was busy in the kitchen, and even though the presence of everyone at the gathering had been comforting, Wendy was relieved to be alone at last. She went upstairs to her parents' room. Nobody had touched it since they'd died a week before. The bed was partially made. A pair of her mom's flip-flops was strewn on the floor. A half-empty glass of water sat on the nightstand along with a pair of reading glasses, a lamp, and an old e-tablet. Her dad's side was tidier: a lamp, an old-fashioned analog alarm clock, and a coaster.

Wendy stared at the room for a long moment before finally bursting into tears. She crawled onto the bed and hugged the pillows, squeezing them until her face was red and damp. *They can't be gone. It's impossible. This can't be happening.*

She lay there, crying softly and then sobbing with every muscle in her body until her bones ached. After that she wept quietly until she finally wore herself out.

- 5 -

Drivers

Swenson, Colorado

"Well, that was awkward." Major Nichols leaned back with one arm dangling out of the open window and a grin on his face. He didn't feel awkward at all.

Colonel Michael Kell gave him a sideways glance but didn't respond. He kept his eyes on the road.

But Nichols continued. "I didn't realize Watson had such a big family. All those brothers and sisters with their horde of kids. Did you know they all flew in from Texas?" He shook his head. "Texas. Who knew? Watson didn't even have an accent."

Kell gritted his teeth. Nichols didn't know when to shut up.

They turned onto the highway that would take them through the countryside that led to Carter Air Force Base. Nichols's open window was letting in all the warm air.

"Air conditioning, set temperature to twenty-four degrees. Roll up passenger window," Kell said.

Nichols yanked his arm into the car as the window rose. He frowned and eyed Kell but didn't say anything. He wasn't about to mouth off to his commanding officer, and with Kell, you couldn't even joke around.

They drove at a comfortable sixty miles per hour. Nichols rubbed his hands together as the air conditioning cooled the inside of the car. He preferred the outside heat to the frigid cooling system.

"You hear about the new Tesla model 23k?" he said.

Kell shifted in his seat. Nichols was always trying to make small talk.

Nichols continued. "There's no driver's seat. No steering wheel. No manual drive. This baby is pure automatic."

Kell rolled his eyes. Now they were making cars with no manual driving system. He'd learned to drive before driverless cars had hit the market, and he'd been on the brink of thirty when they had exploded onto the roads. He had driven manually for years. He still always sat in the driver's seat and always kept his eyes on the road. It was partially out of habit, but mostly he wanted to be in control. He figured if cars ever went fully automated, he'd get himself a motorcycle. They didn't have motion sensors, but they also didn't drive themselves, and some of the three wheelers were fully enclosed with all the luxury and comfort of any car.

"They've got these emergency buttons on every seat in the vehicle. You know, just in case." Nichols shook his head. "Just in case what? There are maybe two or three driverless car accidents a year." He paused. "I guess Tom Watson and his wife are going to be counted among those statistics now. I wonder how many other accidents weren't really—"

"That's enough." Kell's voice was stern as they pulled into the base, and the car eased into a parking spot.

"Yes, sir," Nichols said, sitting upright. He turned his face away from Kell and rolled his eyes as he exited the vehicle.

They walked through the base to the main office building. It was after five, and the day shift was off duty, leaving the sparse night shift. They passed a single guard on patrol and a civil engineer who was rushing toward the parking lot and talking into a com.

Kell checked the personnel app on his wristcom to see who was inside and around the main office building.

"We're clear," he said.

The two men passed the double doors that led into the building and walked around back. Nichols glanced around as they approached a door with construction and warning signs on it. Kell entered a code in the security panel beside the door and then unlocked it with an old-fashioned key card. They navigated through corridors and construction tape until they reached a plain door marked with hazard signs.

Kell removed a clean white handkerchief from his pocket and then pressed his finger against the DNA security panel. When the green light illuminated, he removed his finger and pressed it into the handkerchief as he stepped aside.

"Go ahead," Kell said, his lips tight.

Nichols frowned and stepped forward. He hated the DNA protocol and was pretty sure it had left a permanent scar on his fingertip. When the green light clicked on, and the door slid open, he stuck his finger in his mouth and followed Kell through the door and into another elevator.

"That's hardly sanitary," Kell said, eyeing Nichols, who still had his finger in his mouth.

Nichols said nothing as he pulled his finger out of his mouth and tried to dry it subtly on his pants.

"Don't let me see you doing that again," Kell said.

"Yes, sir," Nichols said as Kell pressed the elevator button.

"Did you decide what to do about Smith?" Nichols asked as they descended to the lower levels.

"What makes you think anything needs to be done about Smith?"

Nichols shrugged. "You asked what I thought about him a couple of weeks ago when you were reviewing his file. That's what you do when you're recruiting for ROMANS."

Kell frowned. "Smith's status is unchanged."

Nichols shook his head. "I can't get a read on that guy. He looks good on paper, but is he pro or con? Hot or cold? Red or blue? I can't figure him out."

Kell couldn't get a vibe on Smith either, but he wasn't about to tell Nichols that. He was slightly relieved. Nichols usually had a good eye for recruits, and the fact that he couldn't get a read on Smith confirmed Kell's own sense of the man— Smith was vague. But Kell had never been good at reading people. It was an undesirable weakness, especially in a leader. He kept it well hidden.

He regarded Nichols's reflection in the metallic walls of the elevator and frowned. He'd been certain that Nichols would be right for his inner circle. And while Nichols had completed his duties diligently, the man was annoying, always flapping his jaw, always chattering and probing. Kell had grown to dislike him, which wasn't unusual; he disliked most people once he got to know them. He'd been considering Smith as a possible replacement, but he suspected that in a year or two he'd grow to dislike him as well.

Things would be better if he could work alone. Then he could get things done right and without any hassle. But that was impossible. He needed a team, people to do the things he couldn't do, and he needed someone who was willing to get his hands dirty. Nichols was still the best man for the job.

The elevator doors opened, and they walked down a short hallway that opened onto the second-floor catwalk that wrapped around the secret underground MOTH compound. The staff looked up from their workstations on the floor below as Kell and Nichols walked along the catwalk to their offices.

"I want you to follow up on the investigation in DC," Kell said. "Make sure they're following the trail we left for them to find."

"Will do," Nichols said. *The trail we left.* He snorted as he stepped into his office. Kell had given the order. Nichols had done all the work, and he hadn't left any trail whatsoever.

Kell entered his own office. He took a seat at his desk, turned on the smartscreen, and opened the daily reports. As usual he couldn't make heads or tails of Dr. Walsh's reports because they were comprised of medical jargon. The man was maddening in his refusal to cooperate.

Kell tapped his wristcom and pinged Nichols. "Infirmary, now," Kell said. "Wait for me when you get there."

Nichols received the message, shook his head, and then got up and headed downstairs. He lingered outside of the infirmary, waiting for Kell to show up.

It didn't take long. Kell approached briskly and pulled on the door handle, but it didn't give. It was locked.

Nichols tapped the sheet of e-paper that was affixed to the door. Kell hadn't noticed it. It read, "Sterile environment. No admittance."

Kell snorted. There were no surgeries scheduled for today. Why did Walsh need a sterile environment? He turned and took a few paces down the corridor, entering the next door. Nichols followed him up a short flight of stairs and into the dimly lit observation room.

They moved to the front of the room and stood before the large window that looked down on the infirmary below, which resembled a hospital room.

Dr. Walsh was bent over the hospital bed, checking the subject's vital signs and surgical wounds. His assistant, Dr. Sommers, was sitting on a stool in front of a panel of monitors, making notes on an e-tablet.

Kell pressed the intercom button. "Dr. Walsh, what's the prototype's status?"

Dr. Walsh froze for an instant before straightening his back and standing upright, unobstructing the view of the hospital bed. Kell frowned as Captain Dessa Rae Andrews's face came into his line of vision. Her head had been shaved, and she looked a little paler than usual, though her complexion was still dark due to her being African American. She seemed to be sleeping peacefully, but Kell knew she was in a deep, medically induced coma.

He gritted his teeth. He had to stop thinking of her as Captain Dessa Rae Andrews. She was someone—*something*—else now.

"I sent a full report this morning," Dr. Walsh said. "I suggest you review it. I'll make an update in a couple of hours, once we're done here."

"Your report is nothing but a bunch of scientific jargon," Kell said. "I told you—"

Dr. Walsh cut him off. "There's a layman's version of the report included. Just click the button at the top of the report, and you'll get the nonscientific version." Dr. Walsh rolled his eyes and shook his head, and then he bent over his patient.

Kell could see Nichols's reflection in the observation window. His eyes had gone wide, and his mouth was slightly ajar. Nobody rolled their eyes at Colonel Kell. Nobody. Kell felt his face growing hot.

Nichols cleared his throat. "Looks like she's on the road to a fast recovery."

Kell didn't answer.

"So what do we call her?" Nichols said.

"What?" Kell was annoyed and not in the mood to answer stupid questions.

"Well, she's not Dessa Rae Andrews anymore, right? So what do we call her?"

Kell snorted. "What does it matter? Call her *the prototype*."

"Do you know how many people would love to get their hands on this project?" Nichols said, leaning back against one of the theater chairs and crossing his arms over his chest. "The air force has been trying to build a supersoldier for decades, and here it is, right under their noses."

Kell closed his eyes. Why did Nichols insist on making unnecessary remarks?

"If this goes well, what are we looking at, three years to deployment?"

"I'm hoping for one," Kell said, his voice tight.

"Glory days," Nichols said.

Kell turned to Nichols. "What did you say?"

"Glory days, sir."

"What's that supposed to mean?"

Nichols shrugged. "Once we gain control of the federal budget, it's going to be glory days for all of us."

Kell frowned, and his face grew hard. He stepped forward, his face inches away from Nichols's. "You think this is about glory? We're not making a political move. We're making a practical move. We'll make sure the military is adequately funded—not overfunded but adequately funded, and the rest goes back to the elected officials." Kell snorted. "They can do whatever they want with it."

"Yes, sir," Nichols said.

Kell glared at Nichols before taking a step back and easing off. He turned toward the glass and watched the doctors poring over medical reports.

"We're done here," Kell said, and then he turned and walked to the door.

Nichols took one last look at the room below. "It's kind of a waste," he said. "I always thought she was hot." Then he turned and followed Kell out of the observation room.

When the door had closed behind them, Lieutenant Smith shifted in his seat and sat up. He'd been scrunched down at the back of the observation room, hidden by the shadows.

- 6 -

The Programmer

Shermer Apartments
Cambridge, Massachusetts

Eli Levine sat at the kitchen counter in his apartment, watching his new dombot prepare his meal. He had recently purchased the basic model of the latest domestic robot and already regretted it. He had figured it would be sufficient. It cooked, cleaned, and provided simple home maintenance and security. But it looked like a twisted tin can, and it lacked personality. As it set a plate of beer-battered fish and chips with a side of coleslaw on the counter in front of him, Eli made up his mind to exchange it for the deluxe model, which had a humanoid body, a face that featured more than a hundred different expressions, and a personality.

The dombot set a chocolate milkshake beside his plate and then tackled cleanup as Eli tucked in to his meal.

Wendy had been gone for a week, and Eli still hadn't heard from her. He didn't know what to make of that. Wendy was more dedicated to her work than anyone he knew, including himself. She often stayed at the lab late into the night and throughout the weekends. Yet she hadn't called once to check in. Even in the midst of tragedy, it was hard to imagine that she could put her work aside so completely. On the other hand, he couldn't imagine what she was going through. The shocking death of her parents had jolted him to the core, and he'd never even met them.

His own parents were alive and well, living in a suburb just outside of Los Angeles. He had called them almost every day for the past seven days. However, he hadn't called or texted Wendy since she'd left Massachusetts. He didn't want to be a bother, and he didn't know what to say. *I'm sorry about your parents. Is there anything I can do?* All those lines seemed canned and generic, and none of them captured what he really wanted to say. But no matter how many times he stared at his com, trying to put his feelings into words, he couldn't do it. Nothing was adequate. So he hadn't called—he'd sent flowers instead.

Eli forked his last bite of fish, dipped it into a saucer of malted vinegar, and swallowed it. Then he drained the last of the milkshake. The dombot had retreated to its charging station, and he had to send it a command to clear the dishes, which was another reason to trade up—the deluxe models were proactive, even when they were charging.

He swiveled around in his chair and went to the kitchen sink to wash his hands, counting as he did so. He got to forty before he realized he was done, and then he turned off the tap, dried his hands, and headed to the back of his apartment, leaving the dombot and his dirty dishes behind.

Eli had converted the second bedroom into a home office, his sacred space. He plucked a yo-yo from a long, narrow shelf, and then he settled into his comfy executive office chair and turned on the old laptop that was sitting on the left side of his massive wraparound desk. As he waited for the system to boot up, he swiveled around and scanned the room to see if it needed cleaning.

A worktable was pushed up against the opposite wall, topped with shelves where supplies were neatly organized in bins—all clearly labeled. A cozy two-seater sofa provided a space for respite and reading while a tall bookshelf held his antique comic books, graphic novels, and other rare texts. Only special editions were printed nowadays, so he treasured the old prints he'd accumulated. The books were categorized and interspersed with antique action figures: Iron Man, Blink, and Mystique.

Everything was in order, so Eli turned back to his work, relieved that he wouldn't have to bring the dombot in.

The laptop was about fifteen years old. Eli had modified it countless times, and he'd installed a custom, tracer-free modem, purchased on Blacknet and imported from India. The laptop connected wirelessly to a small, black pyramid-shaped device, which was hidden in a secret compartment in the back of his desk. The pyramid was a bli-fi unit, which accessed the Internet through a satellite and a series of proxy servers, Wi-Fi towers, and anonymous IP addresses.

All mainstream electronics carried tracers—nonremovable microchips and software that were embedded in their systems. Every manufacturer used them—and, of course, sent user data to the government and anyone else who was willing to pay for it. The only way to retain one's privacy was to use a bli-fi network and black-market electronics.

He was just about to log in to Blacknet when his phone beeped.

It was Wendy's friend, Jane. She'd been calling and texting Eli almost every day, keeping him posted on everything that was going on with Wendy, but this was the first time she'd made a video call.

He snapped his com off his wrist and pressed the lower third of it against the surface of his desk. The rest of it propped upright on its own, establishing a small viewing screen.

"Answer call," Eli said.

Jane's image filled the screen. She had a broad, bronze face, and her long black hair was twisted into a knot on top of her head. But what stood out most were her eyes—they were almost golden. She looked tired. Her brow was creased, and he could make out a faint outline of bags under her eyes. She was seated on an airplane, twirling a drink in her hand.

"Hey," she said, leaning her head back against the seat.

"Hey."

"So, the funeral was today."

Eli swallowed. He tried to think of something to say, but nothing came to mind, so he just nodded and felt like an idiot.

"It was the saddest funeral I've ever been to." She choked on her words, and her eyes welled up with tears. "I thought Wendy was going to hyperventilate when the coffins went into the ground."

Eli tried to imagine the coffins descending into the earth—how he would feel if his parents were sinking into the ground forever. He opened his mouth, but nothing came out, so he closed it again.

Jane watched him on the vidscreen and then took a sip of her drink. "What are you doing?"

"Me?"

"No, that doll on the shelf behind you. Of course you."

Eli turned and looked behind him. She was referring to one of the action figures on his bookshelf.

"Those aren't dolls," he said.

Jane shrugged. "Semantics," she said.

"I was just about to check my e-mail." That was only partially true. "Did Wendy get my flowers?"

Jane cocked her head a little and studied Eli's face again. "Yes. She cried when she opened the card. They arrived during the gathering at her house after the funeral."

"Oh no," Eli said. He hadn't meant to make Wendy cry.

"No, it was good. She was touched. She said she hasn't talked to you all week. I think she felt bad about it."

"That wasn't my intention," Eli said.

"It meant a lot to her. While she was putting the flowers in a vase, she said you and I are her two closest friends."

Eli's jaw dropped. "She did?"

"Well, she spends all day every day with you. I think she would have fired you by now if she didn't like being around you." Jane twirled her drink again and then swallowed the rest. "You got the hots for her?"

"What? The hots? Me? No. No—it's not like that at all."

Of course Eli had considered it. Wendy was an attractive woman. But he knew she wasn't the right kind of woman for him, and he knew it was a bad idea to get involved with someone when you knew it wasn't going to go anywhere. Besides, it would destroy their working relationship and ruin their friendship. And it wasn't like Wendy would ever consider dating a guy like him. She was bright and professional; he was nerdy and awkward.

"Why? You already got a girlfriend?"

"What? No. Why are you asking me these questions?"

Jane shrugged. "Just getting to know you. That's what people do. Ask questions."

Eli became annoyed that Jane was putting him in the hot seat. Without thinking, he said, "Do you have a boyfriend?"

"Nah." She sighed and set her empty cup down somewhere out of the camera's line of sight, and her eyes scanned the aisle of the airplane. Then she turned back to her com. "It's been a while since I've been in a relationship. I'm too busy for that right now. Maybe next year."

Eli found that odd. Most people he knew wanted to be in relationships, himself included. But he was picky and not willing to settle. By all accounts he should consider himself lucky if a girl even considered dating him. But he didn't feel that way at all. He wanted someone he could talk to, play video games and watch movies with—a companion, someone like his ex-girlfriend but not too much like her.

"Plane's landing in about twenty minutes," Jane said. "I can't wait to get home and crawl into bed. I'm going to sleep until noon."

"Are you going by Wendy's tomorrow?"

"Yeah, I need to water her plants. I haven't been there in two days, so the mail is probably piling up too. She receives an awful lot of packages."

Eli grinned. "Parts for the BIM," he said. "She has them sent to her house because the lab's mailbox is on the other side of campus. You should have said something. I would have picked up the deliveries and watered her plants."

"I thought about it, but I figured two days is no big deal."

"Did Wendy say when she's coming home?"

Jane raised an eyebrow. "You know she inherited her parents' house?"

"So?" Eli stared at the screen and absorbed what Jane had just said. "Are you saying she's going to move there?"

"Oh no. No way. I think it's hard for her to be there. But she has to make arrangements, settle the estate. She said she wants to be back in Boston in a week, no later."

Eli sighed with relief. With a jolt he realized how important Wendy was to him. She was the only person he spent much time with outside of his friends on the net. He wasn't sure what he'd do if she stayed in Colorado. Suddenly the prospect of losing the grant was much more daunting. He had understood that without funding, they might have to terminate the BIM project, but it hadn't occurred to him that if that happened, he and Wendy would probably go their separate ways.

"Hello? Anybody home?" Jane said.

Eli shook himself out of his daze. "Sorry," he said. "I was

just…I don't know…" He couldn't explain it.

"Don't worry about it," she said. "There's a lot of that going around lately. Anyway, I better go. I have a couple more calls to make before I land. All three of us should get together when Wen gets back."

"Sure," Eli said, even as he squirmed at the thought of it.

"I think you'll hear from her within a day or two."

Eli nodded.

"Bye," Jane said.

"Bye."

Eli stared at the com and wondered if Jane thought he was an utter idiot.

After a minute or so his discomfort passed, and he snapped the com back onto his wrist. He felt terrible that his flowers had made Wendy cry, and now he was worried about whether they'd get that grant money.

The BIM was his only link to Wendy, and he had just realized that she was the only real friend he had in the world.

- 7 -

The Treehouse

City Outskirts
Swenson, Colorado

Wendy shocked herself by sleeping until noon. She woke in her parents' bed, her eyes and throat raw from crying. Getting up was an act of sheer willpower. She rinsed her face in the bathroom and then drifted downstairs and found Aunt Louise in the kitchen.

Aunt Louise's eyes went dark with worry when she saw Wendy. "I'll make you breakfast, dear," she said, reaching for a skillet.

"No, I'm not hungry. But thanks."

Aunt Louise nodded, set down the skillet, and then picked up a rag. She kept an eye on Wendy as she wiped the counters.

Wendy put the teapot on and said, "What day is it?"

"It's Saturday." Wendy barely noticed the concern on her aunt's face.

Wendy frowned. "I was supposed to find out whether I received the grant for the BIM yesterday. But instead I buried my parents."

Aunt Louise left the rag on the counter and put her arms around Wendy. "None of this is fair," she said.

Wendy fought back the tears and nodded, clutching her aunt until the teakettle whistled. Then Aunt Louise rinsed the rag as Wendy poured hot water over a bag of herbal tea. She squeezed Aunt Louise's arm on the way out to the front porch, where Wendy set her steaming mug on the railing to steep and eased into the porch swing. She looked out over the fields.

She'd never felt so empty. Over the last few days, she'd poured everything out of herself, drained every thought and every emotion. Now she was just a spent body, looking out at her parents' property—her property now: the modest lawn and the big oak tree at the far edge with her tire swing hanging there, swaying gently in the breeze.

Beyond the lawn stretched a vast field. Wendy and her mother used to sit together on the couch, looking out the big picture window in the living room, watching for deer and rabbits. Sometimes a feral cat would run by with a mouse between its teeth. Occasionally, late at night, the coyotes would prowl around. Wendy remembered hearing the screams of a coyote's kill, her mother trying to comfort her, and her dad's solemn words about nature and the food chain. The next day he had taken her out to the field and taught her about wildlife. He had showed her how to shoot a gun, hunt, and clean and prepare fowl. The whole thing had disgusted her. Wendy shook her head at the memory. He had just wanted her to be strong and capable.

Her mother used to take her through the field, picking herbs and berries and piling them into a battered old basket. Later the herbs would dry up on the kitchen counter, filling the house with a strange mix of delicious scents as Wendy and her mom munched on fresh forest fruit, the juices dripping onto whatever book Wendy was reading and staining her mother's notes. Wendy remembered her mother's feet were always dirty because she walked the field barefoot—something Wendy never did after stepping on a rusty nail and getting a tetanus shot at age four.

In the distance, past the field, Wendy saw the wooded area where she had loved to play as a child. One summer her father had built her a treehouse in a great oak near the center of the grove.

Wendy blinked and sat upright. She hadn't been to the treehouse in years.

She left her cup of tea sitting on the rail. The sky above was filled with sunshine, and the breeze was warm. As she walked across the field in her slippers, the wrong shoes for this expedition, her skin dampened, and strands of hair stuck to her forehead and cheeks. She crossed the tree line and walked with caution, taking care not to step on any large rocks or rusty nails.

By the time she reached the tree, her head was brimming with memories—her and her dad dragging lumber out here, eating a picnic lunch with her mom while her dad hammered up in the treehouse, and the three of them celebrating with cider and cookies when it was finally completed. When she was older, she had brought her friends to the treehouse, and later, her boyfriend.

After kicking off her slippers, Wendy shimmied up the trunk and onto the lowest, thickest branch. She used to bird-watch from this branch. She reached up and grabbed the next limb, jackknifed her body, and brought her legs up and over the branch before pushing herself up and onto her feet—she tore her pajama bottoms in the process and scraped one of her palms. It had been a long time since she had attempted that maneuver.

She walked along the branch gingerly and then took an easy step onto a slightly higher branch. From there she looked down at the platform that comprised the roof of her treehouse;

her dad used to call it the star-watch platform.

Wendy dropped to the platform and opened a hatch in the roof, revealing the interior of the treehouse below. She lowered herself onto the wooden ladder and descended into her childhood getaway place.

Wendy and her dad had carefully measured every board. The treehouse was five and a half by six feet. It seemed so small and cramped. How had she fit in here with her dad? How had she squeezed half a dozen of her friends inside?

Sturdy beams held up the roof, and the windows were shuttered. Wendy couldn't stand upright now that she was a full-grown adult. She crawled around, opening the shutters and letting the warm breeze push the stale air out.

Finally, she looked around. She was surrounded by wood and greenery. Her things were still there—an old set of com speakers and an antique milking stool with her favorite childhood stuffed giraffe sitting on it. Old scarves were draped around the windows, adding to its rustic charm.

She moved to the back of the treehouse, nearest the trunk of the great old tree, and ran her fingers over the boards that comprised the wall. When her fingers detected an anomaly, she pressed hard against the board, triggering a hidden mechanism, and then a piece of the floor popped up. Her father had built this secret hiding place for her, but of course she had never hidden anything secret there since he knew about it.

She lifted the floorboard and looked inside. It was still there. She reached into the crevice and pulled out a wooden box, slightly shorter and wider than a shoebox. She dusted it off and set it on her lap. She hadn't forgotten the combination to the tiny lock, and a moment later she popped the lid open.

Inside there was a dried flower from her high school sweetheart, a tiny notebook, a dried-up pen, and a butterfly pin she'd gotten when her mother had taken her to Japan for a feature story her mom was working on during Wendy's teenage years. She ran her finger along the butterfly's wing and then fastened it to her shirt.

Wendy sat there for a while, taking in the fresh air and reminiscing. Eventually it occurred to her that Aunt Louise might be wondering where she'd gone. It was time to get back to the house.

She put her things back in the wooden box and knelt over the crevice in the floor. She was about to tuck the box back into its hiding place when she noticed an envelope. She leaned in to grab it and realized the envelope was sitting on top of a soft, black object.

Wendy picked up the envelope and felt something small and hard inside. She held it up and read the writing on the outside: "Yoshi: safekeeping."

It was written in her father's handwriting.

She racked her brain—she couldn't remember seeing Yoshi Kobayashi at the service or the gathering afterward.

Wendy knew him as Sensei from the days when she'd taken judo lessons at his dojo in town. She'd been a little girl then, just six years old when her father had first brought her there "to learn how to be strong," he'd said. Her father had met the sensei when he himself had gone for lessons after taking a few of the classes that Yoshi taught on the base in the evenings.

But why hadn't Yoshi been at the funeral? Her father and Yoshi had always joked that they were like brothers, since both of them had left big families and lots of brothers and sisters behind—Yoshi having come from Japan and Wendy's dad having come from Texas.

She stared at the envelope for a moment, wondering why Yoshi hadn't been at the funeral, and then she set it aside. She reached into the hole and pulled out a large, black canvas bag. She leaned over and looked in the hole. It had been just deep enough to hold her little wooden box. Someone—most likely her father—had enlarged her secret hiding place.

She unzipped the bag and discovered that it held a large silver case, similar to a briefcase but thicker and with rounded corners. Wendy looked for a way to open it, but there were no hinges, locks, or clasps—just a handle and a faint seam. She shook it gently. It was heavy, although nothing rattled inside. Whatever was in there, it was tightly packed.

Her first thought was that this had something to do with her father's work. He had worked on top-secret projects for the air force, but he had never brought his work home, and he would certainly never leave it sitting anywhere that someone could find it, especially not in a treehouse. He had been meticulous with the secrets entrusted to him.

Wendy tucked the envelope into her waistband and put the silver case back in the canvas bag. She set her wooden box back in the hole and gently closed the floorboards. Then she pushed the bag out of the treehouse, setting it on the roof, and climbed out. With the canvas bag slung uncomfortably across one shoulder, she shimmied down the tree and headed back to her family home.

As she made her way across the field, Wendy took the envelope out and examined it. It wasn't yellowed or aged. There was no way to tell how old it was. Had it been sitting in the treehouse for years? Weeks? Days? Why hadn't her father given it to Yoshi? Why had he enlarged the secret hiding space beneath the floor of her treehouse? And what was inside the strange silver case?

Back at the house, Wendy retrieved her now-cold cup of tea from the porch railing and took it inside. She found her aunt dozing on the sofa in the living room. Wendy crept upstairs and stashed the items she'd found under her bed. Then she went to the kitchen, where she washed the cup and set it in the dish rack. Her stomach rumbled, and she suddenly felt like she hadn't eaten in a week. In fact she had eaten very little in the past week.

She had pulled a selection of fruit out of the fridge and was slicing up a fruit salad when her aunt walked in, yawning.

"Hey," Wendy said, trying to sound casual.

"Oh hi, dear," Aunt Louise said through a yawn. She eyed the fruit. "I'm glad to see you've got an appetite."

"There's plenty," Wendy said, "and it's fresh."

"Oh no. I already ate." Aunt Louise patted her stomach. "I was about to take a bath, but I took a nap instead." She took a pitcher of iced tea out of the fridge and poured herself a glass.

"You must have needed the rest," Wendy said. Suddenly it occurred to her that she'd been in a fog for days. She hadn't stopped to think about how all this was affecting Aunt Louise. "How are you holding up?"

"As well as can be expected," Aunt Louise said with a sad smile.

Wendy set the knife down and looked at her aunt. "I'm so sorry. I've been acting like all of this is happening to me and only me."

Her aunt gave her a sympathetic look. "You have a right to mourn."

"So do you. He was your brother."

"And she was my sister-in-law. I mourn better when I keep busy," Aunt Louise said. "Now I'd better go see about that bath." She turned to leave.

"Aunt Louise, do you know if anyone contacted Yoshi? Why wasn't he at the funeral?"

Aunt Louise froze in place before she turned around, her mouth agape and her eyes wide. She clasped her hand over her mouth.

"I didn't even think of it," she mumbled through her fingers. "I guess with all the commotion, I forgot to call him." She set her glass down on the counter. "And your father always said Yoshi was like a brother to him."

"Yoshi still lives in town, doesn't he? How could he not

have heard about it? This is a small town. Word gets around fast."

"Yes, and even if nobody told him, there was a story about it in the paper and then the obituary. And last I heard, Yoshi was still teaching classes at the base. Someone there certainly would have told him." Aunt Louise buried her face in her hands and shook her head. "It's all my fault," she muttered.

"It's not anybody's fault, especially not yours." Wendy squeezed her aunt's shoulder. "He could be out of town. He travels to Japan every few years to visit his family, and when he goes there, he usually stays for several weeks."

Aunt Louise frowned and shook her head. Wendy wasn't surprised by her reaction. Her aunt was as meticulous as her father, in her own way.

"I'm going to go into town and check on him," Wendy said.

"Oh no, let me call him—"

"I'll take care of it," Wendy said. "It's been a while, and I'd really like to see him."

Aunt Louise nodded. "All right. Please tell him I'm sorry."

"You have nothing to be sorry about," Wendy said, hugging her aunt.

"You're a good girl," Aunt Louise said, cupping her hand under Wendy's chin. "All right, I'll go see about that bath." With that, she shuffled off toward the guest bathroom, shaking her head and muttering about how forgetful she was becoming.

- 8 -

The Warrior

Downtown
Swenson, Colorado

Devin Ford stood on the busy corner of Oak and Second Streets, waiting to cross. He had grown up in Swenson and had spent much of his childhood trying to blend in. Now he stood out. He was tall at six foot four, and he was toned, with a lean, muscular frame. His Irish, Hawaiian, and Native American heritages blended into his features: a broad face with a strong jawline, slightly hooded green eyes, and a light spattering of freckles across his nose. Long, thick dreadlocks were tied back at the nape of his neck. He was an imposing figure.

When the light turned green, Devin crossed the street and entered a run-down auto repair shop on the other side.

His old blue VW bus was in the same place he'd left it a few days earlier.

"Hello?" he called. "Anyone here?"

A man riddled with grime slid out from beneath a solar-powered Tesla sedan.

"I'm here," he said. "How can I help you?"

"That's my bus," Devin said, nodding at his vehicle. "I'm supposed to pick it up today."

The man pushed himself to a standing position, sizing up Devin. He looked from Devin to the VW and back again.

"It's a hippy train if I ever saw one," he said.

Devin knew he was being prodded. "Is it ready?" he asked.

The guy stared at him for a beat and then grinned and held out his hand. "Yeah, it's ready. I'm Joe, by the way. This is my place."

"Hi Joe," Devin said, shaking the man's hand and feeling like he'd passed some kind of test.

"This is the first time I've seen a real hippy bus in person," Joe said. "Even with the upgrades to solar power and driverless systems, that thing's a real antique. I reckon it's almost a hundred years old."

Devin nodded. People were always making remarks about his unusual vehicle.

"Jackson must have helped you out the other day. I had to go to Boulder, pick up some supplies."

"Jackson, yeah. That was the guy who helped me."

"He's at lunch." The man headed toward a grungy, old oak desk in the corner. "Come on," he said. "I'll have you out of here in no time."

The desk was covered with e-paper and scraps, several fast-food containers, a dirty ashtray, and an ancient smartscreen streaked with grease.

"Have a seat," Joe said.

Devin sat in an old black vinyl chair beside the desk, and Joe eased into a wooden chair on wheels with a tattered purple cushion on its seat. It resembled an old-fashioned teacher's chair, and it looked older than Devin's bus, but Devin didn't say so.

"Got your estimate?" Joe asked.

Devin leaned back in his chair and sprawled his legs out so

he could reach into his front pocket. He pulled out a cardcom, accessed the estimate, and handed the com to Joe, who looked it over, nodding. "Jackson's good. This is right on the money." He handed the com back to Devin and looked at him expectantly until Devin pulled a slim wallet out of his other front pocket and then counted out the bills—all hundreds.

The man gave him an odd look. "We take e-payments," he said.

"I don't use e-payments," Devin responded.

Joe looked thoughtful. "Ever thought of upgrading her with a newer driverless system?"

"The system works fine, but thanks," Devin said. He glanced at the door, hoping Joe would realize he was in a hurry.

"They're talking about outlawing those old systems, you know," Joe said.

"Maybe next time."

Joe nodded and shuffled through the items on his desk, unearthing a keyboard, and started typing with two fingers.

"Ford's your last name?"

"Yep."

Joe pulled his eyes away from the smartscreen and studied Devin's face. Then he shook his head and said, "Nah, couldn't be."

But a moment later he glanced at Devin again.

"Guy named Ford used to come in here all the time. Airman Ford, I used to call him. I think he was a sergeant, maybe a lieutenant. He had an old brown Buick. Brought it in almost every other month. Man, that thing was a piece of shit."

"My father," Devin said.

"Damn, I remember you. Quiet kid, always rode in the backseat." Joe glanced at the tattoo on Devin's arm. "Marines?" he asked.

Devin nodded.

"You ever see any action?"

"War's over, man," Devin said. "Like, really over." There hadn't been a war since before Devin was born.

"Right," Joe said, nodding and rolling his eyes. "There hasn't been a war in more than thirty years." He gave Devin a sideways glance. "That doesn't mean there's no action."

"I was special ops," Devin said with a curt nod.

Joe nodded. "I thought so. I did one tour in the Middle East back in the day. I was just a kid. Didn't see much action, but I was there long enough to know it wasn't for me. I got out as soon I could."

"I know the feeling," Devin said.

Joe nodded. "These kids nowadays join up, they have no idea what the military's all about. There's no more war, so they think they'll just join the military, get an education and a career on Uncle Sam's dime. Everybody thinks war's a thing of the past. Government's downsizing the military because hey, we don't need it anymore! Fucking idiots."

Devin wasn't sure if the idiots Joe referred to were the people downsizing the military or the kids joining up. He assumed both.

"Every one of them's either a bully or a hero. All that crap about honor and dignity. Honor doesn't mean shit when your buddy gets blown to bits right in front of your eyes."

Joe was right, of course. The wars had ended decades ago, and the kids joining these days were of a different ilk. They used the military as an alternative to college, a path to adventure, a career avenue. Joining the service was relatively safe. It was still grueling, but the military produced the finest and most skilled professionals in the nation, from engineers to pilots, doctors, and scientists. Devin thought it was a fine program.

"I know what you mean," Devin said.

"What'd you do when you got out?" Joe asked.

"Came back here, stayed with a friend—a mentor, really.

Then traveled for a few years. Ran a dojo in Florida for a bit, but that didn't work out."

"A dojo? Like the one a few blocks east of here?"

"Not exactly like that, but that one was where I got my start."

Joe nodded. "I never met the old man who runs the place, but over the years lots of my customers have spoken highly of him. He's the mentor you mentioned, I guess?"

"Yep," Devin said.

"His name's Sensei Kabashu or something, right?"

"Yoshi Kobayashi. Sensei is a title."

"Sorry, man," Joe said.

Devin shrugged it off and wished Joe would focus more on the paperwork and less on the personal details of Devin's life.

"I always wanted to travel, but I got an ex-wife and two kids. Never could afford it. Whereabouts did you get to?"

Joe was still two-finger typing and looking back and forth from the keyboard to the screen and then to Devin. Devin suddenly pitied the man, stuck inside a filthy garage all day, barely making ends meet from the looks of things. There was a shinier, big-box chain garage closer to the center of town that was likely a constant threat to Joe's business, but they didn't handle rare or vintage models. Devin guessed that was what kept Joe in business.

"Hawaii, Uruguay, India, Bali. Spent a little time in South Africa and Europe." Devin shrugged. Europe hadn't been the right place for him.

"Impressive," Joe said. "I don't think I could find half of those on a map. What brought you back here?"

That was a question Devin didn't want to answer. He had been a quiet kid who had grown into a private man.

He looked at Joe, who was still glancing from the keyboard to the screen and back again. Joe had kind eyes, bright blue and cheerful, set in a dingy, weathered face.

"Just visiting Yoshi," Devin said. "I'll be moving on again eventually."

Joe pressed a key with a flourish, and Devin's comcard beeped.

"Your receipt," Joe said, angling his eyes at Devin's comcard and beaming at Devin with crooked teeth. "I think what you're doing is great. Travel while you're young. See the world. Figure out who you are. Settle down later. There are days I wish I'd done exactly what you're doing."

Devin doubted that. He found that most people, whether they admitted it or not, were doing exactly what they wanted to be doing. But he smiled politely and said nothing.

Ten minutes and almost six thousand dollars later, Devin pulled his battered blue VW bus out of the garage.

When he pulled up to the dojo a few minutes later, he found a redheaded woman peering in the windows and knocking on the door. Devin parked the bus and approached the building.

"Can I help you?" he asked.

The woman turned and seemed startled to see Devin standing there. Her smile was awkward. "No, thanks."

"OK," Devin said. He went to the door and started to unlock it.

"Wait," the woman said. "Are you—is this—I'm sorry. Is this still Yoshi Kobayashi's dojo?"

Devin clicked the lock open. "Yup," he said.

"Is he here? I mean, is he home?"

Devin studied the woman's face. She was pale and freckled. There were dark circles under her eyes. She looked familiar somehow.

"Who are you?" he asked.

"My name's Wendy Watson," she said. "I'm Tom Watson's daughter."

Devin's face relaxed when she said that. "Tom Watson…"

he muttered.

"Yes, I have some important news for the sensei—for Yoshi—about my father."

Devin's brow furrowed. "Why don't you come in?" he said, holding the door open. "We should talk."

He left the door unlocked. The Saturday afternoon class was starting in less than an hour, and the kids would be arriving soon. He led Wendy to a futon and a couple of old, secondhand chairs at the back of the studio, where parents of the youngest students watched and waited for their kids to finish their martial arts classes.

"Please," Devin said. "Have a seat."

Wendy eyed him as she took a seat in one of the chairs.

"Do I know you?" she asked.

Devin shrugged. "You look familiar to me too. I've known your father for a long time, so maybe we've met before."

Wendy frowned, and a look of abject sorrow settled into her eyes. Devin wasn't sure what he'd said, but he was sure it had upset her.

"How did you know my father?"

"He and Yoshi are close friends. Yoshi's like a father to me."

"Oh," Wendy said, her face registering understanding. "You're—I'm sorry. I've forgotten your name, but I remember something about a boy living with Yoshi for a couple of years. His apprentice. That must have been you. Yes, I think we met once or twice."

"It would have been a long time ago."

"It was right around the time I was graduating high school," she said. "Wow, it's nice to meet you. I've actually heard a lot about you. Yoshi used to rave about what an adept student you were."

Devin nodded but didn't say anything.

"Is he here? Can I see him?"

"I've been meaning to call your father—" Devin's voice cracked and he bent his head for a moment. "Yoshi's not well," he said.

Wendy stared at Devin in disbelief. "Is it serious?"

He nodded.

"What is it?" she asked.

"Cancer."

"But cancer is—"

"They discovered it too late," Devin said. "I've been here for the last couple of months, teaching his classes and taking care of him."

Wendy cast her eyes downward, and her eyes glazed over. "I don't believe it," she whispered.

It was hard for Devin to believe too, but he didn't say that. Yoshi spent all his time in bed now. He slept a lot. The doctors had started him on heavy painkillers a few days ago, and when he was awake, he was groggy. He tried to speak sometimes, and there were moments when he made sense, but most of the time he was pretty out of it.

Wendy buried her face in her hands. Devin wasn't surprised anyone from Tom Watson's family would react in such a manner. Yoshi had known them for almost thirty years. But what Wendy said next shocked him.

"My parents are dead."

Devin's jaw dropped as Wendy raised her head. Her cheeks were streaked with tears.

"It was a car accident, eight days ago. The funeral was yesterday, and Yoshi wasn't there. I thought maybe he was in Japan or something."

"I'm sorry," Devin said. The news was jarring, and Yoshi would be heartbroken.

Wendy studied Devin's face. "Then he doesn't know about the accident?"

Devin shook his head. "No."

"I guess he's not in any condition to hear about this."

Devin thought about that. "I think he'd want to know. But I don't know when he'll be alert enough…" Devin's voice trailed off as he thought about Sensei's condition.

"Can I see him?" Wendy asked. "I won't say anything about my parents."

Devin nodded slowly. "Yeah. If he seems sharp, and you think it's the right time, you should tell him. If he's in pain or groggy, then it would be better to wait." He didn't tell Wendy that even if she told Yoshi what had happened, he would probably forget when he got his next dose of medication.

Devin rose from the futon and headed to a door at the back of the dojo that led to a staircase and the apartment upstairs.

"Did my father know Yoshi is sick?" Wendy asked as they climbed to the second floor.

"No. I'm not sure what happened." Devin opened the door to the apartment, and they both stepped inside. He lowered his voice. "Yoshi was diagnosed about a year ago. He told me maybe eight months ago. He went to see his family in Japan about six months ago. And it was about two months ago—shortly after I got here—he said it was time to tell Tom. It was starting to show. He was losing weight. His skin color wasn't right."

Devin stared at the floor and shook his head, remembering the shock of how Yoshi had looked. He was a small man but a strong and limber one, with a peaceful but intense energy. All that had faded, leaving behind a wisp of the man he had once been.

"He invited your dad to dinner. He was going to tell him about the cancer, but something happened. Your dad was nervous, distracted. I didn't see him that night, so I can't be more specific. All I know is when I asked Yoshi if he'd told Tom, he said he couldn't because something was wrong. Tom was upset about something, and Yoshi didn't want to make it worse. He said, 'Tom's got enough on his mind right now.' Right after that Yoshi started deteriorating—fast."

Wendy stared at Devin and digested everything he'd said.

"I guess he had no idea what might have been bothering my father?" Wendy said.

Devin shook his head. "If he did, he never said anything to me about it."

They were quiet for a moment, and then Devin said, "Are you ready to see him?"

Wendy nodded and followed Devin to the bedroom at the back of the apartment.

- 9 -

Tabula Rasa

Carter Air Force Base
Swenson, Colorado

She sensed the bright lights before she opened her eyes. There were sounds—voices and a machine beeping. Feet shuffling. Someone breathing nearby.

"She's coming to."

"How long is this going to take?"

This didn't seem right. She wasn't where she was supposed to be. She was lying in a bed, but it wasn't her bed—at least she didn't think it was her bed. The covers were too light, and the clothing she wore felt too thin. The lights, the sounds, the sensations. It was all wrong. She figured she was in a hospital, but why?

Her eyes opened slowly.

"There she is."

"Take it easy now."

"Can't you speed this up?"

She squinted against the bright light directly overhead.

"Sommers, get the light."

As she blinked, the light dimmed, and she took in her surroundings. It was definitely a hospital room, although the big window in the wall was strange. There was another room on the other side. She saw chairs lined up as if it were a theater. Three men stood in her line of vision. Two wore white coats, and one was wearing an air force uniform. He was a high-ranking officer. She looked at his rank insignia. He was a colonel. How did she know that?

She ran her dry tongue across the roof of her mouth and tried to swallow, but her throat was parched.

"Here, sip this."

One of the men in white coats held a cup with a straw to her mouth, and she took a long drink.

"Not too much," he said, pulling it away. "Let's sit you up."

She felt the top half of the bed rise, moving her body into a sitting position. There was a fourth man by the door and a fifth sitting at a desk in the corner. He appeared to be working on some kind of computer housed in a black case. Both wore air force uniforms. They were all staring intently at her.

"Where the hell am I?" she asked.

"You're in the infirmary," one of the white coats said. He was a small man with a pointy nose and frizzy gray hair, and he wore small, round, old-fashioned spectacles.

"Are you my doctor?"

"Yes, I'm Dr. Walsh. This is my assistant, Dr. Sommers." He indicated the other man in the white coat. Dr. Sommers was much younger and taller than Dr. Walsh.

She eyed the man standing at the foot of her bed. Something about him made her uncomfortable.

"That's Colonel Kell," said Dr. Walsh. "He's your commanding officer."

It didn't occur to her to hide the frown that appeared on her face. Commanding officer? That meant she was in the military.

"Do you remember him?" Dr. Walsh asked. "Do you remember anyone in this room?"

She looked around, studying each of them. "I don't know." She did a double take when her eyes passed over the man at the desk. He was handsomest man in the room, with dark hair and mysterious eyes that were looking at her intently. "I think I might know him," she said.

They all looked at the man, and he shrugged in response. "I'm unforgettable," he said.

"What am I doing here?" she asked. It occurred to her that it wasn't normal for there to be five men—three of whom weren't doctors—in a female patient's hospital room, and the desk and computer certainly seemed out of place. The big window in the wall bothered her too. "Why are you all here?"

"All right, let's give her some space. Colonel Kell, Major Nichols, I'm going to have to ask you to move to the observation room."

Her eyes darted to the window in the wall. This definitely wasn't a normal hospital room. Her heartbeat sped up, and it was audible by the beeping on the monitor. Her breath quickened.

The two men didn't move.

"I need to keep her calm," Dr. Walsh said, glancing at the machine and then at the man sitting at the desk with the computer.

"Keep the intercom on," said Colonel Kell. He exited, and the man who had been standing by the door followed him out of the room.

As a wave of relaxation swept over her, she stared at the doctor and then at the window. After a few seconds, the two men appeared there and seated themselves. Their presence rattled her, and the relaxation gave way to tension.

"What the hell is going on? Why are they watching me

from up there?" She sat up and moved to get off the bed, but her body was weak and her head fogged. Plus she was connected to a bunch of tubes.

"Please, I'll explain everything, but I need you to keep calm. You were in an accident, but you're going to be fine."

She stared into the doctor's eyes. He wasn't lying, but he was hiding something. She was sure of it.

"Please," he said.

She swung her feet back onto the bed and leaned back. "This is some creepy-ass shit," she said.

"I'm sure waking up here like this is unnerving," he said, picking up an e-tablet. "I'd like to ask you a few questions."

"When do I get to ask you a few questions?" she said.

"All in good time." He smiled. "Can you tell me the last thing you remember?"

She opened her mouth to answer but clamped it shut when she realized she couldn't answer the question. She searched her memory for the last thing she remembered.

She remembered what the sky looked like, what grass felt like beneath her bare feet. She knew the sensation of sand between her toes. She remembered running and sweating, laughing and dancing. And she remembered flying, soaring through the atmosphere. But the memories were fragmented. She couldn't remember where she had been or who she had been with—just sensations. And facts. She knew things, but she couldn't remember learning them.

"I don't know."

"It's quite all right. You've had a serious head injury, and your memories have been compromised."

"Am I going to get them back?"

He looked up from his tablet. "I wish I could say yes with absolute certainty, but unfortunately there are no guarantees."

A chair skidded, and they both glanced across the room. The man at the desk had shifted his position. She thought he looked annoyed or maybe upset. He kept a straight face, but there was something in his eyes, something familiar.

"Sorry," he said. "Just getting comfortable."

"Who's that?" she whispered to the doctor.

"That's Lieutenant Smith."

"Why is he here?"

"He's helping us monitor your progress."

"Is he a doctor?"

"No. Let's return to the task at hand. Do you know your name?"

She opened her mouth again but ended up biting her lip and shaking her head. She had a name, she was certain of it. But she didn't know what it was. Panic rose in her chest, but it settled quickly.

That didn't feel right, she thought. *I should be damn nervous.*

"What the hell is going on here?" she asked.

The two doctors exchanged a glance.

"As I said, you suffered a head injury."

"Why do I feel..." She searched for the words.

"What? What is it that you feel?"

"Nothing, that's what. I feel nothing." As she spoke, she started feeling angry. "I might not remember my name or anything else, but I do remember feeling things."

The anger flared and then subsided.

"See? There. It just happened again. My feelings just went away."

"What do you mean your feelings went away?"

"I was getting scared. Then I was getting mad. Both times it just went away. For no reason. I should be scared right now. I may not remember my name, but I do remember that someone who can't remember anything should be scared out of their wits."

The doctor locked eyes with the man behind the desk and gave him a curt nod.

"I'm sure it's a side effect of the medication we've given you. Your injuries were extensive. You've been unconscious for the better part of three weeks, and you've undergone several surgeries."

The fear returned, but it was dulled somehow.

"What injuries? What surgeries? I want to know what happened to me."

"Sommers," the doctor said, and the other man in the white coat reached for an IV bag that was hanging by her bedside.

"What's my name?" she asked. The fear was growing now, getting stronger. The man unhooked the tube from the IV bag and connected it to a different bag.

"What's that?" she asked. "What are you giving me? Why won't you answer my questions?"

The man at the desk inhaled sharply, and she stared at him. He was so familiar. "Who are you?" she asked, her voice rising. "Why won't you tell me my name?" Now her heart was racing, and she was breaking out in a sweat.

"Scale it back, Lieutenant Smith," Dr. Walsh said.

She felt the fear and anger subside almost instantly.

"It'll only be a couple more seconds," the other doctor said.

As her body calmed, and she slipped into unconsciousness, she heard Dr. Walsh saying, "We've got more work to do."

- 10 -

Strange Characters

Cambridge, Massachusetts

Wendy spent three hours at Yoshi's bedside, but he barely stirred the entire time she sat there. The days that followed were filled with settling her parents' estate and organizing their personal belongings. Wendy packed some of their things but couldn't bring herself to donate or throw any of it away. So she decided she'd come back at the end of summer. Surely she'd feel stronger by then.

Before she knew it, she was hugging Aunt Louise at the airport and saying good-bye. When she got home, exhausted, she crumpled into bed and overslept, which was radically out of character for her. She scurried to get ready for work, but everything took longer than normal. Even the simple act of brushing her teeth seemed to take an eternity.

On her way to the lab, Wendy sent Devin a text message: "How's Yoshi doing?"

It took Devin a few minutes to respond. Wendy's car was pulling into the parking lot when his message finally came through: "Not so good. It'll be soon."

Wendy frowned and responded: "Anything I can do? For him or you?"

There was a long pause before he finally answered: "Thanks. I don't think there's anything anyone can do."

She replied, "I'll keep you both in my thoughts. Stay in touch."

"Thanks."

She walked into the lab almost an hour late. Eli was already there, hunched over his computer with his earbuds cranked up. She could hear the buzz of his loud music from across the room.

She set her things down by her desk, approached his workstation, and tapped him on the shoulder.

Eli almost jumped out of his chair. He snapped off his earbuds as he turned around, and then he exhaled and collected himself.

"Sorry," Wendy said. "I didn't mean to startle you." She offered him a sad smile. "Thanks for the flowers."

There were dark circles under her eyes, and she was noticeably thinner. Her shirt was wrinkled, and her hair was slightly unkempt. This wasn't the Wendy Watson he knew.

Eli stood up, feeling uncomfortable. He had been dreading this moment, anxious that he'd say or do the wrong thing.

"I'm so sorry about your parents" came blurting out of his mouth, not quite as he had rehearsed. He opened his arms awkwardly and hugged her.

"I'm sorry I didn't call you right away," Wendy said over his shoulder. "The first week—both weeks have been a nightmare."

Eli's nose tingled, and he felt tears welling up in his eyes. He couldn't imagine what Wendy was going through. Wendy rubbed Eli's back as though she were the one consoling him.

The hug ended just as awkwardly as it had started.

"Listen, before we get started today, I was wondering if

you could help me with something," she said.

"Sure, anything."

Wendy pulled a silver capsule out of her pocket and held it up.

"This was my dad's," she said. She pulled on it, and a cap came off, revealing a connector. "It's a hard drive. There's some kind of security system built into it. I was wondering if you could override it."

Eli took the drive and examined it. With everyone using the cloud, hard drives were a rarity. They were mostly used by governments, large corporations, and people who were paranoid. Eli owned several, but none looked like this. It was smooth and rounded, smaller than his thumb. There were no markings on it.

"Your dad worked for the military, right?"

"Yeah, but this has nothing to do with that."

"Do you know what's on it?"

Wendy shook her head no.

"Then how do you know it's not related to his work?"

"My dad had a strict rule about bringing his work home. He'd stay at the lab overnight before he'd bring anything back to the house." Wendy eyed the drive. "I found this in the treehouse he built for me when I was a kid. Plus it was addressed to a friend of his who is not in the military. There's no way this has anything to do with his work." Wendy chewed on her bottom lip.

Eli stared at her. "You have a treehouse?"

She nodded.

"So if this was addressed to his friend, then wouldn't it belong to the friend?"

Wendy shook her head. "It wasn't really addressed to him. It said, 'Yoshi: safekeeping.' I went to see Yoshi. I was going to show it to him and ask him about it, but he's not well." She shook her head, and her eyes fell to the floor. "Actually he's very sick. Dying." Eli's eyes went wide when she said that. "There was nobody else…" She shrugged. "I finally opened it."

"Hm," Eli said. He scratched at his temple. "All right, let's take a look."

He sat down at his workstation, and Wendy rolled her chair over so she could watch. He set the drive beside his keyboard and opened a web browser.

"What are you doing?" Wendy pointed at the drive. "You need to plug that in."

"First I want to find out what company made this drive." It bothered him that there were no markings on it. He knew every hardware manufacturer on the planet and owned devices made by almost all of them. He'd never encountered one that didn't plaster its brand name on all of its products.

"Does it matter?"

Eli shrugged. "It might."

They sat in silence as he perused manufacturers and models. Eli searched locally and then internationally, but nothing matched.

"Maybe it's some obscure brand," Wendy said. "It could even be custom made. My dad is—was—an engineer."

"Or maybe it's military issue," Eli said. "You said he didn't bring his work home, but maybe he used one of their drives for personal stuff."

Wendy shook her head. "That doesn't sound like something my father would do. Like I said, he was meticulous about his work, and he would never steal military property."

Eli nodded. Wendy was a stickler for rules and procedures. She must have gotten it from her father.

"Maybe there was an emergency. You said it was marked 'safekeeping.'"

Wendy thought about what Devin Ford had said: her dad had been acting so unusual that Yoshi hadn't wanted to burden him with the sad news of his illness. But she didn't say anything about that.

"Did you try to open it?" Eli asked.

"Yes. I couldn't even see the files."

"When was this?"

"I've been trying for almost a week."

"And a SWAT team hasn't shown up?"

She shook her head.

"All right." Eli plugged the drive into a small box below his smartscreen. He opened a directory, found the drive, and clicked on it. Nothing happened. Eli opened a command prompt and entered a command, but still nothing happened. Then he tried another and another. It wasn't until he'd made more than a dozen attempts that his screen filled with code and strange characters. He scanned it briefly and then yanked the drive out of the console.

"What happened?" Wendy said.

"I don't know if it's military or not, but this is some of the most sophisticated code I've ever seen." Eli put the cap back on the drive. "We shouldn't do this here."

"Why not?"

"We need a machine that's off the grid. I know you said it's not related to your father's work, but just in case—if there's the smallest chance—it's better to be safe than sorry."

Wendy nodded as she took the drive and cradled it in her palm. "Off the grid? You mean a computer without tracers?"

"Yeah, which means an older computer that was manufactured before tracers became standard and that is not and has never been connected to the net. Completely off grid." Eli fidgeted in his seat and then reached for a yo-yo that was sitting on his desk. An imported, black-market machine would work too, but he didn't say anything about that.

"So where do we get a machine that's off the grid?"

"I have a few at my apartment." Eli shrugged. "I can take the drive home with me and see what I can do from there." He rolled the yo-yo around in his palm.

Wendy frowned. She didn't want to let the drive out of her sight. "Would it be OK if I came with you?"

That caught Eli off guard. He wasn't used to having guests at his apartment.

Wendy leaned forward. "I'll get us a pizza."

"Yes, of course," Eli said, suddenly realizing how rude he was being. "I mean, you don't have to get a pizza, but of course you can come over."

"Right after work?" she asked.

"Sounds good."

That seemed to cheer her up a little. She rolled back to her desk and tucked the drive into her bag. From his workstation, Eli gave her a nervous glance. He unwound the yo-yo without looking at it and straightened the string, and then he turned toward his desk.

Wendy tapped her wristcom and sent over two weeks' worth of messages to her smartscreen. When she saw the long list of unread messages, she groaned.

Eli snapped his head around. "Is everything all right?"

She closed her eyes and nodded. "I turned off all my work-related notifications almost two weeks ago." She sighed and glanced at him. "There are several hundred messages in my inbox."

Eli blinked. She was about to find the letter from the grant committee. It was much too soon for that. She wasn't ready. He tried to think of a way to divert her.

"You don't have to go through them now," he said, trying to sound casual. "If you want, I can sort them for you, get rid of the junk, prioritize the other stuff."

She cracked a slight grin and gave him a sideways glance before turning her focus back to the screen. "Thanks, but I think I can handle—"

Wendy froze, her eyes locked on the screen, and Eli knew

she'd seen the message—the message he'd read several days ago when he'd hacked into the grant committee's system.

"The letter from the grant committee came," she whispered.

"Oh yeah?" Eli said, trying to act nonchalant. He had no idea how Wendy would react if she knew he'd already accessed the message, but he was certain she would not approve.

Wendy swallowed and clicked on the e-mail. Eli gritted his teeth and braced himself.

It took only a second or two for her to react. Her face fell, and her shoulders dropped. She stared at the screen in a daze for a long moment.

"We didn't get it," she said.

Eli's eyes darted around the lab. He had no idea what to say, but words came tumbling out of his mouth anyway. "It's OK. We'll figure something out."

She didn't respond. Eli cringed, expecting her to break out in sobs at any second. He had no idea what to do if that happened.

But instead she sighed and stood up.

"Let's go," she said.

"Where are we going?"

"To your apartment."

Eli glanced at the ancient clock on the wall. It was one of those old analog schoolroom clocks, a hundred-year-old hand-me-down from some classroom on the campus. "It's not even ten o'clock," he said.

Wendy shrugged and collected her things. "I don't feel like being here."

Eli frowned. Wendy had never missed a day—had never missed a minute—of work until her parents had died two weeks earlier. She lived for her work. She worked nights and weekends. She worked when she was sick. Now she was blowing it off to look at the files on her father's hard drive?

"Don't we need to…"

"What?"

"I don't know. Get some work done?"

She shook her head. "Not today. I've been gone for two weeks. One more day won't make any difference. Come on. Get your stuff."

"OK," Eli said.

* * *

Wendy stood in the entryway of Eli's apartment, looking around. The kitchen was small but orderly and fitted with the latest smart appliances—a rarity in apartments. Beyond, there was a cherry dining table with matching chairs.

"You can set your things on one of the chairs," Eli said. "I guess I need to get a coat rack."

Wendy gave him an odd look as she set her bag on a chair.

The living area was cozy, with a plush red couch and a faux-leather recliner. A coffee table sat in front of the couch, and there was a low, wide bowl sitting on it. Wendy bent over the bowl, examining it. There was a thick stick wrapped with some kind of fabric sitting inside the bowl.

"It's a Tibetan singing bowl," Eli said. He picked up the stick and rubbed it around the rim of the bowl, and a lovely chime rang throughout the apartment.

"That's pretty," Wendy said.

"I never play it. I just like how it looks."

Against the opposite wall was a massive smartscreen, below which sat an entertainment panel. A low, wide gaming chair was positioned in front of the screen. Speakers were artfully placed throughout the room, interspersed with artwork. And there were several plants—some hanging, some on stands. One was more of a tree than a plant—it took up an entire corner of the room.

"Your place is really nice," Wendy said, looking around at everything. It looked like it had been decorated by an interior designer, and everything from the furniture to the electronics was clearly top of the line. She did a double take when she saw the dombot charging in the corner and wondered how he afforded such expensive things on his lab salary, but asking would have been rude, so she bit her tongue.

"Thanks," he said. "Let's go take a look at that drive."

Wendy retrieved the drive from her bag and followed Eli into his office. It was as posh as the rest of the apartment.

"Impressive," Wendy said, eyeing the computer array on the wraparound desk.

"Thanks. Here, have a seat." Eli pulled a stool out from underneath a high worktable along the far wall, and Wendy sat down.

Eli opened the closet, which was lined with shelves and neatly stocked with an assortment of electronics, some of which looked quite old.

"You collect old electronics?" Wendy asked.

"Yeah, it's kind of a neurosis I have," he said absentmindedly as he looked through the contents of the shelves.

"My dad did too," she said. Eli could hear the sorrow in her voice. "Not stuff like that. He collected antique record players, vintage microscopes, old clocks, those kinds of things."

"That's pretty cool," Eli said. He pulled a laptop from the top shelf and then picked up a small handheld solar generator from the floor of the closet. He set the laptop on the worktable.

"Wow, that thing looks ancient," she said, eyeing the laptop.

"It's about fifty years old," he replied as he connected the generator to the laptop.

"What's that for?" Wendy said, nodding at the generator.

"I like to keep off-grid devices completely off-grid. That includes plugging them into the walls."

Wendy smirked. "You think data can be transmitted through the electrical system?"

Eli stared at her for a moment without answering. Then he opened the laptop and powered it up.

Within seconds he'd brought the strange code back up on the screen. Then he hunched his shoulders, bent over the keyboard, and furiously hacked at it. Wendy watched in amazement. It was one of the things she liked about working with him; once he committed to a project, he threw himself into it, much like she did.

His fingers flew over the keys, and the code scrolled up and down the screen.

Suddenly he stopped.

"This isn't possible," Eli said. "This thing holds five petabytes of data."

"Five petabytes? On that little thing? No way."

"That's what I'm saying: no way. A device this small can't hold that much data, but it says here that's how much it holds. And it's eighty-five percent full."

"It must be a glitch," Wendy said.

"Maybe." But Eli didn't think so. The code was more sophisticated than he'd first thought. He knew some of it was military, but there were other bits that were almost alien.

"Look at this," he said, tilting the laptop so she could see better. "See those strange characters?"

Wendy examined the screen and nodded. "What is that? Is it some other language?"

Eli shrugged. "I have no idea. I've never seen anything like it before." Then he pulled the laptop toward himself and went back to work.

Wendy retrieved her e-glasses from her bag and conducted

research on languages, alphabets, and hieroglyphics but found nothing resembling the strange characters Eli had shown her. Then she moved on to researching metal briefcases like the one she'd found in her treehouse. There was a vintage Halliburton that came close, but it wasn't a match for the mysterious case that was tucked beneath her bed.

A couple of hours after they had started, Eli's stomach rumbled, and he sat up, his face turning red.

"I'm hungry, too," Wendy said, pulling off her e-glasses. "I'll go get us some lunch."

She returned half an hour later with a pizza and found Eli pacing his office while throwing his yo-yo. It wasn't a good sign. He did that only when he was nervous or stumped.

Eli led Wendy back to the dining table. He was nitpicky about things like that. Wendy almost always ate at her desk, working as she nibbled on her meal, but Eli would take his food to the small counter in the kitchenette, clear off a wide space, and eat away from his work.

After lunch, Eli went back to work, and Wendy resumed looking at languages and alphabets from around the world and throughout history. Eventually dinnertime came, and they ate the rest of the pizza quickly and quietly. After that, the hours sped by, and suddenly it was after midnight. Eli still hadn't made any real headway.

"Oh well, it was worth a try," she said, taking the drive from Eli.

"I'm not done," Eli said. "I'm going to crack that thing."

Wendy raised her brow at the determination in his voice.

"OK, but we need to get back to work tomorrow." She glanced at the time. "Or today, rather."

Eli nodded. "I can take the drive—" But he paused when he saw the look on Wendy's face. She wasn't letting that thing out of her sight. "We can come back here after work tomorrow," he said.

"OK," she said with a cheerful smile, but her eyes were full of disappointment.

- 11 -

Father Figure

Dojo
Swenson, Colorado

He was too far out. The waves were rising, reaching higher each time they rolled onto the beach. He ducked under the water and held his breath. When he came up for a gulp of air, a wave engulfed him, and his surfboard slipped from his fingers. He flailed his arms, reaching for the board, but the raging water swept it away. He choked, spewing water out of his lungs and treading furiously. The shore—which way was the shore?

"Mr. Ford?"

Something gripped his shoulder. It was green and sinewy. Its head was enormous, and its eyes were red and mean. It opened its mouth, revealing sharp, jagged teeth. He opened his mouth to scream, but no sound came out. The beast roared.

"Mr. Ford?"

Devin lurched and blinked his eyes open.

"Mr. Ford..."

He looked around the room and found the source of the voice. It was the hospice worker. Darla? No, Carla. She had the afternoon shift.

"Devin." He rubbed his eyes. "Call me Devin."

"Oh right. Yes. Devin," she said.

"Good afternoon, my boy." That wasn't Carla. It was a man's voice.

Devin straightened his back and blinked at Yoshi. The old man was sitting upright, smiling at him. His eyes were alert, and he looked healthy.

"Sensei," Devin whispered.

"Devin, may I have a word?" Carla said.

He opened his mouth to protest, but she cut him off.

"It will only take a moment. He'll be fine."

"Go on, son," Yoshi said, smiling.

Devin rose and followed Carla out of the room and down the short corridor that led to the kitchen, where she filled a glass with water and handed it to him.

"Thanks," he said, realizing his mouth was dry. He lifted the glass to his lips and gulped. When he was done, she took the glass from his hand and refilled it.

"Do you want to sit down?" she said as she set the glass on the counter in front of him.

"No, I'm good," he said. "Yoshi...he looks..."

"He looks better." She took a deep breath. "But he's not."

"Oh." Devin's eyes fell, and he stared into the water glass.

"Are you sure you don't want to sit down?"

Devin shook his head.

"Very well. Mr. Ford—Devin. I wanted to prepare you—"

"Isn't that what you've been doing? Isn't that what hospice does?"

She stepped forward and rested a hand on his arm. "The truth is nothing can prepare you, not really. Some deaths are more shocking than others. Some are more painful than others. You can be prepared but never fully prepared."

He nodded. "I understand."

"Sometimes, shortly before they pass, a person will become alert. Yoshi has been alert for…" She glanced at her wristcom. "Almost twenty minutes now. It can be misleading. He's been talking, eating, and it seems like he's getting better."

"But he's not."

"No, he's not. In fact it usually means the end is near."

"How long?"

"A day or two."

A day or two. That wasn't much time. Not much time at all. And then what? He would be alone again, just like the twelve-year-old boy he'd been when Yoshi had opened his doors and welcomed Devin into his life.

"Devin, maybe you should sit down."

He snapped himself out of it. "What? No. I'm fine. Was that all?"

"Yes," she said. "Is there anything I can do? Anything you need?"

She couldn't give him what he needed. "No, thanks," he said. "I'm going to go sit with him now."

She nodded. "I'll give you some privacy, but I'll be here in case you need me."

"Thanks," he said, and then he left the kitchen and headed back to the bedroom.

Yoshi was sitting up, looking around the room when Devin entered.

"Devin, my boy," Yoshi said. He held out his arm.

Devin stepped to Yoshi's bedside and knelt beside him.

"Did she tell you I'll be gone soon?" Yoshi said.

Devin gulped and nodded as he gripped Yoshi's hand and swallowed the sob that was rising in his throat.

"I would tell you not to grieve for me, but grief is inevitable. I have known it many times throughout my life." He gave Devin a sorrowful look. "Grieve then, but try to find some comfort in knowing that I will be free." His eyes twinkled. "I will know the great unknown."

Devin felt a tear escape, and he bowed his head. Yoshi rested his hand on Devin's shoulder and held him for a moment. When Devin had recomposed himself, he lifted his face.

Yoshi cupped Devin's cheek. "Devin," he said.

"Yes, Sensei?"

"How long has it been?"

"How long since what?"

"Since we last spoke."

"You've been asleep for several days. Before that, you were slipping in and out for weeks."

"Weeks…" Yoshi's eyes drifted away from Devin's. Then he gathered himself and met Devin's eyes again.

"Tell me, has Tom been by?"

Devin swallowed and looked away. "Tom?"

"Yes, Tom Watson. Does he know about my illness?"

Devin shook his head. "No."

Yoshi sat up a little straighter. "I must see him right away."

Devin's body tensed.

"Please, Devin, I need to see him immediately. You must call him."

Devin stared into Yoshi's eyes. "He's—it's not possible."

Yoshi looked confused. "Not possible?"

Devin searched for something to say.

"Son, whatever it is you have to say, say it. I'm already dying. It's not going to kill me."

Devin nodded. "OK. You're right. It's just—" He took a deep breath and gripped Yoshi's hand even tighter. "Tom Watson is dead."

The old man's eyes went wide. "Dead?"

Devin nodded.

"Are you sure?"

"Yes, I'm sure."

"Oh dear." Yoshi brought his hands up to his face. His eyes darted around. "Oh how terrible. Poor Claudia. And Wendy..."

Devin cleared his throat. "Claudia was killed too."

Yoshi's eyes widened again. "Killed? How? Tell me what happened."

"They were killed in a car accident."

Yoshi was silent and thoughtful as he took in what Devin was saying. Then he raised his eyes to Devin's. His voice was strong and firm. "Tom Watson was not killed in a car accident."

Devin was about to respond, to confirm that it had been a car accident, but Yoshi continued.

"When did you learn about this?"

"His daughter, Wendy, came by a few weeks ago."

"Came by here?"

Devin nodded.

"What did she say?"

Devin shrugged. "She was wondering why you weren't at the funeral. They...Tom and his family didn't know you were ill. She sat with you for hours, but you were asleep, and when you roused, you were groggy."

"Young Wendy..." Yoshi said, his eyes wandering off.

"She's not so young," Devin said. "She's a full-grown woman."

"I trained her, you know," Yoshi said. "For six years. She was a tiny little thing. One of my best students. She never knew her own strength. I could see it, the strength and courage inside her. So much like her father. But she was never tested."

Devin looked at Yoshi questioningly.

"You were tested at a very young age," Yoshi said, patting Devin's hand. "Your mother left. Your father, he was cruel. Wendy had a good life. Smart, caring parents. Her life was never difficult. I mean beyond the ordinary difficulties that each of us faces."

"I'm not sure what you mean…"

Yoshi sighed. "There are ordinary hardships in life. Getting up and facing each day. Money. Difficult relationships. But at some point, we all face something that seems insurmountable. A deep pain, a tragedy, something that makes us feel alone, like the world will never be right again. You experienced that as a young child."

"Yeah, I guess I did."

Yoshi was quiet for a moment, and his eyes filled with tears. "I can't believe Tom Watson is dead. Tell me, have you been teaching my classes at the base?"

Devin nodded.

"And Colonel Kell is still in charge there?"

"As of last week, yes."

"Hm." Yoshi scratched his head. "Young Wendy Watson," he muttered. "She's an engineer like her father, very resourceful."

"She was pretty upset," Devin said.

"Yes, of course. She would be distraught. But she is strong. Capable." His eyes drifted across the room. "Tom would not want to involve her."

"Involve her in what?"

But Yoshi wasn't listening. He was lost in thought. "But there is nobody else. And she—we're all in danger anyway. It has to be her. God help me."

He raised his eyes and looked at Devin. "Devin, I need you to do something for me."

"Anything," Devin said. He was confused by Yoshi's remarks but didn't want to push the old man for fear it would strain him.

"The old family lamp on my dresser, I need you to unplug it."

Devin stared at Yoshi.

"I may be dying, but I haven't gone mad. Please, Devin."

Devin nodded and rose to his feet.

"Close and lock the door first," Yoshi said.

Devin paused and turned to stare at him again.

"Be quiet about it," Yoshi whispered.

Devin approached the door, closed it quietly, and then clicked the lock. He went to the dresser, where Yoshi's old family lamp sat. It had been there for as long as Devin could remember, an antique relic from Japan, more than a hundred years old. Devin bent down and unplugged it.

"Good, now remove the base. Just twist it, as if you were removing the lid from a jar."

Devin looked from the lamp to Yoshi and back at the lamp.

"Go ahead," Yoshi said, waving his hand at Devin.

Devin picked up the lamp and twisted the base. It was screwed on tight. He twisted harder and the base came apart from the body of the lamp, and something clattered to the surface of the dresser.

Yoshi's eyes went wide. "Shh," he whispered and nodded at the object that had fallen out of the lamp. "Now put the lamp back together, and bring that to me."

Devin stared at the object. It was a round, flat metallic disk covered with strange engravings. He reassembled the lamp. Then he picked up the disk and carried it to Yoshi.

"It's a medallion," Yoshi said, taking the disk and turning it over in his hands. "That's what Tom called it."

"Tom gave that to you?"

"Yes, he gave it to me the last time I saw him, for safekeeping. And now I must give it to you." He held out the disk, and Devin stared at it for a moment before taking it.

"This is important, my boy. You must guard this with your life. And in a few days when I am gone…"

Devin's hand clenched when Yoshi said that.

"In a few days, when I am gone, you must get this to Wendy Watson. You must not show it to anyone else, and you must not tell anyone about it. Give it to her, and tell her the code word is *treehouse*."

"Treehouse?"

Yoshi nodded. "Treehouse," he said. "She'll know what to do."

He handed the medallion to Devin and then lay back on his pillows with a deep breath.

Devin examined the medallion and then tucked it into his pocket.

Yoshi's hand reached out and gripped Devin's arm. "You must hide it in a safe place."

Devin nodded. "I'll take care of it." He knelt at Yoshi's bedside. The old man was growing tired again. His eyes had been bright and alert just a moment ago, but now they were glossy, and his lids were drooping.

"I know you will," he said.

Devin clutched Yoshi's hand, and Yoshi squeezed back.

"Sensei, I..." But what was there to say?

"It's all right. Death comes upon all of us."

Devin looked into Yoshi's eyes and nodded.

"Many times I have said you are like a son to me."

"And you are like a father to me," Devin said.

"But you are not like a son," Yoshi said. "You are my son."

Devin's eyes burned.

"I love you," Yoshi said.

"I love you, too." Devin said.

- 12 -

Legal Advice

Shermer Apartments
Cambridge, Massachusetts

Wendy brought the flash drive to Eli's house almost every night after work and on weekends. She sat in his office with him, conducting research for the BIM and looking for ways to raise money to keep the lab open. Sometimes she felt like giving up—on the BIM, the flash drive, the mysterious silver case, everything, but Eli insisted they would figure it all out.

It was a Friday night, three weeks after she had asked him to open the files on the flash drive. Wendy had dozed off in front of Eli's home theater, watching a documentary about emerging hologram technologies.

"Wendy! Wake up!" Eli shook her shoulder. "Wake up. I did it. I cracked the code. We're in."

Wendy blinked her eyes open.

"Get up. You've got to see this." Eli could barely contain his excitement.

She sat upright when she realized what was happening.

"Come on." He rushed off to his den, and Wendy

followed, yawning and stretching as she made her way through Eli's apartment.

"We're going to need coffee," he said as Wendy slid into a chair, blinking and rubbing her eyes. He tapped his wristcom and ordered the dombot to make two espressos. "It'll be ready in five minutes," he said, vaguely chastising himself because he'd meant to exchange the dombot for a better model but hadn't gotten around to it yet.

"What time is it?" she asked.

"A little after ten thirty."

"It feels a lot later. What did you find?"

Eli positioned the laptop so it was directly between them. He took a deep breath.

"There are two partitions: USAF and TW-LOG. I know you said this has nothing to do with your dad's work, but I'm thinking USAF is the United States Air Force. TW—your father's initials. That must be his journal or something."

Wendy sighed. "Turn it off," she said.

"What? Why?"

She shook her head. "It says right there: USAF. I'm not going to poke around in top-secret military files. And I'm definitely not going to drag you into it."

Eli should have known. Of course Wendy wouldn't want to risk it. She was a stickler for following rules. But she was chewing her lip. That meant something was bothering her.

"But we've spent weeks trying to get into this thing. Aren't you the least bit curious?"

"Of course I'm curious. You have no idea how much this bothers me."

"OK, so don't look at the USAF partition. Aren't you at least going to read your dad's log?"

"I'm guessing that's his scientific journal. It's probably a record of the work he did for them. You know—the top-secret work he did."

Eli refrained from rolling his eyes. "What are you going to do with it?" he asked, folding his arms across his chest.

"I guess I should turn it in." Wendy rubbed her eyes and blinked at the screen.

"To them? The air force?"

"It obviously belongs to them."

Eli frowned. He was dying to look through those files. He didn't care about rules. He paid his taxes. As far as he was concerned, the military worked for him.

Wendy looked thoughtful. "Maybe I could ask Jane. She's a lawyer. She'll know what the law says about this kind of thing and whether there's a way around it."

Eli's wristcom beeped, and he glanced at it. "Espresso's ready," he said, getting to his feet. "Come on. You can call Jane from the dining room."

Eli stopped suddenly as they made their way down the hallway, and Wendy almost ran into him.

"Don't tell her what it's about," Eli said.

She gave him a funny look, and he recited, word for word, the notice that appeared whenever anyone booted up a brand new device, including comunits. "All communications are recorded and stored for an indefinite period and are subject to search and seizure..."

"Right..." Wendy said. It wasn't a good idea to discuss the drive over the phone.

"Just tell her to come over here." He nodded at the cups on the dining table, and they both sat down.

"Tell her to come here? It's kind of late." Wendy blew on her coffee.

"Doesn't hurt to ask," Eli said, glancing sideways at his dombot as it retreated to its charging station.

Wendy sipped her espresso and glanced at the time. "She is a night owl," Wendy said. "All right, I'll see if she's available."

Jane arrived half an hour later, looking hip in a green modular minidress. Her thick black hair was twisted into a loose knot at the nape of her neck, and she wore a thin, beaded headband wrapped twice around her forehead.

She hugged Wendy and asked how she was doing and then turned to Eli and held out her hand, offering to shake. She didn't notice the awkward look on Wendy's face. Eli was opposed to handshaking, due to the germs and all. As he stood there, staring at her outstretched hand, Jane studied him. He was overweight—not to the point of being unhealthy, but definitely on the brink. A mop of brown curls protruded from his head. But his features were handsome. He had light blue eyes set above a strong, straight nose, and his lips were full.

Jane finally pulled her hand back and shrugged.

"It's good to meet you in person finally," she said, looking at Eli and then glancing around his apartment. "Nice digs. Got anything to drink?"

Eli was about to offer her a beer when Wendy interrupted.

"Maybe you could have a drink after I explain what's going on."

"Sure, no problem," Jane said.

"Let's show her," Eli said.

He led the way to his office, where Wendy showed Jane the contents of the flash drive and explained what Eli had discovered.

"What's up with this equipment?" Jane said. "It's so twentieth century."

Wendy shrugged.

"This is all twenty-first century technology," Eli said. Then he added, "barely."

"All righty," Jane said. "You want legal advice?" She stared at the screen and then at Wendy. "I need you to tell me everything. How you came into possession of this, what you've done with it, how much of it you've accessed." She sniffed the air. "Is that coffee I smell?"

"Double espresso?" Eli asked.

"Sounds divine," Jane said.

Eli punched it into his wristcom. "It'll be ready in five minutes."

"Excellent," Jane smiled at Eli and then glanced around the room. She went to the wraparound desk and rolled the executive chair over to the worktable. Eli opened his mouth to protest. He didn't like anyone sitting in his chair, but then he clamped his mouth shut because he didn't want to be an asshole either.

The desk chair was lower than the other chairs, but she eased into it and then waved her hand at the two stools, indicating that Eli and Wendy should sit down. They did.

"All right, go. Tell me everything."

Wendy relayed her story. She told Jane about how she'd gone to the treehouse and where she'd found the flash drive. When she mentioned the silver case, Eli interrupted her.

"You never said anything about a silver case," he said.

She shrugged. "I don't know what's in it, and I can't open it."

"But they were together—the drive and the case?" Jane asked, and Wendy nodded.

"A metal case that you can't open and a flash drive containing air force files. I'm thinking they're related," Eli said.

"Let's not speculate," Jane said. "Please continue."

Wendy was staring at Jane with a look of fascination. "You really change when you're in lawyer mode."

Jane smiled. "Thanks. Now go on."

Wendy opened her mouth to continue her story, but she was interrupted by Eli's phone beeping.

"Your espresso's done," he said to Jane.

She stared at him expectantly until he said, "It's already been served in the dining room." Except it came out more like a question than a statement.

Jane threw Wendy a questioning look, but Wendy just shrugged.

Moments later they were seated around the dining table. Jane took a sip of espresso and hissed, "Hot" before setting it down. "Now can I hear the rest of this story?" she said.

When Wendy had finished relaying everything that had happened, Jane nodded, staring into her espresso.

"Do you still have the envelope the drive was in?"

Wendy nodded.

"Eli, do you think the flash drive tracks user activity? Can someone determine how many times the files have been accessed and by whom, that kind of thing?"

"I can't say for sure but probably. I would put something like that on it if it were mine."

"And we can assume it's loaded with military tracers," Jane added as she lifted the espresso and blew on it. She took a small sip and then a bigger one. She set the cup down.

"As your lawyer I advise you to turn the drive over to the air force immediately. You haven't broken any laws. You had valid reason to assume the contents of the drive belonged to your father, not the US military."

They sat there quietly, Jane sipping her espresso and Eli and Wendy absorbing what she'd just said.

Eli couldn't contain himself any longer. The words burst out before he could think about what he was saying. "I disagree. I mean, maybe I'm being selfish. I admit I'm dying to see what's on that drive. I'd like Wendy to take it apart and figure out how someone built a drive that small that holds five petabytes of data. Maybe I'm just curious. But my gut's telling me that turning that thing over to the government is the wrong move."

When he was done, he was surprised to see Wendy and Jane both staring at him with their mouths agape.

"Someone had to say it," he said. "I know you're both thinking the same thing."

"That's not quite what I was thinking," Jane said. "As your lawyer I'm supposed to protect your best interests."

"Technically you're not my lawyer," he said. "And you think turning it over is in Wendy's best interest? Tell me something about all this doesn't stink."

"Do you have any idea how much trouble you could both get in for messing around with confidential military property? The fact that you called me suggests you do."

"We'll get in trouble only if we get caught," Eli retorted.

Wendy was squeezing her temples. "OK, you guys, that's enough. We have to turn it over. I don't want to go prison for treason." She glanced at Eli. "And I'm not going to drag you into this any more than I already have."

"I'm a willing participant!" Eli said.

Wendy muttered something, but it was inaudible.

"What?" Jane and Eli said simultaneously.

"The rules are there for a reason," she repeated, and then she sighed. "That's what my dad always used to say."

"You say it all the time too," Jane said, and Eli had to refrain from laughing. He wasn't the only one who'd noticed it.

"Then your father must have had a good reason for breaking the rules," Eli said. "I mean, he left that stuff in your treehouse. That's not exactly a secure location."

Jane raised her brow and stared into her espresso. Wendy glared at her. "Jane, what do you think I should do?"

Jane shrugged and put on her best innocent expression. "I already advised you."

"You advised me as my lawyer. Now I'm asking you as my friend. What would you do?"

Jane looked into Wendy's eyes for a long time before she

answered.

"You've always been one to follow the rules. I guess you got that from your dad. Me, I live on the edge. And this one," she nodded at Eli. "You'd never guess it, but apparently he does too. You need to do what feels right in your heart. That's my advice, as a friend."

Wendy stood up and started pacing. "Why did my father leave that flash drive in my treehouse when it goes against everything he believed in, everything he ever taught me? Why?"

"Obviously he was hiding it," Eli said.

Wendy stopped pacing and faced him. "From whom?" she asked.

Jane was the one who answered. "The logical answer is that he was hiding it from the air force. Otherwise he would have left it on the base where he worked."

They all fell silent again. Wendy paced the length of the dining area and then stopped suddenly and turned to face her friends.

"I want to know why my father suddenly decided not to follow the rules. I want to know what was bothering him so badly that his best friend couldn't tell him he was dying."

She glared at both of them, daring them to argue with her. "I want to see what's on that drive."

Before Jane or Eli could utter a word in response, Wendy turned and fled to Eli's office.

Jane and Eli stared at each other in shock, and then both of them scrambled out of their chairs and followed Wendy.

She was already at the laptop, tapping frantically on the keys when Eli and Jane entered the room.

"Eli, this thing is locked. How do I open the files on the drive?"

Eli stepped forward to help, but Jane held out her hand and blocked him. "Hold on a sec," she said.

"Wendy, once you see those files, you can't unsee them. If

you do this, there's no turning back."

Wendy stared at Jane for a moment before she responded. "Eli, hurry up. I want to do this before I lose my nerve."

Jane dropped her hand and gave Eli a nod. He stepped to the worktable and keyed in a command. The partitions and directories appeared.

Wendy scanned the screen. "Where should I start?"

Eli and Jane answered simultaneously.

"Your father's logs," Jane said.

"USAF," Eli said.

Wendy turned to look at the two of them.

"You should both leave," she said.

Eli snorted. "Leave? This is my apartment."

"I'm not going anywhere," Jane said. She climbed onto one of the stools. "I'm going to help."

"Me too," Eli said. "I can go through the USAF partition while you two read the log." He caught Jane staring at him through narrowed eyes.

"I think it would be a good idea to stay out of the USAF files for now," Jane said. Now it was Eli's turn to glare at her. "It's nothing personal," she said. "Just taking a precaution. Let's see what's in the log first and then decide how much further to dig."

Wendy nodded. "I agree."

"OK, so I'll help you read the logs," Eli said.

"How are we all going to read them at the same time?" Wendy asked, eyeing the old laptop.

"I'll show you," Eli said.

He brought out an old tablet, a computer monitor, two keyboards, and a touchpad. Within minutes he had set up two additional workstations.

"We can all access the drive," he said. "The laptop is functioning as a server with these other devices accessing its network."

Wendy was already scrolling through the files in the log. "It looks like my dad created a log for every year going back to when he was at the university. Where should we start?" Wendy asked.

"At the beginning, I guess," Jane said. Wendy nodded in agreement and sorted the files by date. "I'll take the first year. Jane, you take the second year—"

"And I'll take year three," Eli said.

Wendy nodded and clicked open the first file.

They worked in silence for more than an hour. Tom Watson had made the first entry just before he'd started college. It gave a brief recount of his five years in the air force before he had been injured and honorably discharged. His commanding officer had pulled some strings and gotten him on a fast track to getting accepted to university with an undeclared major. His passion for science blossomed during his first semester, and a year later he'd declared a major in engineering.

Very little in the journal was personal—a line here about going home to Texas for the holidays, a line there about how his friends took him out to celebrate his birthday, a short paragraph about the lovely woman he'd met. She was a journalism major.

Wendy's eyes welled up with tears. "Mom," she whispered.

Tom Watson had just graduated from university when Wendy noted the time. "It's getting late," she said. "Maybe we should go. I don't want to keep you guys up all night with this."

"I'm fine," Eli said without taking his eyes off the monitor.

Jane glanced at her screen. "How much data did you say this thing holds?"

"Five petabytes," Eli said.

"How long do you think it's going to take us to get through all of it?"

Eli peeled his eyes away from his work and stared at her over the monitors. "A long time. Weeks, probably."

"That's only if we look at everything," Wendy said. "Right now we just need to see if there's anything in here that will tell us why my dad hid this stuff in my treehouse."

Jane glanced at the clock on her wristcom. It was just after midnight. "I don't know about you guys, but I'm not tired. I could go for another hour or two," she said. "But Wendy, I think maybe we should change our tactics. You keep working from the beginning. Eli, you jump ahead to the middle years. I'll start at the end and work my way backward."

"Good idea," Wendy said.

Jane opened the last file in the directory and leaned forward to read it. A moment later she sat upright. The sudden motion caused Wendy and Eli to look up from their work.

"I think I found something," Jane said.

- 13 -

The Candidate

Carter Air Force Base
Swenson, Colorado

Major Nichols was in his office watching a hockey game on his com when he received a message from Colonel Kell: "Get Lt. Smith and come to my office. Now."

Nichols rolled his eyes. "Yeah, I'm going to go all the way downstairs and *get* Lieutenant Smith to bring him to your office, which is right next door to where I'm sitting," he said to nobody in particular. Then his eyes darted to the wall on his right. It seemed like Kell had eyes and ears everywhere. Nichols shook his head and forwarded the message to Smith, adding, "Stop by my office first."

He flipped back to the game and growled as his team missed an easy goal. A minute later there was a knock at his door. He used his com to open it.

Smith strolled in. "Something wrong?" he asked.

Nichols shrugged. "It's Kell. Something's always wrong. You watching the game?"

"What game?"

"Hockey."

Smith shook his head. "I don't watch sports. Besides, some of us have work to do."

Nichols eyed him and then put his com in sleep mode. "All right, let's go see what he wants," he said.

A minute later Nichols found himself sitting on a rickety metal folding chair beside Smith. They were both facing Colonel Kell, who was sitting behind his desk, flipping through the daily reports.

Kell finally put his e-tablet down and looked from Nichols to Smith.

"I understand there's a delay with the prototype," Kell said to Smith.

Nichols relaxed. This didn't involve him. He didn't work directly on the MOTH project, or any project for that matter, since he was neither a scientist nor an engineer. At one time he'd been a pilot, but he'd put those days behind him and traded up for the drudgery of doing Kell's dirty work. Which meant he was here strictly as an observer.

"I wouldn't call it a delay," Smith said. "Her—its—" He leaned forward. "I'm sorry sir, what pronoun are we supposed to use?"

"We need to give it a name," Nichols said. "Dr. Walsh said—"

"I don't give a damn what Walsh said. I don't care if you say *it* or *her*. Call it *the prototype* and just give me a status update."

"Well, sir, we're fine-tuning its—her—whatever. We're still adjusting access to memories and ability to experience emotion."

He paused. Kell raised his eyebrows and nodded, so Smith continued.

"Human memories and emotions are highly complex. Science doesn't fully understand how either operates, so it's been a game of trial and error. We make an adjustment to the emotions, and they flare up. We make another adjustment, and total insensitivity sets in, and I mean physical insensitivity, as in she—or it—or whatever—can't feel a pin prick on the finger. Another adjustment, and childhood memories return. Scale that back and she—it—no, she. Sorry sir, neither *she* nor *it* seems quite right. Anyway, scale that back, and knowledge is lost—knowledge of something as basic as, say, how to tie one's shoes."

Kell blew a breath of air out of his nose and gave the e-tablet a little shove across his desk. "Dr. Walsh could have said as much."

Nichols had to refrain from snickering. He had read Walsh's report and concluded exactly what Smith had just described. It wasn't elementary reading, but it wasn't written at the PhD level either. He had figured out months ago that Kell hated to read. Kell had a tendency to scan text rather than read it. And when he did read, his eyes wandered off the page, and he ended up staring into space. That's why he always demanded verbal status reports.

"And you're working on this directly?"

"Sort of. I wrote a program that Doctors Walsh and Sommers can use to toggle the prototype's memories and emotions, so mostly they're experimenting with the settings, trying to find the right balance, but I'm called in every few days to update the program."

"And what are you working on the rest of the time?" Kell said.

"Housekeeping, mostly. Cleaning up the code, working with Lieutenant Tripp on the documentation."

"The code isn't clean?"

"The code is fine. Cleaning it up just means we're aligning, spacing, making it look pretty, which is to say we're making it clearer and easier to work with."

"I see," Kell said. "What else is on your desk?"

Smith shrugged and leaned back in his chair. "I'm still monitoring the security software I wrote for the MOTH facility. I spend about thirty minutes a day on that."

"I assume it's in good working order?"

"It sure is."

"Nichols, are the barracks ready?"

Nichols almost jumped out of his chair. He hadn't expected Kell to call on him.

"The barracks?"

"Yes, housing for our first batch of MOTHs?"

"Sir, we haven't even started testing the prototype. We don't need the barracks for another—"

"Just answer the question."

"No, sir. But I can get started right away."

"I want to see a detailed project plan, including a line-item budget, by the end of the week. And keep it simple."

"Yes, sir," Nichols said.

Kell shifted in his chair as he crossed his legs and leaned back. He was studying Smith's face. "Would you be able to move faster if you had more funding?" he said.

Nichols raised his eyebrow. Kell was prodding Smith, which meant he was considering Smith for the inner circle.

But Smith shook his head. "Not for this phase of the project. We're in unchartered territory. There's no other way to do it but trial and error."

Wrong answer, Nichols thought.

Kell nodded and frowned, his eyes never leaving Smith's face.

"Permission to speak freely, sir?" Smith said.

Kell's brow went up again, and Nichols could see he was intrigued. Nichols was curious too and found himself angling toward Smith to see what he was about to say.

"Permission granted," Kell said.

"Well, as long as we're on the subject of funding…I'm probably just blowing steam, but I wish the AI team had a heartier budget," Smith said. "And I'm not one to complain, but we're all—the entire base is—underfunded."

It was an interesting remark, all things considered. Kell stared at Smith without blinking.

"Is your equipment insufficient for you to do your job?"

Smith shook his head. "No, it's not that. I can do my job on a Commodore 64." He snickered and caught Kell's blank stare. Smith shot a glance at Nichols. "That's a joke. I can't really…"

He shook his head and turned back to Kell. "Anyway, the equipment is sufficient, but it's outdated. I can do my job with what I've got, but I could do it faster if the equipment were newer. Not this business with emotions and memories but almost everything else could be going faster."

"You've been ahead of schedule for the duration of Project MOTH," Kell said. "I'm not worried about your speed."

Smith licked his lips. "Sorry for being blunt, sir, but doesn't it piss you off?"

Kell looked surprised. "Doesn't what piss me off?"

"The scraps we get from the federal budget."

Nichols and Kell stared at Lieutenant Smith, who waved his arm and looked around Kell's office. "I mean look at this. Florescent lights, metal folding chairs, that desk must be at least a hundred years old."

Nichols exchanged a look with Kell. Most of the furniture and equipment in the MOTH compound were old castoffs, so the air force would never notice they were missing. And while MOTH had a decent budget, they had to be selective when they moved large items in and out, and they had to be careful to make it look like they were operating within a standard military budget, which was always tight these days.

"We're the military. We're here to protect the nation, and

we're sitting on metal folding chairs, sir. Meanwhile prison inmates are sleeping on feather mattresses." Smith leaned back in his chair and folded his arms across his chest. "It just doesn't seem right."

Kell smiled, and Nichols had to stifle a laugh. Kell always looked like he was in pain when he was smiling. Like it actually hurt him to express joy.

"The tight budget affects us all," Kell said. "Most of our department heads have complained about it."

Smith nodded, his gaze fixed on the ground. Then he raised his eyes to meet Kell's. "It's those damn politicians," he said. "Throwing all that money away on schools, social programs, and health care. Meanwhile the military is struggling."

Nichols eyed Smith. He was saying all the right things, and suddenly Nichols wasn't sure he wanted Smith to get an invitation to join the inner circle.

Kell closed his eyes and nodded. "Go on," he said.

"Oh, sure," Smith said. "We built the WASP, and we're on the verge of producing the world's first supersoldier, but we're doing it on a bootstrap budget. The WASP should have flown twenty years ago. If we weren't underfunded, maybe it wouldn't have crashed. And the supersoldiers should have had their boots on the ground a decade ago." He shook his head. "We move slow, we've got poor working conditions, and— well, let's face it, the pay could be better too." He laughed and then stopped abruptly. "Sorry, sir; I didn't mean to rant."

"No apology necessary." A chilly grin made its way to Kell's lips.

You've done it now, Nichols thought. *Now you can suffer with the rest of us.*

"For what it's worth, I agree with you," Kell said. "Every other sector of government is enjoying progress, and we're decades behind where we should be."

Smith nodded and grinned. "If the voters would get their heads screwed on straight, maybe they would elect some leaders who would set things right. If there were a war or even a major conflict, they'd wake up damn fast."

Kell nodded and let his eyes wander off. "By then it would probably be too late," he said, watching Smith closely in his peripheral vision.

Smith's eyes were fixed on Kell. "Somebody should do something about it," he said. "But I guess our hands are tied."

Kell nodded and straightened his posture. "We'll just have to see what happens. Change is inevitable." He tried to smile at Smith, but the expression he made looked more like he had just sucked on a lemon wedge. "I'm glad we had this little chat."

"Thanks, sir. I appreciate it."

"You're dismissed."

Smith got to his feet and headed back out to the catwalk. Nichols and Kell stared at each other as they listened to the sound of Smith's shoes tapping against the metal walkway and fading into the distance.

Kell tapped his com, and the door slid shut. He leaned back in his chair.

"I think he's a candidate," Kell said, and Nichols nodded in agreement even though he had doubts about Smith. There was something about the man that didn't sit right with him.

"I'll send the recommendation up the chain," Kell said.

- 14 -

The Journal

Shermer Apartments
Cambridge, Massachusetts

"Listen to this," Jane said. "It's from the day before the accident." She read aloud from Tom Watson's personal log:

> I found a bug in my car, and I'm being followed. I can only hope it's someone from the Pentagon, but I suspect Kell and Nichols are behind it. I sent the evidence to DC almost a week ago. Why haven't the authorities acted on it?
>
> I'm trying to maintain some semblance of normalcy, but I am growing concerned for my safety.
>
> Upon completing this entry, I am going dark. I will hide my sensitive materials, including this journal, until this blows over. I have taken precautionary measures in case something happens to me.

The room was quiet as all three of them processed this information.

"He was concerned for his safety." Wendy's voice was shaking. "And he died the next day."

"The implications of that are serious," Jane said.

"Who are Kell and Nichols?" Eli asked.

"Colonel Kell is the commander of the base where my father worked," Wendy said. "I don't know anyone named Nichols."

"Kell? He spoke at your parents' funeral, didn't he? Pasty old guy with no lips?" Jane asked.

Wendy nodded.

"Why would the commander of the base be following your dad?" Eli asked.

Jane answered, "Your father turned evidence over to the Pentagon a week before he died. I'm guessing it had something do with this Kell guy. He must have been engaged in illegal activities."

"Maybe there's more information in the journal," Eli said.

Wendy stared at him and then looked at Jane. Jane gave her a nod, and Wendy opened the previous file in the directory. She scanned the first few lines and gasped.

"What?" Jane and Eli answered simultaneously.

"This one was written about a week earlier," Wendy said.

My suspicions have been confirmed: I have obtained proof that Kell and Nichols are engaging in treasonous activities. I believe they are organizing a coup d'etat.

They discussed taking control of the government and restoring the military, and they reviewed the precautions they were taking in order to continue their work undetected. It seems their work is centered around something called Project MOTH. They did not discuss the specifics of the project, but they did say it would be instrumental in taking control of the military budget.

I have sent the evidence I collected to my contact at the Pentagon.

P.S. I made a horrible blunder while I was recording their conversation. Nichols was pacing around Kell's office, and he almost walked into me. I managed to get out of his way, but I bumped into a chair. They both heard the noise and were suspicious, but I'm hoping they'll dismiss it. If they find out I've discovered what they're doing—if they find out about my "personal research"—I will be in grave danger.

Wendy gripped the sides of her head and buried her face in her hands. "I can't believe this is happening."

"I'm confused," Eli said. "How did your dad sit in on a conversation—and move around the room—without their knowledge?"

Jane opened and read the previous file and then the one before that and the one before that. She read aloud, going back until Tom Watson first suspected something was amiss with his commander, but there wasn't much more information. Three months before he and his wife were killed, Tom Watson had realized that the commander of the base, Colonel Kell, was engaging in unusual activities. He had been shocked when it became clear that Kell and his right-hand man, Nichols, were traitors.

It was late. Wendy's eyes were bloodshot, and she felt like she was reliving the two weeks right after her parents' death, except this time it was even more horrific.

"Murder? Treason? I can't believe this," she whispered.

Jane wrapped an arm around Wendy's shoulders. "We're going to figure this out."

"How about another round of espresso?" Eli said.

Five minutes later they were back at Eli's dining table, drinking espresso. Wendy stared into her cup with a blank look on her face.

"I don't understand why we can't drink this in the den," Jane said.

Eli sighed. "The den is for working. The dining room is for eating and drinking."

"Even during an emergency?"

"Always."

"He does it at work too," Wendy said, rubbing her temples.

"It's not healthy to eat while you work," Eli pointed out. "Besides, it's good to take a break. That's when you come up with your best ideas."

Jane frowned. "Speak for yourself." She stared at Eli as she sipped her coffee. "All right, let's review," she said. "Your dad collected evidence implicating these guys, Kell and Nichols, in organizing a coup. His journal indicated it was some kind of recording, and he sent it to the Pentagon about six weeks ago."

"Do you think they killed my parents?" Wendy's voice was small. She sounded like a child.

Jane and Eli exchanged a glance.

"If your father was correct—if those men were committing treason and found out he knew about it—then I think it's a possibility," Jane said.

"Why didn't the Pentagon act on it?" Eli said.

"That's a good question," Jane said.

"We should turn my dad's journal over to the authorities," Wendy said.

Jane shook her head. "Your dad's journal isn't evidence. And he's not here for them to question. All they'd do is question Kell and Nichols, and we'd be right back where we started, except you'd possibly be facing trial for accessing those files, and we'll have lost everything your father left behind."

"Then what do we do?"

"Whatever evidence your dad collected, we need to find it." Jane said.

"It's got to be an audio or video file," Eli said. "It's probably sitting on that hard drive."

"Or in the silver case," Wendy said.

"Or somewhere else altogether," Jane added.

Wendy rubbed her eyes and pressed her fingers into her temples. "This really isn't a job for the three of us," she said.

"Who else is going to do it?" Eli said.

Jane set her coffee on the table. "Eli, we need to figure out if Mr. Watson saved the recording he made to that drive, and we need to do it quickly."

"I should be able to narrow it down. Pull out any files that were saved to the drive in the designated time frame and isolate audio and video files."

Jane turned to Wendy. "You need to figure out a way to open that silver case you found."

"I'll take it to the lab and see what I can do," Wendy said. "At the very least, I should be able to find out what it's made from."

Jane glanced at her wristcom. "It's pretty late. Maybe we should all get some rest."

"We just drank espresso," Eli said.

"I can't sleep," Wendy said.

"Eli, how long will it take you to sort out those files?"

"Not long," he said. "An hour, tops."

"OK, let's check out those files. After that we'll call it a night. Tomorrow we'll meet at the lab and look at that case."

"You guys don't need to come to the lab," Wendy said.

"We'll be there," Jane said, "Right, Eli?"

"Right? Oh yeah, right. We'll be there."

As they walked back to Eli's office, Jane nudged him. "What is it?" she whispered.

"What's what?"

"You seem distracted."

A few paces ahead, Wendy disappeared into the office. Eli paused and turned to Jane. "I'd like to find out how Wendy's dad was in an office with those guys but they couldn't see him."

Jane looked thoughtful. "Yeah, me too."

* * *

Back in Eli's office, they settled into their previous positions. Wendy and Jane continued reading Tom Watson's logs, and Eli ran a program he'd written to isolate files on the drive that matched his criterion.

"It's done," he said.

"Really?" Jane said, looking up from her reading. "You said it would take an hour."

"I said an hour, tops."

"What did you find?" Wendy said.

"There's nothing here that matches. The only files your father added to this drive in the three weeks before he died were the journals you already read. I'm sorry. "

Wendy closed her eyes and took a deep breath. "Did you check the other partition?" she asked.

Eli nodded. "I searched the entire drive."

"Then we're back at square one," Jane said, standing up. "We need to regroup. We still have the silver case, and it's possible Mr. Watson stored whatever evidence he collected in there."

"And we have the other files on the drive," Eli said. "The recording he made might not be on the drive, but maybe there's something else."

"Like what?" Jane said.

"Like whatever made Wendy's dad suspicious in the first place."

"You're talking about the USAF partition," Wendy said.

Eli shrugged. Jane stared at him, and Wendy rubbed her eyes.

"Let's discuss it tomorrow," Jane said. "Wendy, you need to get some rest."

* * *

The next morning Wendy brought bagels and cream cheese to the lab. Jane brought orange juice and coffee, and Eli contributed a box of donuts.

Wendy set the silver case on the long workbench in the center of the lab. "This is it," she said, picking up a coffee.

Eli reached for it, but Jane beat him to the punch.

"May I?" she said.

"Go ahead." Wendy was rifling through the cabinets, gathering supplies.

Jane pulled the case toward her and examined it. "It's just like you said: no hinges or clasps; the seam is barely visible."

Eli leaned over and ran his hand over the surface of the case. "Did you notice this depression?" he said.

Wendy set an armful of equipment on the table. "What?"

"I only noticed it because of the angle of the light. Run your hand over it."

She reached across the table and let her palm skim the surface of the case. "That's weird," she said.

Eli shrugged, and Jane felt the irregularity. "Maybe it got damaged."

"I don't think so," Eli said, rubbing his hand over the depression. "It's a perfect circle."

Wendy slid the case across the worktable and positioned it in front of herself.

"Anything I can do to help?" Jane asked.

"No, you guys sit tight while I run these tests."

Jane took a seat across from Wendy and reached for a bagel. Eli loaded a plate with a few donuts, grabbed an orange juice, and headed for the counter in the kitchenette.

"We don't have cooties," Jane said as Eli sat on the stool at the counter.

"He won't eat over here," Wendy said.

"Don't you think eating in a scientific laboratory is a bad idea?" Eli asked.

Wendy shrugged. "I don't eat near the BIM."

"Speaking of your glorious machine, I'm going to go check it out. I haven't seen it since last year," Jane said, sliding off her chair and heading for the BIM.

Wendy nodded but didn't say anything. She eyed Eli and wondered if he'd told anyone that they hadn't gotten the grant. She hadn't.

She powered up the alloy scanner and set it on top of the case; then she leaned back in her chair and sipped her coffee as she watched the scanner roll across the surface. When it was done, she clicked for a reading, and her jaw dropped. She quickly clamped it shut.

"I should have known," she said.

"What is it?" Eli said.

"Unknown compound." She sighed.

"What about the components?"

"It identified a few of them," she said. "I'll have to run it through the university's database—"

"You can't do that," Eli said as Jane returned from the BIM room.

"Can't do what?" Jane asked.

"Hello? Ever heard of tracers? The NSA? If this is made of

materials unique to the military, they'll pick it right up."

Wendy sighed. "I don't really care what it's made of. But there has to be a way to open this thing."

Her com dinged and she glanced at it. It was a message from Devin. She clicked and read it: "He's gone."

Wendy swallowed hard as the color drained from her face.

"What is it?" Jane asked. "What's wrong?"

Eli looked up from his keyboard. Over the past few weeks, he'd seen Wendy exhausted, frail, and defeated. But it looked like she had sunk to a new depth. It was like she wasn't even inhabiting her body anymore, she looked so distant.

"It's a message from Devin," Wendy said. "Sensei—he's dead."

"Sensei?" Eli asked. "Like a martial arts instructor?"

"Oh, honey," Jane said. She got up, went to Wendy, and wrapped her arms around her.

"He was Mr. Watson's best friend." Jane said to Eli. "Wendy studied judo with him when she was little."

"You know judo?" Eli said.

Wendy didn't answer, but Jane nodded.

"Is his name Yoshi?" Eli asked, recalling the name on the envelope in which Wendy had found the flash drive.

Jane nodded and gave Wendy a squeeze before letting go and stepping back.

Eli swallowed hard and wished he knew what to say. He jammed his hand into his pocket and gripped his yo-yo.

Wendy blinked a couple of times. She read the message again and then responded: "I'm so sorry. He was one of the most caring and wisest people I've ever known. I'll be there soon. Let me know if there's anything I can do for you."

She stared at the screen in a daze until Devin's final reply came through: "Thanks."

Eli and Jane were silent, waiting for a cue from Wendy. She stared at her wristcom for a long moment and then said, "I'll have to go back to Colorado right away for the funeral." She shook her head and squeezed her temples. "I can't believe this is happening."

Jane stepped forward and rubbed Wendy's shoulder. *"Mi amiga,"* she whispered.

Wendy shook her head. She was too tired, too tapped out, to cry. She felt spent, like every ounce of emotion had been drained from her body. She tried to process what had happened, to her parents and now Yoshi, but she couldn't. Her mind could not come to grips with it. She knew they were dead, but it all seemed so far away. She needed to latch on to something closer, something immediate. Something she could work with.

"I'll try to get a flight out tomorrow," she said.

"How long do you think you'll be gone?" Eli asked, and Jane glared at him.

"I don't know," Wendy said. "I guess it depends on when the funeral is. I don't think Devin really has anyone. I'd like to help him if he'll let me. That's what my father would want. He and Yoshi were like brothers."

But she was haunted by the fact that her father and Yoshi hadn't seen much of each other in the months before her father's death. Whatever had happened at the base had wrenched her father out of his normal routine, even pulled him away from his dearest friend.

"We'll have to put all this on hold for a while," she said, surveying the equipment spread out on the table.

"We don't have to put it on hold. I can keep working on the case, start going through the files on the drive. There must be something there that would help us," Eli said, trying to contain the desperation in his voice. He really wanted to dig into those USAF files.

Wendy shook her head, but Jane reached out and gripped Wendy's arm. "He's right," she said. "I'm sorry, Wen. If this were just about your father, I'd go along with putting it on hold. But if your father was right and these men are planning a coup, then national security is at stake."

"So you think I should stay here?"

Jane shook her head.

"I can make a copy of the drive," Eli said. "I'll keep it at my place, and you can take the other one with you to Colorado. It's probably a good idea to keep a backup anyway."

Jane nodded. "I agree with him."

Wendy thought about it and nodded. "OK. I don't like it, but you're right. We shouldn't stop working on this."

"Do you want me to go with you?" Jane asked.

"No. My aunt will be there, and so will Devin."

"You hardly know him," Eli pointed out.

Wendy shrugged. "We spent a few hours together when I went to see Yoshi, and we've kept in touch since then." She eyed her wristcom. "Besides, Jane's going to Mexico in a few days."

"You're going to Mexico?" Eli asked. This was the first he'd heard about it.

"I'm on sabbatical," she said. "I'm supposed to go to Mexico for a few weeks to train activists, but…"

"I don't want you canceling your trip on account of all this," Wendy said. "I know how much it means to you."

"It doesn't mean more than you or your family, or national security, for that matter. It's not a big deal. I'll make it up next year."

Eli blinked. Jane was full of surprises. "Are you some kind of political activist?" he said.

Jane flashed him a big smile and nodded. "Sure am. You wanna go hug a tree with me sometime?"

"And you travel around, training people?"

"I teach them the art of civil disobedience," she said.

Eli stared at her.

"I teach them about the laws regarding the right to assemble, the right to free speech, and the penalties for civil disobedience.

"Like protests and stuff like that?" Eli said.

"Yeah, stuff like that," Jane said.

"Why don't you just do the training online? The Internet is the best place for activism."

Jane turned to Wendy. "I thought you said he wasn't political?"

Wendy just shrugged.

"I do vote, you know," Eli said.

"Well, that's a start," Jane said.

- 15 -

Roswell

Shermer Apartments
Cambridge, Massachusetts

Jane was sitting at the worktable in Eli's apartment, going through the files on the USAF partition. She had endured boring videos of staff meetings, listened to dull audio recordings of scientific jargon she couldn't make any sense of, and perused a variety of documents ranging from blueprints to jumbled equations. She marked anything that was heavy on the science so Wendy could take a look later. She had just opened a spec sheet on military goggles when her wristcom beeped.

"It's an e-mail from Wendy," Jane said, tapping her com. She frowned and read the message. "The funeral's tomorrow, and she's thinking about staying a few more days. She has some business to attend to regarding her parents' estate."

"Yeah, I got the same e-mail," Eli said without looking up. He was at his desk on the other side of his home office, and Jane wasn't sure whether he was checking his personal e-mail or working on something related to the drive.

"I'm worried about her," Jane said.

Eli was absorbed in his work and didn't hear her.

"Hello? Yoo-hoo, over here. I'm talking to you."

Eli looked around and then looked at Jane. "Huh?"

"I'm worried about Wendy," she said.

"Yeah, so am I," he said.

"What are you working on over there?"

"Some of the files on the hard drive have extensions I've never seen. I'm trying to figure out which programs will open them."

Jane leaned over, glanced at Eli's screen, and saw a search engine on his monitor. "Do you think that's a good idea?" she asked.

"What?"

"Searching the net for information on those file extensions. If they're as secretive as that flash drive, you might attract unwanted attention."

"Nah," Eli said. "This system can't be tracked."

As soon as the words were out of his mouth, his eyes went wide, and his mouth fell open. All net activity was tracked. Sure, you could use an old device that wasn't connected to the net, but as soon as you went online, everything you did was recorded, and everyone knew it. He glanced at Jane out of the corner of his eye. She was staring at him intently.

"Are you using bli-fi?" she said.

"Uh." Eli looked around helplessly.

"You're really paranoid, aren't you?" she said.

Eli scratched his head and reached for a yo-yo.

Jane shrugged. "It's not a big deal. I use it too."

"You use bli-fi?"

"I'm a lawyer. I have to use bli-fi to protect my clients' confidentiality. Damn thing cost a fortune."

"I didn't know lawyers used them," he said, "but I guess it makes sense."

"Well, they're not illegal, you know."

"True, but they're pretty hard to get in the States," Eli said.

"All the lawyers know where to get them. Custom built. The guy I bought it from was wearing a ten-thousand-dollar suit. I can only imagine the markup."

"Custom built?" Eli shook his head. "I bet they import them from India—"

"That's illegal. There's an embargo on Indian bli-fi units."

"So they route them through China. Make a few modifications and resell them to upscale clients like yourself." Eli tossed his yo-yo and wondered why he hadn't thought of it.

"It's lowdown, but that's business," Jane said, returning to the files she had been scrolling through. The next one was a video. She clicked it and braced herself for utter boredom and confusion, but this video was different. It was black and white, and the footage had been filmed in a rural location at night. Army officers were milling around the wreckage of some kind of crash. It looked like a plane crash, but the lighting was poor, and it was hard to see. She watched as two medics passed in front of the camera, carrying a stretcher with a body on it.

"Holy shit!" she screamed.

Eli nearly flew out of his chair. "What? What is it?"

"I think you'd better come look at this."

"Did you find the evidence?"

Jane's face had paled, and her mouth was hanging open. She shook her head.

"This better be good," Eli said, rising from his chair and trying to catch his breath. Jane's outburst had scared the hell out of him.

Jane rewound the video and let it play. When it got to the medics with the stretcher, Eli leaned in closer to the screen.

"Is that what I think it is?" Jane said, her voice shaking.

Eli grabbed the laptop and pulled it in front of him. He minimized the screen and checked the file.

"Roswell," he said. "You found a file named Roswell, and

you didn't say anything?"

"I...I didn't think about it."

"Look at the timestamp: 1947." He opened the video again, and they watched as two men in army uniforms zipped a body bag over the face of what had to be an alien.

"I knew it," Eli whispered.

"Do you think it's real?" Jane said.

Eli turned his head and glared at her. "I don't think the air force deals in science fiction."

Eli closed the video and looked at the directory. He clicked on the next folder and found the first video. There was no audio. An alien was strapped to an operating table. Men wearing surgical masks and scrubs were poking and prodding it. The alien squirmed and twitched. One of the doctors injected it with something.

"It looks terrified," Jane said. "What are they doing to it?"

They gave it another injection, and the alien's movements slowed.

"I think they're sedating it," Eli said.

The next video showed an alien carcass undergoing an autopsy.

"Gross," Jane said. She reached out and closed the file.

Eli frowned at her and scurried around the table to the other workstation. Within seconds he had opened the Roswell file. Jane was clicking through the subdirectories, trying to figure out how the information was organized.

"There's a whole folder of photographs," she said, scrolling through the images. "They look like...well...aliens."

"The grays," Eli said, scrolling through the files. "That's what people call them. And you're right. The descriptions of the Roswell aliens have been pretty spot-on."

The creatures had small, thin bodies with large, egg-shaped heads. Their lips were so thin, they were indistinguishable from the rest of their faces, and their eyes were large and dark.

Contrary to typical descriptions, the aliens had been clothed when they were discovered at the crash site.

"I just found a psychology profile on the alien's behavior," Jane said, but Eli was busy reading one of the discovery reports.

"They found four dead aliens. Two more were alive," he said.

Jane looked up at him. "What happened to them?"

Eli scanned the report. "They cut up two of the dead ones. A third was frozen." He clicked to another page. "One dead alien and one live alien seem to have disappeared," he said. "The record just sort of trails off after that."

Jane stared at him. She was at a loss for words.

"It could still be alive," Eli said. "The live one that disappeared."

"That was like a hundred years ago," Jane said.

"We don't know how long aliens live. We humans keep extending our life expectancy. How long do you think they live if they're so advanced they can actually travel from their world to ours?"

Jane thought about that.

"Maybe it's still out there, living in Roswell," Eli said.

"I certainly hope not," Jane said. "And what about the live one that didn't disappear?"

Eli shook his head. "This report doesn't say anything about that, but…" He clicked through the contents of the Roswell folder. "There are thousands of files here."

Jane stared at the screen in awe. "And why was Wendy's dad involved in this? He wasn't even born yet."

"Let me do a quick search," Eli said. He scanned the Roswell directory for Tom Watson's name. "Here it is. Project files." He scanned a few documents as Jane clicked through photos of the wreckage. She found herself fascinated by the shots of the aliens.

"Wow," Eli said. "Tom Watson was reverse engineering technology found on the aliens' ship. His first assignment was to develop an infrared film that was stuck to the alien ship's windows. It looks like he was using the technology to develop infrared goggles."

"Oh right, I saw something about goggles in a different folder," Jane said.

"Later he was working the tech into contact lenses. This stuff is very advanced," he said. "It hasn't hit the market yet."

Jane found the folder Eli was reviewing and read an inventory file. "Get this," she said. "Two months after the Roswell crash, the air force was established as a military branch separate from the army."

"Yeah, I knew that," Eli said.

Jane read a few paragraphs and then said, "Did you know that originally they weren't going to go through with it? It was just a proposal, but things were calm after World War II, so they were going to keep everything under the army."

"Let me guess: After Roswell, they realized they needed a branch dedicated to air and space?"

Jane nodded. "And there are plans here for something else…United States Space Force."

"Better late than never, I guess," Eli said.

"Yeah, I guess that's long overdue," Jane said.

"Hey," Eli said. "I found an inventory sheet. It looks like Wendy's dad put this together. The first column lists all items that were inventoried at the site of the crash. Each column after that shows an updated inventory. He consolidated decades' worth of inventories into one spreadsheet." He scanned the columns. "Damn," he whispered.

"What?"

"They lost a lot of stuff."

"How do you lose stuff like that?" Jane said.

Eli shrugged. Then he sat up and looked at Jane. "We've

just stumbled into the greatest discovery in the entire history of humanity. Aliens. Alien technology. There's no telling what we could do with it." He clicked through photos of the alien tech. "I'd love to get my hands on some of this stuff."

Jane ignored him. She was focused on her com, tapping and swiping the screen.

"What are you doing?" Eli said.

"Calling Wendy."

Eli's eyes went wide. "You can't talk about this over the phone!"

"Oh right," Jane said. She frowned and looked at the laptop. Then she started tapping and swiping her wristcom again.

"Now what are you doing?"

"Booking a flight," she said. "We need to bring this to Wendy."

"Now?"

"Well, like you said, we can't exactly call her and say, 'Hey Wen, we just found a bunch of videos and photos of aliens on your father's top-secret air force hard drive along with his confidential work in reverse engineering alien technology.'"

"So you're just going to hop on a plane—"

"No, *we're* going to hop on a plane. You're coming too. Go pack your things."

Eli shook his head. "I can't. I can't just pack up and leave right now."

"Why?"

"I don't do that. I don't…I don't travel," he said.

"Don't your parents live in California?"

"I go see them twice a year. I plan those trips for weeks."

Jane gave him a funny look. He was getting pretty worked up.

"OK," she said, her voice soft. "Don't worry about it. You stay here, keep working on that." She eyed the laptop. "I'll fly out and tell her what's happening." Jane stared at her wristcom. "We need a better way to communicate. It's ridiculous that I have to fly across the country just to tell her what's going on."

"You don't have to. It can wait."

"It can't wait. She would want to know. Wouldn't you?"

Eli sighed and stared at the floor. The he got up and headed for the door.

"Where are you going?" Jane said.

"I'm going to go pack," he said.

- 16 -

The Medallion

Swenson, Colorado

"Wendy, have you tried one of these kebabs? They're quite tasty."

Wendy shook her head. "No thanks, I'm not hungry."

Yoshi's funeral had brought back memories of her parents' funeral—memories that were still fresh, and Wendy had lost her appetite.

"I wish you'd eat something," Aunt Louise said. "I know how hard this is for you, but you've got to take care of yourself."

Wendy started to protest, but Aunt Louise was right. She reached for a veggie kebab and a napkin. "I'll try," she said.

Aunt Louise smiled and then turned away from the buffet table, scanning the crowd. "This is the biggest funeral I've ever been to."

"His students loved him," Wendy said, sniffing the kebob. It smelled zesty.

"It seems like the entire town has come to pay their respects, including all the folks from the base," Aunt Louise said. "But I don't see any of his family."

"Most of them are in Japan," Wendy said. "Devin is going to bring Yoshi's ashes home in a few weeks, and they'll have a service for him there."

"That will be difficult for Devin," Aunt Louise said, crumpling her napkin and tossing it in a nearby trashcan. "Going through all this twice."

Wendy nodded. She knew the feeling.

Yoshi's service had been so packed that people had spilled out into the street. But now the crowd was thinning out. Some of Yoshi's teenaged students were starting to clean up, gathering plates, folding and stacking chairs, and collecting tablecloths.

"We should get going," Wendy said. "I don't want to linger."

"Let's go pay our respects to Devin," Aunt Louise said. "He's grown into such an unusual man, don't you think?"

Wendy shrugged. "I don't know him that well."

"I've had dinner with him and Yoshi on several occasions," Aunt Louise said, "at your parents' house. He's quite somber, but I always liked him."

They gathered their things and approached the door, where Devin was receiving hugs and condolences as people left. He looked sad and uncomfortable. Wendy felt a tug on her heart as she remembered feeling the same way at her parents' funeral.

Aunt Louise reached out and grasped Devin's hand. "Tom always said Yoshi was like a brother to him. I'm so sorry for your loss."

Devin reached in his pocket and pulled out a card with a number handwritten on it. He gave it to Aunt Louise and then gripped her hands in his. "Tom was family, and that means you are, too. If you ever need anything, call me."

Aunt Louise glanced at the card. "Thank you," she said.

She gave his hands a squeeze, and then she stepped aside to wait for Wendy.

"He was a remarkable man." Wendy almost choked as she spoke. "He won't be forgotten."

"No, he won't," Devin said. "Thank you for coming."

"Listen, if you need anything...if you want to talk or just sit with someone, I'll be around for a few more days."

Devin gave her a sad smile. "Thanks, that means a lot."

"You know where my parents' house is?" she asked.

Devin nodded.

"Stop by if you want."

"OK, thanks."

Wendy reached out to give his arm a squeeze, and then she walked off with Aunt Louise.

* * *

An hour later Wendy's car turned into the long drive that led to her parents' house. The sun was setting, casting a pale pink glow across the western horizon. As the car rounded the last bend past a knot of trees, Wendy saw a strange car in the drive. It was a nondescript black sedan that she didn't recognize. She thought about the silver case tucked into the attic space above her closet, and her heart started to pound. What if someone had come looking for it? She was tempted to turn around and make a run for it, but she decided to check it out first.

"Slow to fifteen kilometers and drive around the house," she said. "And lock doors."

The locks clicked, and the car slowed and swerved gently to the right. Wendy entered 9-1-1 on her wristcom and readied herself to engage the call if she saw anything—or anyone—who didn't belong there.

As the front porch came into view, Wendy saw two

shadowy figures sitting on the steps. One of them stood up and waved. Wendy squinted against the light, and then she sighed. It was Jane.

She pulled the car into the garage and came around to the front of the house, where Eli and Jane were sitting amid a mess of luggage.

"You guys gave me a scare," she said. Her breath was still coming fast. "What are you doing here?"

Eli frowned and dropped his eyes to the ground. Jane stepped up and gave Wendy a hug. "Oh right, like you're not happy to see us."

Wendy cracked a weak smile. "I'm always happy to see you." She glanced at Eli. "Both of you. But why are you here?" She gasped. "Did you find something? The evidence?"

"No, we didn't find the evidence," Jane said. "But we found something else, and we thought you should see it."

Eli rose to his feet and brushed off his pants. There was dirt everywhere. Dirt, grass, trees. It was filthy. He'd never realized how much he appreciated urban living.

"OK, let's get inside, and you can tell me about it," Wendy said.

She helped them carry their luggage into the house. "How much did you two pack?" she said, rolling one of Jane's suitcases into the entryway. "And how long are you planning on staying?"

"We had to bring all the equipment," Eli said, stacking one of his boxes on top of another. He eyed Jane. "She insisted."

"And we'll stay as long as we need to," Jane said. "Or until you kick us out."

"But you're supposed to be on a plane to Mexico in a couple of days."

Jane shook her head. "I don't want to hear another word about Mexico. I already canceled."

Wendy opened her mouth to argue, but Jane held up her

hand and wagged a finger in Wendy's face. "Not another word." She looked around at the crates and suitcases. "Is that everything?"

"That's everything," Eli said, shoving his hands into his pockets. He gripped his yo-yo but didn't pull it out.

Wendy nodded and shut the front door. "Come on," she said. "Let's go in the kitchen, and I'll get you guys something to drink."

"I thought you'd never ask," Jane said with a big smile. She turned to Eli. "Got the tablet?"

"Oh, right," he said. He opened a small carryon satchel and retrieved a tablet, and then he followed Wendy and Jane into the kitchen.

"Sorry, it's stuffy in here," Wendy said as she went around opening windows. "I've been keeping it locked up pretty tight when I'm out." She pushed the back door open and clicked the screen door into place.

"Worried about our friends from the base?"

Wendy shrugged and took a pitcher of iced tea out of the fridge. "Kind of." She poured three glasses and brought them to the table, where Eli and Jane had already seated themselves.

"Iced tea?" Jane said, staring at the glass.

"Sorry, we're fresh out of booze," Wendy said.

Jane sighed. "Oh well. Bottoms up." She took a long drink.

"So what do you guys want to show me?" Wendy said.

Eli held out the tablet, and Wendy stared at the photograph he was showing her.

"What is that?" she said.

Instead of answering, he swiped the surface of the tablet, and a second photo appeared. He swiped again and again, scrolling through the images.

"May I?" she said, and he gingerly handed the tablet to her. She swiped through about a dozen more photos and then set the tablet on the table.

"Well?" Jane said.

"Aliens," Wendy said. "Those are aliens." She bit her bottom lip and stared into her iced tea.

"You don't seem surprised," Eli said with a confused look on his face.

"Well…"

Jane was eyeing Wendy suspiciously. "She already knew," Jane said.

Wendy shrugged. "Not really. I mean, kind of."

"You knew there were aliens, and you didn't say anything?" Eli said.

"Hello?" Jane said. "Military secret."

"I don't know much," Wendy said. "When I was sixteen, my boyfriend and I got in a fight at school. At lunchtime I left and came home."

Jane's eyes went wide. "You cut class?"

Wendy nodded. "It was the one and only time." She looked at Eli. His mouth was hanging open.

"Even I never cut class," he said.

"You're not a real rebel," Jane said to him. She turned to Wendy. "Go on, Wen."

"I came home and sat in my treehouse for a couple of hours. Around the time school would have been getting out, I headed for the house. My father was out there, near the tree line, talking on the phone. I don't remember exactly what he said—something about Roswell, aliens, and materials or something. I definitely got the gist of what was going on and what it meant. He would have been mortified if he knew I had overheard him, so I never said anything."

"You didn't tell him?" Jane said.

Wendy shook her head. "I thought it was some kind of punishment the universe was dishing out because I'd cut school. I kept the whole incident to myself."

"But surely over the years you've wondered…"

Wendy grinned. "Yeah, I've wondered." She picked up the tablet and swiped through a few of the photos. "If all this other stuff wasn't happening, I'd be a lot more excited."

"Well, it's all there," Eli said. "Photos, videos, reports, inventories. Everything about the Roswell crash, the aliens, your dad's work. He was reverse engineering their technology."

"Wow," Wendy said. The hint of a sparkle gleamed in her eyes, but then it passed. "But that doesn't have anything to do with the evidence or the coup, does it? Did you guys find a connection?"

Eli and Jane got quiet for a minute, and then Eli shook his head, and Jane said, "No."

"It's OK," Wendy said. She picked up the tablet and examined the photo. "I can understand why you guys wanted to come out here and show me this. But we're not supposed to be messing around with this stuff. We need to stay focused on finding out how Kell and that guy Nichols are planning to overthrow the government."

There was a loud crack outside, and all three of them stiffened. Wendy turned and looked at the windows. They were all open.

"Keep talking," she mouthed at Jane.

Jane nodded and said, "Anyway, the flight was a total drag. Do you know what they charge for a glass of wine?"

Wendy got up and crept to the kitchen door. In one swift movement, she snapped on the outdoor light and flung open the screen door. A few meters from the door, Wendy saw the back of a large, bulky figure with big hair.

"Devin?" she said.

He turned around with an uncomfortable look on his face. "Hey," he said.

Wendy stepped closer to him. "What are you doing here?" she said.

He looked surprised. "You said to stop by anytime. I didn't

realize you had company. I didn't want to interrupt."

He was stoic, but there was sorrow in his eyes. "You're not interrupting," Wendy said. "Please, come in."

"I don't want to intrude," he said.

"You're not intruding," Wendy said. She wondered how much he had heard. "You came all the way out here. At least have a glass of iced tea."

He nodded and then followed her inside. When Devin entered the kitchen, Eli's jaw dropped, and Jane eyed him from head to toe. She gave Wendy an approving nod and a thumbs-up, but Wendy ignored her.

"Devin, this is my friend, Jane," Wendy said.

"Nice to meet you," Devin said.

"The pleasure is all mine," Jane said, shaking Devin's hand.

Wendy gave her a look and led Devin to Eli. "And this is Eli, my friend and colleague."

Devin offered his hand to Eli.

"He doesn't shake," Jane said.

"Oh," Devin said. He pulled his hand back. "Well, it's nice to meet you."

"Right," Eli said. "I mean, you too."

The four of them were silent for a long, awkward moment.

"Well, Eli and I should really get settled in," Jane said suddenly. "I'll show him around the house?"

"Yeah, that would be great," Wendy said. "He can take the guest room, and you can stay with me in my room."

"Ooh, slumber party," Jane said with a wink. "I love it. Come on, Eli. Devin, it was nice meeting you."

Devin nodded. "You too."

Eli and Jane exited the kitchen and started hauling their luggage upstairs.

"Can I get you some iced tea?" Wendy said.

"Sure, that would be great."

She grabbed a glass, filled it, and handed it to him.

"How are you holding up?" she said.

He shrugged. "I'm holding up. Thanks for asking." He sipped the tea. "Did your aunt make this?"

"Yeah, how did you know?"

"I've been here for dinner with Yoshi a couple of times when your aunt was here. It's the best iced tea I've ever had. I'd recognize it anywhere."

Wendy nodded. "She spikes it with lemonade. My aunt mentioned that you'd had dinner here." It was strange to think of people she didn't know in her family home. Then she leaned against a chair and eyed Devin.

"So, how long were you standing out there on the porch before I saw you?"

Devin scratched at the back of his neck and raised his eyebrows. "Not long."

"Did you hear anything interesting?"

Devin studied her face. "I didn't mean to eavesdrop," he said. "That's not why I came here."

"I know," Wendy said. "But what did you hear?"

Devin shifted uncomfortably. "Something about aliens, a coup, and Colonel Kell and Major Nichols planning to overthrow the government."

"It's not what it sounds like," she said. She stared at the floor for a moment. "Actually, it's exactly what it sounds like, but—"

"You don't have to explain anything to me. That's not why I'm here. I came to give you something."

"Oh?"

He turned and scanned the open windows. "Can we go somewhere more private?" he asked.

She raised her brow at that. "Yeah, sure. Let's go to my father's study."

"Cool," Devin said. He followed Wendy out of the kitchen and down a short hall that led to a wood-paneled study.

Devin glanced around the room and then went to the window and closed the blinds.

Wendy watched him curiously but didn't say anything.

Devin came around the big mahogany desk. He placed his hands on its surface and bent over it. "Lift up the back of my shirt," he said.

"Excuse me?" Wendy said. "Are you—"

"I'm not trying to get fresh with you, I promise. Just lift up my shirt. I had to hide it in a safe place."

Wendy took a deep breath. "OK," she said. She stepped forward and pushed his shirt up. His skin was dark and smooth, and there was a large, square bandage right in the middle of his back.

"Are you hurt?" she asked.

"No. Take off the bandage," he said.

"I…uh. All right," she said.

She gently peeled the medical tape from his skin and immediately realized there was something hard and flat embedded in the gauze. When she had removed it, she turned the bandage over, revealing a round, metal disk in a clear plastic bag.

"What is this?" she asked.

Devin stood upright, pulled his shirt down, and turned around.

"I don't know," he said. "Your father gave this to Yoshi the last time they saw each other."

He leaned back against the desk and folded his arms over his chest. "A few days before he—" Devin's voice caught, and he swallowed hard. "A few days before he died, Yoshi became alert. He was just like his old self, smiling and talking and eating. It lasted only a couple of hours. He wanted to see your father right away. He insisted on it."

"Did you tell him what happened to my parents?"

Devin nodded. "I had to. He was devastated, very worried

about you."

Wendy's eyes filled with tears.

"He said your father gave him this medallion for safekeeping the last time they saw each other." He leaned forward and looked Wendy in the eye. "He told me to guard it with my life until I could give it to you."

Wendy was confused. She glanced at the disk. "I've never seen this before."

"Also he was torn up about giving it to you, like it was a last resort."

Wendy removed the medallion from the baggie and examined it. "My father gave this to him the last time they saw each other. How long ago was that?"

Devin shrugged. "About three months before your father passed away."

"That's right around the time my father found out about the coup."

"I don't know anything about a coup," Devin said. "But Yoshi said to tell you the code word is *treehouse*."

Wendy gasped, and her eyes went wide and lit up. She thrust the medallion into Devin's hand. "Hold this," she said. "I'll be right back." Then she scurried off.

She returned a few minutes later, carrying a big, black duffel bag, with Jane and Eli trailing behind.

Wendy set the bag on the floor and cleared a space on the desk. Then she opened the bag and removed the silver case, setting it gently on the desk.

"May I?" she said to Devin as she eyed the medallion.

He handed it to her, and she turned to face the others.

"I think this is a key," she said.

"It doesn't look like a key," Jane said.

"It fits the depression in the case," Eli said.

Wendy nodded. "Right. My father stopped working on his 'personal research' right around the time he found out what

Kell and Nichols were up to. That must have been when he hid the case in my treehouse and gave the medallion to Yoshi for safekeeping. I think this contains his 'personal research,' whatever that means. I can't figure out why he put it in quotes, like maybe it was a code for something else. And remember in his log he said he didn't want to think about what would happen if anyone got a hold of his 'personal research?'"

"Well, go on and open it, then," Jane said.

Wendy turned to the case and ran her fingers over its surface. "Wrong side," she said. She hefted the case, turned it over, and then checked for the depression. "There it is," she whispered. She pressed the medallion against the case, but nothing happened. She slid it around and jiggled the case.

"Try turning it over," Eli said.

Wendy glanced at him then at the case.

"Not the case, the disk," he said.

"Oh right."

She flipped the medallion over and pressed it against the side of the case.

There was a loud click, and the case popped open.

- 17 -

Stabilized

Carter Air Force Base
Swenson, Colorado

This time when she woke, she wasn't confused. She was prepared. She had no substantial memories. The fear and anger had abated. She felt nothing.

She could still recall the grass, the sand, the sea, and most of all, soaring through the sky, but the vagueness of these fleeting visions no longer troubled her.

Her eyes snapped open, and she sat up. No rousing, yawning, stretching, or blinking. It occurred to her that it was an unusual way to wake.

There was a man—Dr. Sommers—sitting in a chair near her bed, reading something on his e-glasses. Another man, the one who was familiar to her and who they called Lieutenant Smith, was in his usual position at the desk in the far corner.

Dr. Sommers removed his e-glasses and stared at her as he tapped his wristcom and spoke into it. "She's awake."

Dr. Walsh's tinny voice responded. "I'm on my way."

Dr. Sommers approached her and reached for a cup that

was sitting on the tray beside the bed.

"Thirsty?" he said.

She nodded and stared at Lieutenant Smith as Dr. Sommers brought the cup up to her face, as if she were a child. She took it from his hands and gave him a curt nod, as if to excuse him, and then she sipped from the straw. Water. It was lukewarm, and she was certain it was from the tap. She sucked down the entire cup.

"Very good," Sommers said, eyeing her carefully. He turned to Smith. "How do things look on your end?"

Lieutenant Smith gave Dr. Sommers a thumbs-up accompanied by a sarcastic smile.

She set the empty cup on the bedside tray and moved to get out of the bed. As she attempted to swing her legs around, she realized that her body was weak and stiff. It felt unfamiliar.

"Oh no, we'll need you stay there a while longer." Dr. Sommers pointed to an IV bag dangling behind her, and she realized she was connected to it by tubes that tapped into her veins.

"Dr. Walsh will be in to check on you momentarily. If all goes well, we might get you out of that bed today."

He beamed at her, flashing his bright, white teeth. She squinted and examined his eyes. They were not smiling. The smile on this man's mouth was false. Why? What purpose did he have in deceiving her? Maybe he was just being polite.

She glanced at Smith again, but he was bent over a black hard-shell case that was propped open on his desk. He tapped and swiped at it.

The door opened, and Dr. Walsh scurried in, his eyes alert. He looked over his shoulder, as if someone was following him, but nobody was there. He glanced up at the observation window. The room was empty. He sighed, and then he approached her.

"Hello there." He was slightly winded.

She stared at him.

"Hello?" he said again.

"Hello?" she said.

The two doctors exchanged a glance.

"Basic social skills compromised?" Sommers said.

"The tests will tell us more," Dr. Walsh answered. He entered a note on his tablet.

She blinked. *Social skills compromised.* That didn't sound good. Out of the corner of her eye, she saw Lieutenant Smith staring at her and frowning.

"How do you feel?" Dr. Walsh said.

"I am in good condition," she said. "I am ready to go."

"Oh?" he said. "Ready to go where?"

"Away from this bed." She eyed the door. "Beyond this room."

The two doctors looked at each other.

"Expression of desire?" Dr. Sommers said, throwing a hard look at Smith.

But Dr. Walsh focused on her. "You want to leave this room?" he said.

"I want to walk. Move."

"Ah yes, that's good. Very good." He nodded and tapped something on his tablet. To Dr. Sommers he said, "Standard physiological impulse." He turned back toward her. "Other than that, how do you feel?"

"I do not understand the question."

"Besides wanting to walk, to move, how do you feel?"

"I answered your question in full."

"Is your body sore or weak?" he asked.

She considered the question. "That is why I want to move," she said.

"OK, good," he said, tapping his tablet again.

Dr. Sommers was looking at her with a funny expression on his face, and Lieutenant Smith's brow was furrowed.

"Language and speech patterns seem to be altered," Dr. Sommers said. "Her movements seem stiff."

Dr. Walsh nodded. "A side effect." He turned to Smith. "Lieutenant Smith, we'll need to discuss that in more detail later." Smith nodded as Dr. Walsh made a note on his tablet.

Dr. Walsh scurried around, checking the monitors and machines, and then he returned to her bedside and started unhooking the tubes from her wrists.

"You're stabilized," he said. "Which means we can get you off this machine and out into the world—well, out beyond this room, anyway."

There was a noise from above. All four of them turned and saw a man come into view through the observation window. It was the man who had been at the foot of her bed the first time she'd woken in this room—Colonel Kell.

Another man appeared beside him. Major Nichols. He was stout, with a ruddy face, and he stood with his feet squared, his hands clasped behind his back, and his eyes fixed on her.

Dr. Walsh turned back to her. "As you know, you were in a serious accident. Phase one of your treatment, which consisted mostly of surgeries, is now complete, although we may need to perform additional operations, depending on how your recovery goes. The next phase involves rehabilitation."

"Rehabilitation? To restore my memories?"

The doctor frowned. "You have retained most of your memories. You can walk and talk, and you know all the things you knew before. Tell me, can you pilot an aircraft?"

She thought about it and said, "Yes."

"The purpose of rehabilitation is to maximize your mental and physical performance. We'll start by testing you to assess your current condition, and then you'll begin training and therapy. But first we need to get you settled in your new quarters."

Dr. Walsh retrieved a stack of clothes from a duffel bag

and set it on the foot of the bed.

"Can you stand up?" he said.

She nodded and moved to swing her legs around to the side of the bed. As she pushed herself to her feet, she thought her knees were going to buckle, and for an instant she felt lightheaded.

"Take it easy." Dr. Walsh steadied her by gripping her arm gently. "You've been immobile for some time."

He looked over at Dr. Sommers. "We may need to bring in a nurse to assist her. Is the wheelchair on hand?"

She held up her hand. "That won't be necessary," she said.

She concentrated on her body and took a step and then another. Her head cleared, but she still felt fragile, and that troubled her. She slowly pulled her arm away from Dr. Walsh's grip and took a few more steps.

"Impressive," Dr. Sommers said.

"I didn't expect her to be so steady on her feet," Dr. Walsh said, making another note on his e-tablet. He patted the stack of clothes he had set on the bed. "You can get dressed now. You do remember how to get dressed?"

She glanced at the stack of clothes, thought about it for a moment, and then said, "Yes."

"Good," he said. He tapped his wristcom and said, "Come in, Tia."

The door opened, and a woman carrying a rifle entered. She was dressed in dark fatigues and wore her hair pulled back in a tight bun at the nape of her neck.

"This is Tia," Dr. Walsh said.

There was a long pause. Everyone was staring expectantly. She remembered what Dr. Sommers had said: *social skills*. "Hello Tia," she finally said, but her eyes were on the gun the woman was carrying.

"She's here to protect you." Dr. Walsh pointed at the gun. "It's not real. It's a tranquilizer gun."

141

"What do I need to be protected from?" she said.

Dr. Walsh smiled. His smile was just as fake as the other doctor's. "It's just a safety precaution." He nodded at the stack of clothes on the bed. "We'll leave you to it, then."

Lieutenant Smith snapped his black case shut as Dr. Walsh turned and walked toward the door, stepping aside so the other two men could exit before him. Dr. Sommers went through first and stood in the corridor. Lieutenant Smith followed, glancing over his shoulder at her as he walked out the door. When she made eye contact with Smith, a flash filled her mind—it was an image of him leaning against a doorframe, smiling and tipping his hat to her, and then it was gone. She gave her head a slight shake. Had it been a memory?

Dr. Walsh was looking at her with a curious expression on his face. He pressed a button on the wall and glanced up at the observation window as it dimmed. She watched as Colonel Kell and Major Nichols faded behind the darkening glass. When she turned her attention back to Dr. Walsh, he'd already left the room.

She glanced at Tia and then examined the clothes. Cotton panties, a sports bra, navy blue cargo pants, a white tee shirt, a white tank, and a gray hoodie. Socks and sneakers at the bottom of the pile. Plan, simple, and functional.

She dressed quickly and was about to pull on the socks and shoes when she heard muffled voices beyond the door.

"You said she can't experience emotions." She wasn't sure, but she thought that was the voice of Colonel Kell.

"I never said she cannot experience emotions," Dr. Walsh said. "I said her emotions are suppressed. She needs time and space to adapt. You'll be crowding her. It's bad enough she has to be trailed by two guards, toting guns no less."

"Didn't you just say the guards are here for her protection?" Kell's said.

"We both know why the guards are really here," Dr. Walsh

said. "You're the one who insisted on keeping her under watch."

She turned at looked at Tia, who was staring at her with a blank expression. Then she looked from the door to Tia and realized that Tia couldn't hear the men outside.

"And you would let her roam around freely?"

"I certainly would not, but do you really think she needs to be watched with a gun while she's getting dressed?"

They continued arguing as she tied her shoes. She gave Tia one final glance before she walked toward the door. She moved slowly, still feeling slightly wobbly on her feet.

"She's a prototype. You yourself said she could behave unpredictably."

She waved her hand in front of the door panel, but it didn't open.

"That's exactly why she needs space. And as lead on this project, I must insist that you give us room to work. This phase requires essential personnel only."

There was a long silence. She waved her hand in front of the panel again, and when nothing happened, she knocked on the door. She thought it unusual that she remembered how to operate a door but she couldn't remember her name. There was another stretch of silence.

"Major Nichols and I will wait in the barracks common area," Kell said, and then she heard two pairs of footsteps fading away.

The door slid open, and Dr. Walsh stood there, looking frazzled.

Lieutenant Smith and Dr. Sommers were waiting in the corridor behind Dr. Walsh. Another man whom she did not recognize was with them, dressed in fatigues and carrying a gun like Tia.

"Ah, there you are," Dr. Walsh said, looking her up and down. "I see everything fits. Are you comfortable?"

"These clothes are adequate," she said.

"Good, very good. We'll escort you to your quarters now," he said.

They made their way down the corridor, with the man in fatigues leading the way and Dr. Sommers trailing him followed by Dr. Walsh, who walked beside her. Tia was behind them, with Lieutenant Smith at the rear. At the end of the corridor, they huddled into an elevator that took them down to a lower level and opened into a large, round common area sparsely furnished with dingy couches, chairs, and tables. Various corridors stretched out from the central room. Colonel Kell and Major Nichols were sitting in two chairs that were positioned kitty-corner from each other. When the group stepped off the elevator, they rose to their feet.

Dr. Walsh ignored them and led the group down a corridor on the right and stopped at the first door.

He turned toward her, smiling, and she realized his teeth were yellowed, and they looked brittle. "Your quarters," he said.

He pressed his palm against a panel beside the door and then waved his wristcom in front it. The door slid open.

"Go on," he said, gesturing to the room beyond. "Let's get you settled."

She entered the room and turned around as Dr. Sommers and Lieutenant Smith entered. Dr. Walsh turned to the two guards. "We'll take it from here. You can wait outside," he said. Then he shut the door just as Colonel Kell and Major Nichols approached.

"Have a look around," he said, nodding with enthusiasm. Dr. Sommers lingered by the door, and Lieutenant Smith leaned against a chest of drawers, the black hard-shell case dangling from one hand.

There was a single bed, freshly made, with a small metal nightstand beside it that held a reading lamp. A desk with a smartscreen above it and a chair tucked below it was pushed against the far wall. There were no windows. It was bland and bare.

Dr. Walsh pointed at the dresser that Lieutenant Smith was leaning against. "You'll find clothing stored in the drawers," he said, and then he walked past the dresser and pointed at a second door that sat between the dresser and desk. "The lavatory is through here," he said.

She stared at him.

"Go on. Have a look," he said.

She walked through the door and found a small closet to the left, where a few empty hangers were dangling from a rod. Beyond was a plain bathroom with a concrete floor, a narrow shower, a toilet, and a sink.

She paused as she caught her reflection in the mirror. The woman in the mirror was familiar, yet she seemed like a stranger. She reached up and touched her face. It was round and dark. She ran her hand over her hair. It was cropped close to her scalp. She had big, deep brown eyes. She blinked at herself as Dr. Walsh squeezed in beside her and pulled on the mirror, revealing a medicine cabinet where a toothbrush, toothpaste, soap, and other toiletries were stored.

"It's not fancy, but it's practical." He closed the cabinet and backed out of the bathroom. "Dr. Sommers?"

"Yes?"

"Why don't you show her the testing and training station?"

Dr. Sommers stepped forward and opened the desk drawers, showing her a keyboard, a trackpad, and a stack of e-paper. He removed an e-tablet and handed it to her.

"This is preloaded with testing and training programs as well as a syllabus and schedule that you'll use."

Dr. Walsh chimed in. "It's all part of your rehabilitation and retraining."

Dr. Sommers reached over and activated the e-tablet and

then pointed at an icon labeled "Orientation." "Start there. It will walk you through the other programs. It should be fairly self-explanatory."

Dr. Walsh stepped forward, pulling something out of his pocket. It was a wristcom.

"Hold out your hand," he said.

She did, and he wrapped the com around her wrist.

"I assume you know how to use this?"

She held it up to her face and nodded.

"You'll be able to contact me or Dr. Sommers with that," Dr. Walsh said. "If you have any questions or need anything, use it. One of us will always be nearby."

"I understand," she said.

"We'll leave you to get settled, then," he said, nodding at the e-tablet. "Go ahead and start the orientation program. Someone will be by in a few hours with a meal, and tomorrow we'll begin physical therapy."

As the men filed out of the room, she activated the tablet and examined the icons on the screen. One was familiar—an Internet browser. She tapped it, and the application opened and filled the screen, but with the words "No User Permissions for Internet Access" were displayed across the top.

When she looked up from the tablet, Lieutenant Smith was staring at her.

"Come along, Lieutenant Smith," Dr. Walsh said.

And then she was alone.

- 18 -

The Case

Eli cleared his throat, and they all turned to look at him. He was staring at Wendy. When she made eye contact with him, he gestured at Devin and then stared at the floor. "He's...um..."

Wendy looked back and forth from Devin to Eli. Devin was leaning against the back of a large wingback chair with his legs crossed and his arms folded across his chest.

"He's what?" she said.

"He's here," Eli said, but it came out like a question.

Jane rolled her eyes. "I think what Eli's trying to say is that you don't know Devin very well." She turned to Devin. "No offense."

Devin pushed himself off the chair and stood upright. "None taken. I'm sorry. I should go."

"No," Wendy said. "You can stay. I mean, if you want to stay, you can."

Eli shifted uncomfortably on his feet. An awkward silence filled the room.

"Wendy," Jane whispered. "This could be your dad's work stuff. You know, his top-secret work stuff."

"It's OK," Wendy said. "Devin's like family. I trust him. Besides, he used to be special ops for the marines."

"I don't want to intrude," Devin said. "You and your friends—"

"You're not intruding," Wendy said. She turned to Jane and Eli. "Besides, he already overheard us talking about aliens, the possibility that someone murdered my parents, and the coup that we're trying to stop."

"Oh, well, then he pretty much knows everything," Jane said.

"Not exactly," Devin said.

"Anyway," Wendy continued. "You can stay, but I understand if you'd rather be somewhere else."

Devin considered that and then resumed his position leaning against the chair with a shrug. "I don't have anywhere else to be."

"OK then." Wendy glanced at Eli. "It's settled."

She turned to the case and slowly opened it, spreading it flat on the desk. Both sides were packed with foam inserts. Various objects were embedded in the foam.

"What is all that stuff?" Devin said.

Wendy leaned over and looked at everything. "I have no idea."

There were canisters, tubes, and various instruments and objects packed into the top side of the case. A row of rolled-up fabrics took up most of the bottom. Wendy reached out and touched the foam. It gave easily, creating an indentation exactly the shape of her finger. When she pulled her hand back, the foam restored itself to its original shape. Not a trace of the indentation from her finger remained.

"Wow," she said. Something at the edge of the foam panel caught her eye. It was a latch. Wendy clicked it, and the panel came free, revealing another layer of items below.

She replaced the foam tray and picked up one of the pieces of fabric. It was rolled up tight. She gave it a little shake, and one end came loose, revealing a long and wide swath of material.

"Jane, feel this," she said. "What kind of fabric is it?"

Jane stepped forward and ran her fingers over the fabric. "I'm not sure, but it's soft, isn't it?"

"Light, too," Wendy said. She wrapped the fabric around her hand. "I can barely feel it," she said, looking up at Jane just as Jane's mouth fell open. Behind her Eli's eyes had gone wide.

"What?" Wendy said, looking back and forth from Jane to Eli and back again.

"Wendy," Devin said. Wendy turned to look at him. He looked slightly alarmed. "Your hand."

She looked down at her hand, but it wasn't there. She gasped and jumped back. Her arm seemed to end where the excess fabric dangled from her wrist. She furiously wiggled her fingers. She could feel her hand, but she couldn't see it. Her hand had disappeared.

Wendy let out a short shriek and shook her hand. The fabric fell away and her hand reappeared. Her heart pounded in her chest, and her breath came fast.

"Wow," Jane said.

"It's an invisibility cloak," Eli said excitedly. "Just like in Harry Potter."

"Harry whatter?" Devin said.

Wendy was still trying to catch her breath.

"That's how he did it," Eli said. "That's how your father was in the room with those guys without them seeing him."

"Right," Jane said. "Except if Kell is the commander of the base, he'd know all about this…invisibility fabric."

"Maybe he does," Eli said. "Maybe that's why he got suspicious of Wendy's dad."

Wendy reached out and ran her fingers over the fabric. "But how is this possible?"

"I bet it has something to do with your father reverse engineering the alien technology," Eli said.

Devin raised an eyebrow when Eli said that. "There are a lot of people who would want to get their hands on something like that," he said.

Wendy picked up the fabric and wrapped it around her hand again. They all watched as it tightened itself around her fingers, palm, and wrist and then disappeared.

"It's like the fabric is alive," she said.

Wendy waved her hand around and wiggled her fingers. There was a slight disturbance in her field of vision, but her hand had definitely become invisible. She shook her hand, and the fabric fell away. She let it drop onto the open case.

"We could have a lot of fun with that," Jane said with a grin.

"No kidding," Eli said.

"There are four more," Devin said. He nodded at the case, where four more swatches of fabric were rolled up tightly and tucked into the foam. Wendy bent down and studied them. Each one had a slightly different tint. Wendy picked up the fabric that had made her hand disappear and held it up to the light. It looked black, but there was a red sheen to it.

Jane grinned. "One for each of us, plus an extra."

Wendy turned to look at her.

"Kidding," Jane said.

Wendy picked up the fabric and rolled it up.

"What are you doing?" Eli asked.

"Putting this back. I don't think we should be messing around with this."

Wendy was about to set the fabric back in its place when she noticed something tucked into the foam. She leaned in and saw that it was a flash drive just like the one she'd found in her treehouse. She set the rolled-up fabric on top of it and then closed the case. As the latch clicked, the medallion popped out of the depression on the side of the case. Wendy picked it up and stared at it thoughtfully.

"You think your dad built an invisibility cloak on his own as part of his 'personal research?'" Eli asked, making air quotes.

"That doesn't seem likely," Wendy said, tucking the medallion into her back pocket.

"Then maybe this isn't his personal research," Eli said.

"Or maybe 'personal research' is code for something else," Jane added, "like Wendy said earlier."

"You guys said the flash drive had information about all his work," Wendy said.

"Yeah," Jane said. "I've already gone through every project he's worked on since he received security clearance. I can't say I understood all of it, but fabric that makes people invisible was definitely not on the list." She turned to Devin. "What do you think about all this, big boy?"

Devin scratched at the nape of his neck. "I really don't know what's going on here."

"Oh, I'm sorry," Wendy said. "We need to fill you in."

Devin listened carefully as Wendy relayed all the events since her parents' tragic and untimely death. Jane and Eli piped in, filling in details that Wendy missed. He didn't interrupt or ask any questions until they were done.

"So your main goal is to find the evidence that Tom recorded?" he asked.

"If we can find it, we can send it to the authorities," Wendy said. "And stop them."

"This is pretty serious," Devin said.

"We're not planning on getting into a confrontation," Jane said. "We just want to find the evidence Mr. Watson already collected and turn it over."

Devin looked at Eli and Jane. "You two already searched

the drive and didn't find it, right?"

They nodded.

"And Wendy, it can't be in the case because your father hid the case and gave Yoshi the key before he would have obtained the evidence?"

"Yes. Although—I guess my dad could have had another medallion and accessed the case after he hid it, so the evidence could be in the case, but I think it's unlikely."

"So what's the plan, then?" he said.

"The plan?" Eli said.

"We need to keep digging," Wendy said. "Maybe we'll find whatever made my dad get involved in all this in the first place."

"But that won't do you any good," Devin pointed out. "Does it matter what got him involved? He was involved. He figured it out. Knowing what drew his attention to Kell won't do any good."

"It could lead us to another clue," Eli said.

Jane leaned forward. "Do you have a better idea?"

"Yeah. Actually I do. Why don't I wrap myself up in that magic fabric you've got there, go into the base, and collect new evidence?"

The three of them stared at Devin. Eli's jaw dropped, and Jane grinned, but Wendy frowned.

Devin shrugged and leaned back in the chair. "It would normally be a difficult mission, but that—" He pointed at the fabric in the case. "Would make it easy."

"You don't know that," Wendy said.

"I know infiltrating a military base is less of a challenge if they can't see you."

"Putting that on doesn't mean you can just walk into the base. We don't know what kind of security they have or whether it would get you through a simple metal detector."

"You're an engineer. You can test it first," Devin said.

"Besides, I can get in. I teach judo classes there."

"I don't think that's a good idea," Wendy said.

"Why not?" Jane said.

Wendy gently kicked her under the desk.

"Ow, OK," Jane said.

"Devin, I trust you, but I'm not...I don't want you get in trouble. I would never..." Wendy frowned at him.

"I can take care of myself," Devin said. "Special ops, remember?"

Wendy shook her head. "I'm sorry. It's not going to happen."

- 19 -

What is Justice?

City Outskirts
Swenson, Colorado

That night Wendy's dreams were riddled with strange images. She dreamed of her father and Yoshi, both dressed in *judogis*, squaring off on the mat. When her father turned to look at her, he had the face of an alien. He touched his wrist and disappeared. Yoshi stepped forward, half his face hidden in the shadows. "What is justice?" he said, and then he stepped aside, and her mother was there, swimming through the air like an acrobat. A rabble of butterflies danced in the air, surrounding her. She floated over to the sensei and held out her hand, revealing a white-winged moth. The sensei gingerly cupped his hands around the moth, and then all the butterflies fell out of the air. Her mother screamed.

Wendy woke with a start, the cryptic words from her dream lingering in her mind. *What is justice?* She rolled onto her back, blinked, and then angled her head toward the open window. It was still dark outside, although there was a glowing light on the eastern horizon, where the sun was pushing up into the sky.

She steadied herself with a few deep breaths, and then she got up and dressed quickly before going downstairs and starting the coffee. She listened to the machine percolate for a few minutes, the images from her dream fading in and out of her mind.

The coffee was still brewing when she walked out of the house and headed across the field to the grove. Within minutes she was back inside her treehouse.

As soon as she sat down on the wooden floorboards, she was overwhelmed by memories of her parents and Yoshi. Her sobs came loud and hard. They were almost violent, rocking her entire body to the core. Time slipped away, and she found herself staring at her not-so-secret hiding spot. That was how she'd gotten dragged into all this craziness—coups d'etat, murder, aliens, and the strange, invisible fabric. Why had her father left those items there? She hadn't been to the treehouse in years, but there was always a possibility that she might visit it. Had he left the things there for Wendy to find? Was she part of his backup plan?

It was too much. The sobs recommenced, softer now. She cried herself to exhaustion and fell asleep curled up on the hard floor of the treehouse.

* * *

She woke hours later and felt like she was inside an oven. The sun was high, and she hadn't opened the shutters. Her body was damp with sweat, and she was hot, thirsty, and tired. She climbed out of the treehouse and headed back to the house.

Wendy found Jane and Eli on the front porch, chatting quietly and drinking coffee. As soon as they saw her, Jane breathed a sigh of relief.

"We've been looking everywhere for you," she said.

"I couldn't sleep, so I went for a walk," Wendy said.

Eli and Jane could see that Wendy had been crying, and she looked tattered and exhausted. Jane wrapped an arm around Wendy, and they sank into the porch swing. "Want to talk about it?" she said.

Wendy shook her head.

Jane nodded and decided to change the subject. "So that guy, Devin," she said. "He's a looker."

"I guess," Wendy said.

"Are you sure you're OK with involving him in all this?" Eli said. "You don't know him very well. Are you sure you can trust him?"

"It doesn't matter how well I know him. We have to trust him because he already knows."

"But do you?" Eli asked.

"Do I what?"

"Do you trust him?"

"Yeah," Wendy said. "I guess I do."

"How can you trust someone you barely know?" he asked.

"I don't know," Wendy said. "Part of it is his connection with my family. I knew Yoshi Kobayashi since I was six years old, and I would trust him with my life. He trusted Devin, and he trusted him one hundred percent. My gut says I can trust him too."

Eli looked uncertain, but Jane said, "That's good enough for me."

In the distance they heard the grinding of tires turning onto the dirt road that led to Wendy's house. Wendy rose to her feet as Devin's bus emerged from around the bend.

"Speak of the handsome devil," Jane said.

Eli eyed the ancient jalopy that was rolling up to Wendy's house. "That thing looks like it's about a thousand years old," he said.

156

Wendy walked across the porch to the front railing as Devin parked his bus. He climbed out, opened the side door, and retrieved a large cardboard box and a paper bag.

"What you got there?" Jane asked as he approached the porch.

"Leftovers from the service yesterday," he said. "I thought you guys might be hungry."

Jane smiled and gently nudged Wendy with her elbow. "I knew there was something I liked about him," she said.

"Thanks," Wendy said, taking the bag from Devin. "You didn't have to do that."

"It's no trouble. Besides, I can't eat all of it."

"Here, let me help you with that," Jane said, taking the box from Devin. "Let's eat."

Moments later they were sitting at the kitchen table with a feast of leftovers spread out before them: cheese and cold cuts, kebobs and rice, and a bowl of fruit.

"This hits the spot," Jane said. "I was starving."

"Yeah, thanks," Eli said.

Wendy was quiet through the meal and barely touched her food. When the others were almost done eating, she finally spoke.

"Listen," Wendy said. "We need to stop all this. I think we should send the case and the flash drive to the Pentagon or something—maybe bury it somewhere. I don't know. What we're doing is dangerous. It's not a game. It's serious."

"Chica, we know that," Jane said, and Eli nodded.

"I want you two to think about going back to Massachusetts and putting all this behind you."

"What about you?" Eli said.

"I'm going to stay here for a few days, take care of some business regarding my parents' estate, and then I'll be back."

"No way," Jane said, and Eli shook his head.

Wendy looked to Devin for support.

"Sorry, I'm with them," he said. "I don't think we should walk away from this, not with what's at stake."

"Why do you want to do this? Why do you want to risk yourselves for this?"

Jane answered first. "Wendy Bird, you've always been the good girl." Jane smiled. "Don't get me wrong, I'm a good girl too. But I can also be a bad girl. I break the rules, and I've broken the law when it was the right thing to do. I was getting ready to go show people how to take control of their government through civil disobedience. My job was to teach them how to break the law. And I've done it before, many times. I've stared down a SWAT team while I was chained to a tree. I've been arrested for protesting in front of a public building. I once harbored a whistleblower who was wanted for treason. This is what I do."

Wendy stared at Jane for a long time, and then she said, "Well, when you put it that way..." Jane flashed her a bright smile, and then Wendy turned her attention to Eli. He was staring down at the ground. "What about you?" she said.

Eli blinked and looked out the kitchen window, past the field behind Wendy's house. It was hot, and tiny beads of sweat were emerging on his forehead.

"I want to help you," he said, "because you're my friend. Maybe my only friend." He ran a hand through his hair, and it stuck up and out, a big mess of frizzy curls. "But I'd be lying if I said that was the only reason. There's a part of me that finds this all very exciting. I'm curious about the aliens and their technology, and I'm concerned about what happened to your parents. I want to find the truth."

Wendy looked to Devin. "And you?"

"I'm here for Yoshi and your parents. I think Yoshi and Tom would want me to help you, and if your parents were murdered, they deserve justice. I may not be a soldier anymore, but I can't sit back and do nothing while some traitor tries to take over the country."

"But what we're doing, it could be considered treason."

"It's not treason," Devin said. "We're trying to prevent a coup. How could anyone call that treason?"

"It doesn't matter," Jane said. "What we're doing is illegal."

Eli took a deep breath.

"You can't ask us to walk away from this," Devin said. "Not if they're really planning a coup."

"Wen, if you're not comfortable with this, why don't you hand it over to us?" Jane said. "If you want to walk away, there's no reason you can't. We can take it from here."

But Wendy shook her head. "No, that's not what I want. I just thought it was the right thing to do. I thought we'd find the evidence on that drive, send it off, and be done with it. Instead we've got aliens and invisibility fabric but no evidence."

"I told you I can use that fabric to get the evidence you need," Devin said.

Wendy shifted her eyes to glare at him, but her face softened. "I appreciate that you're willing to take that risk, but I can't go along with that. I don't think we've exhausted all our other options yet."

"So you're not going to shut it down?" Eli asked.

"No," Wendy said. "I don't know how far we'll take it. But we'll keep looking for that evidence." She sighed. "But I want you guys to know that you can drop this and go home at any time, for any reason, and you don't have to say what it is. I'll have no problem with that."

"Well then, let's get to work," Jane said, rising to her feet and picking up her dish.

Devin was quiet, thinking. "Eli, you're a programmer, right?"

"Yeah," Eli said.

"Can you do any hacking?" Devin asked.

Eli's mouth fell open, and his face turned red. Jane cocked her head to one side as she watched him react to Devin's question.

"Why do you ask?" Eli said.

"Well, I was thinking you could find the evidence by hacking into Tom's e-mail. If he sent it to the authorities electronically, it should be there, in his e-mail account. Is that possible?"

Wendy, Eli, and Jane all looked at each other.

"I can't believe I didn't think of that," Eli said.

"It's perfectly legal," Jane said. She turned to Wendy. "As sole inheritor of your parents' estate, you are within your rights to access all their accounts, including e-mail. No hacking required."

Wendy turned to Eli. "Can you do it?"

Eli was still staring at Devin, still assessing this new person who'd been thrust into his life. He nodded.

"How long will it take?"

"A few hours," he said.

- 20 -

Postal

City Outskirts
Swenson, Colorado

Wendy helped Eli get set up in her dad's study while Jane headed into town to pick up groceries, and Devin returned to the dojo to attend to Yoshi's business. They agreed to meet back at Wendy's house at dinnertime.

Wendy wasn't sure what they would do if Eli couldn't get the evidence they needed. She spent a couple of hours going through her father's belongings, searching for another drive or some device where he might have stored the evidence he'd recorded. But her search was fruitless.

During her last trip home, Wendy had avoided the basement and the heart-wrenching memories it was sure to dredge up. But with nothing else to do, she took the silver case down to the basement, which had been converted into an office for her mom.

Metal shelves lining the back wall were filled with boxes, old books, e-tablets, and stacks of e-paper. The opposite wall held a huge smartscreen and an old-fashioned bulletin board.

An old dining table stood at the center of the room. It was strewn with gadgets, handwritten notes, a bucket of styluses and pens, and a variety of other office supplies.

Everything was interspersed with her mother's personal touch: e-frames scrolled through family photos, fake plants were strategically placed to add life to the otherwise drab environment, and bright, digital paintings gave it a light, bright sensibility.

Wendy's eyes filled with tears as she glanced around the room and set the silver case on the table. She set about organizing her mother's things into neat stacks on the shelves, and then she picked up the e-tablet that held the manuscript her mother had been writing.

She scrolled through the first few pages and then flipped to the end. The manuscript was further along than she had realized. She checked the revision tracker and realized that her mother had been working on the third draft of the project. It was almost ready for editing and publication.

Wendy bit her lip and wondered if she should publish it posthumously, and then she nodded. It was a ridiculous question. Of course her mother would want it published. She set the e-tablet aside, deciding to take it home and read it thoroughly once all this insanity was behind her.

Wendy set up an off-grid laptop that Eli had loaned her and spread the silver case open beside it. She carefully set aside the fabric that had made her hand invisible and then reached into the case and removed the flash drive that was hidden beneath it. She expected the contents of the drive to be encrypted like the other one, but there wasn't so much as a password to access the files. Within minutes she found herself studying diagrams and reading about the strange fabric, how it worked, how it was constructed, and what it could do.

She had become lost in her research when she heard the basement door open.

"Wendy?" It was Jane.

"Yeah, I'm down here," Wendy called.

Jane came bounding down the stairs. "What are you doing down here? We've been looking everywhere—" She froze when she noticed the silver case opened on the table beside Wendy.

"Find anything interesting?" she said as she approached slowly.

"I found some files with specs on the fabric." Wendy popped the flash drive out of the laptop and tucked it back into the foam. Then she set the fabric on top of the drive and closed the case.

"Oh," Jane said. "I thought you didn't want to mess with that."

Wendy shrugged. "Curiosity got the better of me."

Jane grinned. "Right. Well, dinner's here, and Eli says he has some new information."

"Did he find the evidence?" Wendy said.

"I don't know. He won't say anything until you're in the room."

Wendy picked up the case, and Jane followed her up the basement stairs.

"Oh, and you might want to call Devin," Jane said as they entered the hallway on the main floor.

"Why?"

"We sent him into the woods to see if you'd gone off to your treehouse again."

"Tell Eli I'll be there in a minute," Wendy said. As Jane walked off toward the kitchen, Wendy ran upstairs. She texted Devin and then hid the silver case in the crawlspace above her closet. By the time she got to the kitchen and glanced out the windows, she could see Devin crossing the field and heading back to the house.

In the kitchen she found Eli inspecting the silverware as he set the table. Jane was opening cartons of Thai food and setting them in the middle of the table.

"You found the evidence?" Wendy said.

"No, not quite," Eli said as Devin entered the house from the kitchen door.

"Hi," Wendy said.

"Hey," he said. "I was looking for you."

"I was in the basement," Wendy said.

Devin raised an eyebrow but didn't say anything.

"Grab a plate," Jane said. "Hope you like Thai."

"I love it," Devin said.

Within seconds they were seated around the table. Jane and Devin busily piled food on their plates while Eli talked, and Wendy sat listening intently to what he was saying.

"Your father had three e-mail accounts that we know about: an old personal e-mail account that he rarely used, his current personal e-mail account, and his work e-mail. I'm assuming he didn't use his work e-mail to send incriminating evidence against his boss to the Pentagon, and, well, hacking into the military's e-mail system is a high-risk activity, so I didn't check that one. I did get into both of his personal accounts, but he didn't send any e-mails with attachments within our timeframe."

"I'm guessing he had other e-mail accounts you don't know about," Jane said, dipping a skewer of chicken satay into a dish of peanut sauce.

"Yeah, he probably did," Wendy said. She scanned the food but wasn't hungry. Still, she helped herself to some rice and curry.

"If he did, I won't be able to find them," Eli said. "Being an engineer he'd know how to hide his tracks. But that doesn't matter. I don't think he sent the evidence by e-mail."

He reached for the coconut milk soup and ladled it into a bowl. "I checked his bank account to see if he paid for drone shipping," Eli said.

Jane started to say something, but Eli held up his hand. "I didn't hack it. Wendy had his login credentials."

"The bank gave them to me when we transferred the estate into my name," Wendy said, pushing rice around on her plate.

Eli continued. "The week before the accident, he paid for drone mail to deliver a package to Washington, DC,"

"Let's stop calling it an accident," Wendy said, "at least until we're sure one way or the other."

"OK," Eli said. "A week before the crash."

"And?"

He frowned and pushed his chair away from the table. He scurried out of the kitchen and returned a moment later with an e-tablet.

"Let's not smear any food on this, OK guys?" Eli looked around at everyone.

Wendy nodded, and Jane rolled her eyes. Devin scooped a forkful of rice into his mouth.

"I found this," Eli said, holding up the tablet, so they could all see. "It's from the security cameras at the post office—"

"Wait a minute," Jane said. She glared at Eli as she set her fork down. "How did you get footage from a security camera at the post office?

Eli gripped the tablet and stared at her. "I just got it," he said. His eyes dropped to the floor, and he shrugged. "It wasn't that hard, and like you said, we're already breaking a bunch of laws, so—"

"OK," Jane said. "You don't have to justify your actions. You did the right thing."

"Even if it gets him thrown in prison?" Wendy said.

"Let's worry about that later," Eli said, his voice shaking. "I need to stay focused."

"Show us what you got," Devin said.

Eli nodded and held up the tablet, and then he tapped the

play button.

Wendy caught her breath when she saw the footage of her dad walking into the small office and handing the clerk a parcel.

"That confirms he sent something," Eli said. "So I accessed the post office tracking database. That parcel was scanned twice—once when it was dropped off and again when it was loaded onto a truck headed for a warehouse for drone distribution. But it disappeared after that. I had to dig into the deleted files to find it. The record was wiped clean. I'm pretty sure the package was intercepted."

"It doesn't make sense," Wendy said. "My dad would have tracked something that important. Why didn't he say anything about it disappearing in his journal?"

"That's the thing," Eli said. "He did track it. It took me a while to figure it out. The database says the package disappeared, but the tracking page that customers access on the Internet says it was delivered."

"How is that possible?" Devin said.

"Yeah, wouldn't the tracking site pull from the database?" Jane said.

Eli nodded. "Yes, it does, but someone hacked it and fed it false information—just for that package—so your dad would think it was delivered. He tracked it three times, and every time the system told him the package was en route to its destination until it was delivered."

They were all quiet for a few minutes. Nobody touched the food.

Devin finally broke the silence. "Don't you think your dad kept a copy somewhere?" he said as he reached for the pitcher of iced tea.

"I'm sure he did," Wendy said. "But I've looked everywhere, and I can't find it."

"Then all we have left is the flash drive and whatever's in

that silver case," Jane said.

"There's more," Eli said. "Your dad did send the package to the Pentagon. To someone named Honorine Bartlett."

"I know her," Wendy said. "I've never met her, but I know who she is. When my dad was in the air force—"

"Your dad was in the air force?" Eli said. "I thought he was a civilian scientist."

"When he was younger, he was an airman. He was injured and honorably discharged. Honorine Bartlett was his commanding officer. After he was injured she pulled some strings to help him get into university. And when my dad graduated, she got him the job here."

"Um," Eli said. He looked at Wendy, and then his eyes dropped to the ground.

"What is it?" Wendy said. "What else did you find?"

"Well, she, um…This woman, Bartlett…she's in a coma."

"What?" Wendy said.

Devin shifted in his chair and sat upright. Jane almost choked on her drink.

"It gets worse," Eli said. "She was attacked in a mugging a few days before the accide—before Wendy's parents died. It was a brutal assault. They're saying it was attempted murder, but they don't have any leads. She was in critical condition for weeks. She could still die."

The silence that filled the room was heavy.

"A mugging that turned into an attempted murder?" Devin said. "And they can't find the guy who did it?"

"Nobody said it was a guy," Jane pointed out.

"I think that's one too many coincidences," Eli said.

Devin nodded. "I agree. It can't be a coincidence."

"But it's not hard evidence," Jane added.

"You guys think Kell tried to have this woman killed? And killed my parents?" Wendy said. Her voice was shaking. "Honorine Bartlett is a decorated general."

"If Kell is planning to overthrow the US government, he's going to be prepared to make sacrifices. In the military that means sacrificing lives," Devin said. "To him it's war."

"But there is no more war," Eli said.

"Depends how you define war," Devin said.

Wendy's eyes glazed over, and she grew distant as they all watched her and waited for her to absorb this new information. When she snapped out of it, she looked around the room at each of them. Her eyes were on fire.

"Then we're going to take that son of a bitch down."

Jane's eyes got big, and Eli's mouth fell open as they stared at Wendy, and then they exchanged looks of worry with each other.

Eli snapped out of it first. "But how are we going to do that?" he said.

"We need a new angle," Jane said, still staring at Wendy.

"You know what I think," Devin said.

"Right," Wendy said, mostly to Devin. "But it's too soon to think about sending one of us in there."

Eli and Jane both snapped their heads around to look at Wendy when she said that. She hadn't mentioned sending Devin in; she had said *one of us*.

Wendy looked around the table, locking eyes with her friends, one by one.

"But I do want to learn more about that fabric. I want to see how it works and if it works, which is why I'm going to try it on and test it.

- 21 -

Hippocratic

Carter Air Force Base
Swenson, Colorado

Dr. Walsh slid a stack of e-paper across his desk. "Lieutenant Smith, I assume you've seen these reports."

Smith picked up the top sheet, glanced at it, and then set it back down.

He nodded. "I have."

"Her progress is nothing short of miraculous. As a doctor, that's not a word I use lightly. *Miraculous.*"

Dr. Sommers leaned forward. "I agree."

Dr. Walsh scanned Smith's deadpan expression. "You don't seem excited."

Smith shrugged.

"Project MOTH is one of the most important scientific breakthroughs in the history of humanity," Dr. Walsh said. "And you played a critical role."

Smith nodded. "Yes, I did."

Dr. Walsh kept his gaze on Lieutenant Smith for a beat, and then he picked up the reports and flipped through them.

"Hearing and eyesight are well beyond the most advanced humans on record. Vital signs are absolutely perfect. Photographic memory. Only four hours of sleep required per night. Half the food the average human of equal size requires—"

"As long as you recharge her every few days," Smith said sarcastically.

Dr. Walsh frowned. "It's astonishing. We've surpassed our expectations on almost every level, and preliminary tests indicate her physical scores will be just as high."

"Official physical testing starts tomorrow," Dr. Sommers said.

"Good. Then I guess we're on track." Smith started to push himself up from his chair, but Dr. Walsh held out his hand.

"There are a couple of issues I wanted to address," Dr. Walsh said.

Smith settled back into his chair. "Oh?"

"Well, of course. If everything was on track, I wouldn't have called this meeting."

Smith glanced at Dr. Sommers, who was scrolling through a tablet, and then he glared at Dr. Walsh. "Meeting? Where's Colonel Kell? I thought he attended all meetings for this project."

Dr. Sommers looked up from his tablet.

"I wanted to discuss her social behavior and speech patterns," Dr. Walsh said, waving his hand in the air. "Kell doesn't need to be present for that."

Smith frowned and shook his head. "Doc, I already told you, if the neurologists haven't figured out how those areas of the brain function, I don't have much to work with. It would also help if I knew what kind of technology you're using to manipulate her brain functions. I don't know if you're using some kind of biotech or microchips—"

"That's need-to-know," Dr. Walsh said. "And you don't need hardware specs in order to write the software. Furthermore, it doesn't explain why she seems to have regressed in certain areas. Her behavior is awkward, her language is stilted, and her movements have become rigid."

"Maybe that's what happens when you turn a human being into a robot," Smith said with a shrug.

Dr. Walsh frowned. "We need you to fix it. It's critical that these supersoldiers blend in with normal troops. I'm sure you'll agree that Colonel Kell has made that quite clear."

"I don't see what's the big deal if the supersoldiers aren't social butterflies." Smith narrowed his eyes at Dr. Walsh. "It almost sounds like we're going to hide the fact that they're supersoldiers."

"I didn't imply any such thing," Dr. Walsh said. "In any case, that's where your focus needs to be. We need her to speak and behave like any other officer before we can move on to the next phase."

The next phase, of course, was to build a team of prototypes and train them to work together. After that they would go into full production. But before any of that could happen, this prototype had to pass muster. She had to be perfect.

Smith sighed. "I'll look into it, but I can't make any promises."

"We don't need promises. We need results," Dr. Walsh said. "And I'm counting on you."

"It might take some time. We may need to bring in another neurologist."

"Do what you can with what you have. We expect to have her in physical training and rehabilitation for a month. If you're unable to make any headway in that time, I'll see about bringing in additional resources."

"Sounds good," Smith said. "Is that it, then?"

"That's it," Dr. Walsh. "Thank you for all your hard work."

Smith gave Walsh a funny look as he rose to his feet and turned toward the door. He turned and exited the room, leaving the two doctors staring after him.

"The man is an enigma," Dr. Walsh said.

Dr. Sommers shook his head. "I don't trust him."

"I do," Dr. Walsh said. "Besides, you don't trust anyone," Dr. Walsh said.

"I trust you."

"That's different," Walsh said, resting his hand on Dr. Sommers's.

"These issues are a minor setback, considering all we have accomplished," Dr. Sommers said. "We saved a body that was totally decimated in a spaceplane crash. That alone is a medical marvel. We not only repaired the body—we enhanced it. Actually, we did more than enhance it. We created the world's first true superhuman."

"We succeeded," Dr. Walsh said.

Doctors Walsh and Sommers had been pursuing human enhancement together for more than two decades, and it was only when they accepted positions within the air force that they finally had the resources they needed to bring the project to realization. And after dozens of failures, Dessa Rae had come through like a champ.

"We did it," Dr. Sommers said, squeezing Dr. Walsh's hand. "We finally did it."

"Kell can't use her if she can't blend in," Dr. Walsh said.

"She will," Dr. Sommers said. "If Lieutenant Smith can't figure it out, we'll bring in the best neurology researchers on the planet. And if nothing else, we'll manually train her."

"That would take months, maybe years," Dr. Walsh said.

"Maybe not. These abilities are already in her mind. Training could very well trigger the return of normal behavior." Dr. Sommers stared off into space. "We know so little about the human brain."

"It's not a bad idea," Dr. Walsh said. "Let's add speech therapy and social behavioral modification to her schedule. We can afford to cut in to her academics. I just don't want any more delays. I'm sick and tired of Colonel Kell harping on me about schedules and deadlines."

"The man's a Neanderthal," Sommers said.

Walsh started to laugh but caught himself.

"Watch what you say," he whispered.

It was common knowledge throughout the MOTH compound that Kell and Walsh didn't get along. They were polar opposites. Kell was tall and lean. Walsh was short and round. Kell was aggressive. Walsh was passive. Kell was a man of action. Walsh was a man of deliberation. Kell was a soldier, not a scientist, and he didn't understand that projects like MOTH couldn't possibly adhere to a schedule because they were discovering the science and creating new technologies, not working within established parameters.

"He never should have been put in charge of this project," Sommers whispered.

Dr. Walsh narrowed his eyes at Dr. Sommers, and then he let out a sigh. He pressed his thumb against his desk drawer, and it popped open. He pulled out a small metal device, clicked the power button, and set it on the desk.

"The dampener," Sommers said, eyeing the device. "You must need to get something off your chest."

"I'm certain he's got every nook and cranny of this place bugged," Dr. Walsh said. "You can't be speaking ill of him." He leaned forward, close to Dr. Sommers's ear. "And you must never let on that you know about ROMANS."

"Well, if you could just hurry up and bring me in—"

"I told you; it's not that simple. I can't recommend you. They would have to feel they need you on the inside, and they don't need you on the inside."

Dr. Walsh leaned back in his chair and swiped his forehead with the palm of his hand. "I never should have told you," he said. "Maybe I never should have signed up for this."

"We wouldn't have come this far without their resources," Dr. Sommers said.

"Oh please. I sold my soul, and you know it," Dr. Walsh said.

Sommers nodded. "You started tossing and turning in your sleep the night you terminated the first failed prototype."

Dr. Walsh's eyes fell to the surface of his desk. "It's regrettable that we have to terminate the failures, but it's not like we can reintegrate them."

"And it would be too costly to keep them alive down in the barracks," Dr. Sommers said. He swiveled his chair so he was facing Dr. Walsh. "Creating a superhuman has been our life's work. Yours and mine. It's what brought us together—"

"Don't you dare say it's what keeps us together," Dr. Walsh said.

"I wasn't going to say that," Dr. Sommers said. "It would have taken decades for us to enhance human potential to this magnitude, but Colonel Kell provided another way, a faster way."

"And I was impatient."

Dr. Sommers reached across the desk and took Walsh's hands in his. "I crawled in right after you. Nobody forced our hands."

"But what's the point?" Dr. Walsh said. "We achieved everything we dreamed of, but nobody will ever know. We'll be on our deathbeds, and someone else will be taking credit for the breakthroughs we developed. There will be no honors or awards, and all of humanity will suffer for decades because these medical advances will be kept secret. How many illnesses will go uncured? How many preventable deaths will occur?"

"You're feeling even guiltier than I thought," Dr. Sommers

said. Then he leaned forward and slid a sheet of e-paper across the desk, placing it in front of Dr. Sommers. It was the summary report on the prototype. A full-body photo of Dessa Rae occupied one side of the report.

"Sacrifices have to be made for all great achievements."

Dr. Walsh shook his head and pushed the report away. "We're doctors. We don't sacrifice lives. In an emergency we may have to make hard choices—save one patient instead of another. It would be one thing to sacrifice a life to save millions, but that's not what we've done. We've broken the oath, Lloyd."

"You're having regrets," Dr. Sommers said.

"We all have regrets," Dr. Walsh said. "But what kind of people would we be if we didn't question our own actions?"

"I don't know," Dr. Sommers said. "What kind of people are we?"

- 22 -

The Demo

City Outskirts
Swenson, Colorado

"Are you sure you want to do that?" Jane asked.

"Can I try one on too?" Eli said.

Devin folded his arms over his chest.

Wendy ignored them. "I've been reading about it, studying the specs, and I understand how it works," Wendy said. "Well, I don't understand how it works, but I understand how to work it, I think."

The others stared at her.

"We don't know how much time we have. If they're planning this coup, then we could have a week or a year. That's why we need to do something. I'm not saying I'm going to put on the suit and walk in there. I just want to test it."

"I thought if anyone went in, it was going to be Devin," Jane said.

"Like I said, we're just testing it." Wendy frowned. "I don't get you guys. One minute you're all pushing me to bend the rules and break the law, and now you're all getting angry

176

because I'm thinking about trying on some suit."

"I thought it was a cloak," Eli said.

"The official name is covert vestment," Wendy said. "It's more like a suit than a cloak. It's not alive, but it behaves like a living thing. It wraps itself around the body and becomes a full bodysuit. You can configure it any number of ways. You can even program pockets and pouches into it."

"So you could configure it to be a cloak?" Eli asked.

"Yeah, I guess you could," Wendy said.

"All right," Jane said, rising to her feet. "Let's see that thing in action."

Devin narrowed his eyes at Jane as Wendy leaped out of her chair, her eyes gleaming.

"First I want to explain how it works. Meet me in the basement in two minutes," she said, and then she scurried out of the room.

"Don't say a word," Jane said when she saw Devin glaring at her. "This isn't easy for her, and she needs our support."

Devin opened his mouth to respond, but Jane held up her hand. "Not a word," she said. "Come on. I'll show you where the basement is."

Eli frowned at the messy table as Jane and Devin left the room. He felt an urge to clean up before following them down to the basement, but he was worried he might miss something important. With a sigh he followed the others.

Upstairs in her room, Wendy climbed onto a chair and removed the silver case from the crawlspace above her closet. She wasn't sure when she had decided to try the suit on, although it seemed like she'd made up her mind the moment she'd realized what the fabric could do. She still wasn't comfortable with the idea of using the invisibility suit to enter the base, but maybe seeing how it worked would help them formulate a plan. Maybe she would let Devin use the suit to infiltrate the base. Maybe she wouldn't. She hadn't decided yet, but she knew it was a decision she would have to make soon. They had run out of options.

The others were waiting for her in the basement, seated around her mother's worktable. She connected Eli's off-grid laptop to a wall projector and opened a drawing program.

"The suit is made of nanites, tiny robots or computers, too small for the human eye to see. These nanites are miraculous by the standards of modern engineering. They're barely visible through one of our microscopes. I would say this tech is at least twenty years ahead of what we've seen in the field of engineering, maybe more."

She made a series of dots across the screen in a toggled grid.

"Did the suit come from the aliens?" Eli said.

Wendy shrugged. "I don't know. There's no information about who built the suit."

"Is there anything that connects it to the Air Force?" Jane said.

Wendy shook her head. "There's nothing that connects it to anything. No information whatsoever about any organization. No names, no places. Just dates and facts. How the suit was built. How it works. How to use it."

"Oh good, another mystery," Eli said.

"Let's worry about where it came from later," Wendy said. She pointed at the projection on the wall. "Most of the nanites in the suit turn the wearer invisible. Beyond that there are several types of nanites that perform unique functions. Think of them as specialists." She doodled over each of the dots, giving each one a unique size and shape.

"These would all look the same under a standard microscope, but a more powerful microscope would show that they are quite different from each other." She tapped the keyboard, and a yellow box appeared around one of the dots, highlighting it. "This one records audio and video."

Wendy clicked the keyboard again, highlighting another nanite. "This one sends and receives data to and from a remote location.

She tapped the keyboard again, and the highlighter moved to the next dot. "This is a binder. It binds other nanites together."

Wendy turned off the projector. "There are hundreds of nanites with special functions, but all of them communicate with each other. This technology is advanced, even for me, but from what I can tell, whoever developed the fabric either couldn't get all the nanites to play nice together or couldn't make them fit in a single piece of fabric." She pointed at the silver case. "That's why there are five swatches. Each one does something different."

"What do the others do?" Devin said.

Wendy bit her bottom lip and stared at the sliver case for a moment before she removed the medallion from her pocket. She pressed it against the side of the case, and it popped open.

She lifted up the invisibility fabric and removed the little flash drive that was tucked beneath it, and then she held it up for the others to see. "Each swatch of fabric has an accompanying flash drive with all the specs, blueprints, instructions, everything you could want to know about it, much of which I barely understand."

She set the flash drive back and laid the invisibility fabric over it, and then she pointed at the next piece of fabric in the case. "Except this one. There's no flash drive. I don't know what this one does."

She indicated another swatch. "This one is a teleportation suit."

Eli's eyes grew wide. "A what?"

"Teleportation suit. Don't get excited just yet. It's broken." She glanced thoughtfully at it. "Actually at first I thought we could use this one. Pop into the base, grab what we need, pop out, but that's not going to happen."

"What about the other two?" Jane said.

Wendy pointed at another piece of fabric. "I'm pretty sure this one is for espionage," Wendy said. "It's basically a disguise."

"What kind of disguise?" Jane said.

"It makes the wearer look like someone else. Face, hair, clothing, everything changes."

"Are you serious?" Jane said, leaning forward. She reached out and touched the fabric, but Wendy swatted her hand away.

"Like I said, I don't understand how it works. We're not going to mess with anything that might reconfigure your face," she said.

Jane nodded but kept her eyes fixed on the swatch.

"And this one," Wendy said, lifting the last piece of fabric from the case. "This one is a full body shield. It emits a force field that repels punches, blows, even bullets. But we have no use for it."

"Why not?" Devin said. "That could come in handy."

"Because we're definitely not entering a top-secret air force base with guns blazing," she said.

She ran her hand across the swatches. "I don't know where they originated, but I don't think my father built them, and I have no idea how he came to be in possession of them or why."

"I bet it has something to do with General Honorine Bartlett," Devin said.

They all looked at him.

"She works at the highest levels of the Pentagon. Maybe she supplied him with these suits so he could find out what those traitors were up to."

"You think my father was working as a spy?"

"I wouldn't put it that way, but yeah, it's possible."

Wendy stared at Devin. Then she blinked and snapped out

of it. "Let's stay focused." She took a breath and turned back to the case. "Now let me show you the accessories," she said.

Wendy removed a layer of foam and set it aside. She removed a pair of goggles.

"Although my dad didn't build the suits, I think he might have been involved in building these goggles, which makes sense, since they're similar—and I use the word *similar* loosely—to what he was working on for the air force."

"What do they do?" Eli asked.

"Everything the ones he developed for the air force couldn't do, including a few things I'd love to incorporate on the BIM." Wendy looked down as a heaviness cast over her eyes. She lifted up the goggles. "They're infrared, with one hundred percent brightness. It looks like broad daylight when you view a nightscape through them. They have built-in sensors, similar to radar, plus X-ray capability. And they can go online, so the view through the goggles can be overlaid with data. Plus they do everything else you'd expect: record audio and video, GPS, and so on. And of course they're coated with nanites, so they are as invisible as the rest of you when you're wearing the suit."

"Nice," Eli said, "May I?" He held out his hand.

"Here you go." Wendy handed him the goggles.

Eli took the goggles and inspected them under a task light.

Next Wendy removed what looked like a case for contact lenses. "These are earbuds," she said. "But they mold themselves to the skin just inside your ear. Full stereo sound." She clicked the case open and held it up for them to see.

"They look like lumps of clay," Jane said.

"That's because they get fitted into the ear. You kind of smoosh them around the earhole."

"How many of those do you have?" Devin asked.

"A whole bunch. This pair is already configured to work with the invisibility suit. The others are not." She closed the case and set it back into the foam. Eli handed her the goggles and she put those away too.

"And the most important accessory…" She reached into the other side of the case and removed a stack of what looked like thin strips of e-paper. "They're wristcoms. Lighter and more flexible than any I've seen. This is what controls the suit, and it's configured to interact with the earbuds and goggles too."

"Amazing," Eli said. "Can I try on the suit after you?"

They all stared at him.

"What?" he said, shrugging and looking around at them. "Like you all don't want to try it on."

"One step at a time," Wendy said. "Like I said, I read the manual, and I know how to work it, but I don't completely understand how it works. If something goes wrong—if it breaks—that's it—we're out of commission. I want to do some tests and experiments with it. Let's see how that goes, OK?"

Jane and Eli nodded but Devin said nothing.

"All right; then let's get started," Wendy said. "Jane, I'll need your help."

Wendy snapped the case closed. She removed the medallion and picked up the case by its handle. Jane followed her upstairs to Wendy's bedroom, where Wendy stripped down to her underwear and bra. She opened the silver case, retrieved the earbuds, and pressed a lump of the claylike material into each ear. Then she strapped the goggles on and pressed the paper-thin wristcom around her wrist.

Finally she lifted the red-sheen fabric from the case and held it up. "Here goes nothing," she said.

She wrapped the fabric around her body like a blanket. Then she raised her arm and tapped the wristcom.

Jane's jaw dropped as she watched the fabric wrap itself around Wendy's body, separating from itself to create new seams and then resealing. Jane shook her head. "Eli and Devin are going to be sorry they missed this." She looked Wendy up and down and grinned. "For a number of reasons."

Wendy blushed as the suit finished fitting itself to her body. She continued taking deep breaths until it was done.

"You look…" Jane was at a loss for words.

"What?" Wendy said.

"You look sexy," Jane said. She tilted her head to one side.

"Don't get any funny ideas," Wendy said.

"Oh please, you're like a sister to me," Jane said.

Wendy grinned and tapped the wristcom again, and she disappeared.

Jane gasped and stood there with her mouth hanging open. She stared at the spot where Wendy had been standing a moment earlier.

"I'm still right in front of you," Wendy said, and Jane almost jumped.

"Let's see what happens if you make contact with the suit while I'm wearing it. Try to touch me," Wendy said.

Jane reached out her arms and took a few steps until her hand came into contact with something soft and fleshy.

"No need to feel me up," Wendy said, jerking back. She tapped the wristcom and reappeared.

Jane laughed. "OK, let's go show the boys."

When they reached the basement, Jane said, "Here she is."

Eli and Devin looked up, dumbfounded when they saw Wendy in a skin-tight shimmery bodysuit.

"How does it feel?" Jane asked.

Wendy raised her arms and waved them around. "Not bad," she said. "I thought it would feel heavier, but it's quite light. I almost feel naked." Without thinking, she reached up to brush her face. "But it feels kind of weird on my face."

"Because you're not used to wearing clothing there," Devin said. "You'll get used to it."

"You kind of look like Catwoman," Eli said.

"Who?" Wendy said.

"Catwoman," Eli repeated.

Wendy shook her head, shrugged, and then she flexed her toes and pivoted her ankles to see how the suit moved with her body.

"You don't know who Catwoman is?" Jane asked.

"Should I?" Wendy said.

The others looked at each other with grins on their faces.

"Actually, yeah," Jane said. "It wouldn't hurt for you to know about her if you're going to go around dressed like that. All you need is a whip."

"You mean a cat-o'-nine-tails," Eli said.

"Even better," Jane said, arching one eyebrow.

Wendy glanced at them, a curious look on her face.

"She's from Batman," Eli said. "If you haven't heard of him…"

"I know who Batman is," Wendy said. Then she added, "I think" under her breath.

She slowly put one foot in front of the other and walked across the room. When she turned and came back, she moved quicker and more naturally.

"I think I've got this," she said. "The bottoms of my feet feel weird. The nanites are constantly moving and adjusting to protect my feet."

"But you're comfortable?" Jane asked.

Wendy flapped her arms and bent her head from side to side. "Yeah, I think I am." Then she looked at Devin, who had been quietly observing. "Let's try some judo," she said.

Wendy spent almost an hour getting used to the suit. She and Devin went out to the field behind the house, and Eli and Jane watched from the porch as they worked through some judo exercises. Then they all followed Wendy into the grove so she could see what climbing a tree would be like.

Next she wanted to test her fine motor movements. Eli

supplied her with a game on one of his electronic tablets.

"Unbelievable," she said as she tapped, swiped, and danced her fingers over the keyboard. "It feels like I'm wearing surgical gloves, thin and flexible, but not as suffocating. Much better, actually."

Finally, she set the game aside and rose to her feet. "Now let's turn it on."

They returned to the basement. Wendy didn't want anyone to see her disappearing in the front yard—or the backyard for that matter.

"Here I go," Wendy said. She raised her arm and swiped the com, and then she disappeared.

"Badass!" Jane yelped.

Eli's stared in awe. "That is the coolest thing I've ever seen," he said.

Devin watched silently, with a thoughtful look on his face.

Wendy's voice seemed to come from a disembodied being. "OK, let's go through it all again, this time while I'm invisible. Devin, you up for sparring against someone you can't see?"

"Let's do it," Devin said.

- 23 -

Risk

City Outskirts
Swenson, Colorado

Later that evening, after Devin had gone home, Eli was still working in the basement, studying the software for the invisibility fabric and its accessories. Wendy and Jane were out on the porch, sitting in the swing. Wendy was sipping an iced tea, and Jane was drinking a Tom Collins.

Wendy spoke quietly. "I'm thinking about going into the base."

Jane sat forward abruptly, and her drink sloshed onto the porch. "I knew it," she said. "Are you crazy? Why would you do something like that when Devin is trained and willing?"

"I can't explain it," Wendy said. "It's something I need to do."

Jane shook her head. "I love you like a sister, but I can't support this. Do you have any idea how much danger you'd be in?"

Wendy nodded. "I do, but I'll have you guys backing me up. Devin can help me prepare."

"Do you really think he'll do that?"

Wendy shrugged. "I hope so."

Jane sighed and swirled her drink. The ice cubes clinked against the side of the glass. "It's a bad idea, Wendy Bird."

"Maybe." Wendy set her glass down and turned to Jane. "When we were in college, and you used to go off on all your protests, I thought you were crazy. I wasn't judging you or anything. I just thought there were better ways—safer ways—for you to try to make the kind of changes you wanted to make."

"There are safer ways," Jane said.

"Right, but you often chose the riskier options. Remember when you went to that rally where the cops were tear gassing the protesters?"

Jane sipped her drink and nodded. "I went to many protests like that."

"Yeah, but you decided to go after they'd started tear gassing. My mother was arrested at a similar protest when she was younger."

"Really? You never told me that."

"It was before I was born," Wendy said. "Back in college you got arrested a bunch of times."

"True, but what you're talking about doing is not like anything I've done. When you get arrested for civil disobedience, half the time they never even fill out the paperwork. They let you go when things cool down. Worst-case scenario, you go to county court and pay a small fine. This is different, Wendy. If you get caught, you'll face trial—maybe a secret trial. I won't be able to represent you because I'm not a criminal lawyer, and it won't matter anyway because you'll be guilty, and you'll go away for a long time—the rest of your life."

"I don't think that's going to happen."

"You don't know what's going to happen."

"You're right, but I need to do this. I can't explain it. Ever since Devin mentioned it, I've been thinking about it nonstop. I've been having strange dreams…"

"Your dreams are telling you to infiltrate a top-secret military base?"

"Not quite," Wendy said. "But I think whatever compelled you to take the risks you took when we were in college is the same thing that's compelling me now."

"I was a rebellious kid who wanted to see justice done."

Wendy nodded. "Exactly."

"Don't get mad, but do you think you're feeling rebellious out of grief?"

"Maybe," Wendy said. "But it doesn't matter. I don't want these guys overthrowing the government, and I want to know the truth about what happened to my parents. If they were killed—murdered—then I want justice for them. You were trying to save the world, and I always admired that about you." Wendy sighed and picked up her iced tea. "But this is personal."

Jane nodded. "I understand that." She leaned back against the swing. "I've never seen you like this," she said.

"Does it bother you?"

"Yes." Jane folded her arms across her chest. "It upsets me that you're suddenly interested in engaging in criminal activity and high-risk behavior. It's the exact opposite of the Wendy I know." She looked at Wendy. "You're the most reliable, consistent person I've ever known. It's a little scary seeing you like this."

Neither of them said anything for a moment.

"You've already made up your mind, haven't you?" Jane finally said.

"Pretty much," Wendy said. "I need your support."

Jane scooted over and wrapped her arms around Wendy. "If you really need to do this, then you'll have my support."

Wendy squeezed Jane. "Thank you. You're the best friend I could ever wish for."

"But there is one condition," Jane said.

"What's that?"

"You're going to test the hell out of that suit before you do anything crazy. I will not only withdraw my support—I will physically stop you from entering that base unless you make sure that suit works perfectly, including getting past security."

"I can agree to that," Wendy said.

They settled back on the swing. "Now I just have to convince Eli and Devin to go along with it," Wendy said.

"Well, the hard part is already over," Jane said. "They're going to be easier to convince than me."

* * *

"I can't believe you're on board with this!" Eli was shouting at Jane. Wendy took a step back. She'd never heard him raise his voice. He barely talked to strangers. And now he was yelling at her best friend, whom he barely knew.

Devin was sitting quietly and scowling at Wendy. It had become his standard expression over the last couple of days.

"She's already made up her mind, and she's going to need our help," Jane said.

"Did you even try to talk her out of it?" Eli said.

"Of course I did," Jane said. "You know how she is once she decides to do something."

Eli turned to Devin. "You can't let her do this."

Devin glared at Wendy. "I can't stop her," he said.

"So you'll help me?" Wendy said.

Devin shook his head. "Yoshi said you were strong. He never said you were stubborn. Or foolish."

"He said I was strong?"

Devin rose out of his chair. "It's a fool's errand. You're

taking an unnecessary risk."

"I have to do something," Wendy said.

"No, you don't. Something has to be done, but you don't have to be the one to do it," Devin said.

"I guess I was wrong about them being easier to convince than I was," Jane said.

"Why would you choose to sneak into the base when I'm trained for missions like this? Why?"

"I have to do this," Wendy said. She got to her feet and looked at Eli and Devin. "I will sit here and argue with you about it all day, if that's what you want. But nothing is going to change my mind." She pointed at the door. "And if you want out, there's the door. I said any of you can leave for any reason, no questions asked. I want your help, but I'm doing this with or without it."

"Your father would not approve of this," Devin said.

"My father's not here," Wendy said. "And if he were, we wouldn't be having this discussion."

"If the first thing I do after losing Yoshi is let something happen to you—"

"You're not letting anything happen to me," Wendy said. "This is my decision. Even if it all goes wrong, it's not your fault or responsibility."

Devin folded his arms across his chest and then leaned against the wall but said nothing.

"I'm not asking you to understand. I'm just asking you to make a decision. Will you help me or not?" Wendy said.

"I do understand," Devin said. "It's not a question of understanding."

"Well, I don't," Eli sputtered. "I think you're acting insane. What kind of friends would we be if we went along with this? It's madness!" His face was red, and he looked like he was about to burst. Instead he shook his head, grabbed his yo-yo, and stormed out of the room.

"I'll go talk to him," Jane said.

"No," Wendy said. "He'll come around. Just give him some time to cool down. He just needs to get used to the idea. Once he realizes how cool it will be, he'll be back."

"You've got this all figured out, don't you?" Devin said.

"No, not yet. That's why I need all of you to help me. So we can figure it out together."

"Right. Then I should go in, not you."

Wendy sighed and eased back into her chair. "You're right," she said. "You should be the one to go in. You're trained for this kind of thing."

Devin perked up a little when she said that.

"But that's not going to happen." Wendy knew her friends would argue, but she hadn't expected their emotions to run so high, and she hadn't expected such a strong reaction from Devin. They barely knew each other. Why was he so adamant?

Devin pulled out a chair and sat down. "Fine," he said. "What do you want me to do?"

"I want you to train me," Wendy said.

"It takes months to train for something like this," Devin said.

"I think we can get through the basics in a couple of weeks," Wendy said.

"What about me?" Jane said.

"You're in charge of logistics. Mission coordinator," Wendy said.

The stairs creaked, and the three of them turned as Eli descended. "And me? What do you want me to do?"

"That was fast," Devin muttered.

Wendy got up and walked over to Eli. "Communications. I need you to be my eyes and ears. Make sure the audio and video work. Communicate with me while I'm inside the base. I figure you can rig something, maybe in Devin's bus."

Eli nodded. "I can do that."

Wendy looked around at her friends. "So you're all on board?"

They all looked at each other.

"We're on board," Jane said.

Eli shrugged.

"I'm willing to help you with training and planning," Devin said. "Let's see how that goes, and then I'll let you know if I'm on board."

Wendy sighed. It was the best she could hope for, but none of them looked happy about it.

- 24 -

Training

City Outskirts
Swenson, Colorado

Wendy pulled the knife back, positioning it above her shoulder, and with a fluid, whipping motion threw it at the target that Devin had pinned to a big oak tree on her parents' property. The knife sailed through the air and hit the target dead center.

Devin walked to the tree and removed the three knives she had thrown, two of which had hit the outer rings of the target.

"Not bad," he said as he walked back to her and handed her the knives.

Not bad. A week ago she hadn't been able to get a knife to land inside the target. Now the knives rarely landed outside of it. Devin had been steadfast in training Wendy, but he had also been steadfast in his refusal to praise her progress. Jane had joked that Devin was as stubborn as Wendy. He had agreed to help, but he still wasn't comfortable with Wendy's plan.

Wendy glanced at her wristcom. "Don't you think that's enough knife throwing for today? I want to get to the city in time for the lunch rush."

"One more set," Devin said.

Wendy nodded. She tucked two of the knives into sheaths on her belt and then threw the third, missing the center target by only an inch.

"Try again," Devin said.

Wendy pulled the next knife from the sheath.

Devin had dubbed their plan the Carter Mission, and he had been training Wendy for a week. They spent mornings practicing weapons. Wendy refused to carry a gun, insisting there was no way she would ever use it. She was going to be invisible, and the need for any weapon was almost nonexistent. The worst-case scenario was that the suit might fail, and she would be exposed. She would let herself be taken into custody before trying to shoot her way out of the base.

So they focused on more traditional weapons: knives, swords, and sparring sticks. Wendy was clumsy with the sparring sticks, so Devin made her spend a lot of time working with them, pointing out that in many situations one could find a stick, a pipe, or some similar object to fight with. "You can pop the leg off a table if you have to," he had said. Wendy didn't see that happening, but she continued to practice with the sticks diligently. Her earlier judo training kicked in, and she made decent progress each day.

She had initially thought sword practice was absurd, outdated, and unrealistic, but Devin had said sword fighting would teach her to be fast, light, and stealthy on her feet. And he was right. Working with the dull, wooden practice swords forced her to be more aware of everything around her, alert to the tiniest motion. She'd been surprised to discover that she quite liked working with swords.

She had reluctantly agreed to carry a blade when she embarked on the mission, so they spent the most time working with knives. Devin taught her about the different blades and showed her a range of throwing techniques.

She threw the next knife and once again hit the target dead center.

A grin crept onto her face. She eyed Devin, but he kept his eyes on the target. "Next," he said.

The third knife landed between the first two.

"That's enough for today," Devin said.

He walked to the target and plucked the knives out of the tree trunk. Wendy packed the knives while Devin rolled up the target. They put the equipment away in the garage, and after a quick lunch of veggie wraps and fruit, they climbed into Devin's bus and headed into Boulder for Wendy's stealth training. It was an hour drive, and they made good use of the time, reviewing their strategy for the upcoming mission.

The plan was as vague as could be, which bothered Devin. Wendy would get inside the base, locate Kell, and shadow him. She would be wearing cameras and audio recording equipment, so if he said or did anything incriminating, they'd have their evidence. Eli was procuring bugs that she could place in strategic locations, and these would give them several days of recordings after Wendy's mission ended.

There was no way of knowing what Kell would do or where he might go, and though they were putting the suit through rigorous testing, Devin felt like they didn't know enough about it. Where had it come from? Who had built it? But it was the best plan they had come up with.

"You're trailing Kell through the base, and a bunch of officers comes up behind you. What do you do?"

Wendy thought about it. "I try to stay between the officers and Kell. If I think they're going to close in, I try to get out of their way and catch up to Kell later."

Devin shook his head, and Wendy sighed. Devin had been testing her by presenting various scenarios, and she had to say what she would do in any given situation. If she gave the wrong answer, he'd drill the correct one into her head.

This is what they did as they drove into Boulder for stealth practice.

"You get in front of Kell," Devin said.

"But he might take an unexpected turn, and then I'll lose him."

"Then you turn around and resume pursuit. You don't want to get stuck in the middle of a moving crowd while you're on the base."

They drove in silence for a few minutes. Today's scenarios were mild. He often gave her scenarios that frightened her. She wasn't sure if he did that because he thought they were plausible or because he wanted to scare her into backing off. It didn't matter. She'd made up her mind.

"When are your friends coming back?" Devin said.

There hadn't been much for Jane and Eli to do while Wendy trained with Devin, so they had flown back to Massachusetts. Jane had returned to work, rescheduling her sabbatical for early the following year. Eli was gathering their equipment—bugs, off-grid coms, and a load of software they could use. Eli and Jane were still meeting in the evenings to review the files on the flash drive. They had insisted they would focus on looking for anything that might lead them to evidence of a coup, but they had both become fascinated with the Roswell files.

Eli had also been tasked with closing up the BIM lab indefinitely. Wendy hoped six weeks would give her enough time to complete the mission, regain her bearings, and then figure out what to do—shut down the project permanently or try to raise more money, which seemed a hopelessly impossible task. And she wasn't sure what to do with the few months of funding they had left—continue their work, try to merge with some other team, or sell it all.

She gnawed on her lower lip as she thought about the BIM.

She had a sinking, persistent feeling that the project she had dedicated her entire career to was over. She couldn't imagine what else she would do with herself, and whenever these thoughts invaded her mind, anxiety consumed her.

However, the thought of breaching Carter Air Force Base did not faze her. It was all part of this new, nightmarish part of her life that felt surreal.

She pushed thoughts of the BIM out of her mind. She needed to stay focused.

"They'll be here two days before the mission," Wendy said. "Eli's going to need at least a day to train us on the equipment he's acquiring."

Devin gave her a sideways glance. "I hope you're ready by then."

Devin told the bus to find a spot in a parking structure near the busiest part of downtown Boulder. Wendy stepped into the back of the bus and slid out of her loose sweatpants and tee shirt, revealing the invisibility suit she wore beneath her clothing.

"You ready?" Devin said as the bus pulled to a stop and the engine switched off.

"Let's do it," Wendy said, and then she tapped her wrist and disappeared.

Devin opened the door and stood by casually as Wendy hopped out. He checked the wristcom that Eli had rigged, which showed Wendy's location as a red dot on a map, so Devin could track her while she was invisible.

"All systems go?" Wendy asked as Devin closed the door.

"We're a go," Devin said. Then he turned and followed the red dot on his com.

Wendy had mixed feelings about their daily stealth training. She had found invisibility to be freeing, even empowering. She lost all sense of inhibition while wearing the suit. But sometimes it made her nervous and uncomfortable. One day she'd overheard a private conversation between a young man and woman. They were discussing a pregnancy, and Wendy had felt as if she'd violated them by simply being in the wrong place and overhearing their very personal conversation. This had made her nervous, and when she got nervous she became clumsy. That day she'd banged her knee into a park bench in downtown Swenson. The man and woman had nearly jumped off the bench because they were so startled.

Wendy checked her own map as she exited the parking garage and turned west toward the business district. After spending a week's worth of afternoons in Swenson, Devin had decided they needed bigger crowds for Wendy to navigate. Today she would be going in and out of businesses to practice entry and exit, and she'd ride at least three elevators and two escalators that were carrying other passengers. Then she'd work her way from the far end of the Boulder's business district back to the parking garage when the evening rush hour was at its height.

She sighed and lumbered forward, snaking around two women dressed in business casual attire. It was going to be a long afternoon.

- 25 -

Physical

Carter Air Force Base
Swenson, Colorado

The sound of her feet hitting the treadmill pounded in her ears. *Boom, boom, boom.* She'd been running for almost three hours, varying her speed every twenty minutes. According to the odometer, she had covered more than 235 kilometers. She quickened her pace, and a screeching sound filled the room.

"That's enough," Colonel Kell said. "We can't afford to burn up another treadmill."

She came to an immediate halt and stood frozen in place while Dr. Walsh took her vitals.

"She barely broke a sweat," Major Nichols said.

She wasn't sure how she knew, but she was certain it was not normal for a group of doctors and air force officers to stand around, watching one person running on a treadmill day after day. They were always watching her. Colonel Kell and Major Nichols often talked about her as if she wasn't there in the same room with them.

She glanced at Lieutenant Smith as Dr. Walsh moved a

handheld scanner over various parts of her body. Smith was quiet, and when he wasn't staring at her, his eyes were darting around at the others.

"Heart rate 166," Dr. Walsh said. "Temperature 37.3, respiration rate 32 BPM, and blood pressure 110/70. Very good. Maximum speed 93 kilometers per hour."

"Can she go faster?" Kell said. "Or has she reached her threshold?"

Dr. Walsh turned off the scanner and handed it to Dr. Sommers. "I believe we've reached the threshold. She can certainly go longer, but her maximum speed has remained steady, between ninety and ninety-five kilometers per hour, for over a week. She can sustain that speed for about forty minutes."

"She's ready," Kell said. "We need to move to the next phase in her physical training."

"She's not ready for hand-to-hand combat yet," Dr. Walsh said.

"She's damn well—" Kell stopped himself and lowered his voice. "We're behind schedule. It's imperative that we're ready to begin phase two—"

"She has at least a week of ethics training to complete before she can engage in any form of combat." Dr. Walsh's voice was stern.

Colonel Kell raised his voice. "Ethics training?"

Dr. Walsh lowered his voice to a whisper. "I'm not going to approve her for combat training until we know she understands the rules of engagement. We know her behavior and speech were affected by the…" He glanced at her and smiled his crooked-toothed smile before turning back to Kell. "We need to make sure her ethics haven't been compromised. She can start in one week. I am not going to risk failure because we overlooked an important detail."

She observed the two men with a disinterested look on her

face, but she was noting every muscle twitch and vocal tone. She had been studying interpersonal interactions due to Dr. Walsh's concern about her social skills.

Dr. Walsh was still smiling with his mouth, but there was something else in his eyes. Anger? Annoyance? She had not yet mastered reading people's emotions.

"Dr. Sommers and I need to speak with her now," Dr. Walsh said. "Alone."

Kell glared at Dr. Walsh. "I will attend all prototype meetings."

"We'll be discussing the female reproductive system."

Major Nichols snickered, and Kell's glare faded to discomfort. "I'll pass," he said.

"We'll see you tomorrow, then?" Dr. Walsh's voice was suddenly chipper.

Kell grunted and left the room without answering. Major Nichols followed him, glancing back at the others with a snide grin on his face.

Lieutenant Smith closed the black box that held his computer and turned to leave the gym.

"You can come with us, Lieutenant Smith," Dr. Walsh said.

Smith paused at the door and nodded.

Dr. Walsh led them out of the gym and to his office down the hall.

"Have a seat." Dr. Walsh approached his desk and sat in the chair behind it. "We're not here to talk about her reproductive system," he said to Lieutenant Smith.

"I figured," Smith said.

Dr. Walsh ran a hand over his mussed hair. "She's already read an advanced college text on human anatomy. It only took her six hours."

"And passed the accompanying tests with flying colors," Dr. Sommers added.

"She knows how the female reproductive system works."

Dr. Walsh looked at her. "Isn't that right?"

"I have studied both male and female reproductive systems thoroughly," she said.

"We need to have a sensitive conversation," Dr. Walsh said to Lieutenant Smith. "Not the kind of thing Colonel Kell excels at."

Lieutenant Smith was looking at Dr. Walsh with interest.

"It's not a secret," Dr. Walsh said. "She's merely being debriefed. It will all be in tomorrow's report. But I'd appreciate it if you could be discreet until then."

"No problem," Lieutenant Smith said.

"I trust you, and I think you should be present for this conversation," Dr. Walsh said. "For observation." He eyed the black box.

"Gotcha," Lieutenant Smith said.

Dr. Walsh turned toward her. "We'd like to share with you some of the details of your accident and the treatments we've administered. You need to understand what—who you are. You see, you're different from other...uh...people. Your studies in human anatomy will certainly be useful, but your anatomy is slightly different from other humans. We haven't given you much detail regarding your injuries or your treatment because we felt it would be emotionally overwhelming."

"I do not experience emotions," she said.

"Yes, well, that wasn't always the case," Dr. Walsh said. "But now we feel you can handle the information." He nodded at Dr. Sommers.

Dr. Sommers tapped his tablet and handed it to her. "Do you know what that is?"

She took the tablet, and Lieutenant Smith leaned over to see what she was looking at.

"It is labeled 'donor form,'" she said. She handed the tablet back to Dr. Sommers. "I cannot read all of it."

"Most of it's redacted," Lieutenant Smith said.

"It's your donor form," Dr. Sommers said. "Well, not yours, but it belonged to the person you used to be."

"Before my accident?"

"Yes."

"I do not understand."

"Sorry?"

"I do not understand how an accident made me a different person."

"Because you died, and when we brought you back to life you became something—someone—else."

What the doctor was saying made no sense. She didn't understand, so she said nothing in response, even though both doctors usually became annoyed when she was unresponsive.

"You were technically dead, so your donor form went into effect," Dr. Walsh said. "Do you understand?"

She considered for a moment. "Some of my parts were donated to patients in need?"

"No," Dr. Walsh said. "This is not a standard donor form. It's military issue. When you sign it, you effectively donate your entire body—your person—to the military upon your death."

"But I am alive."

"Yes, we have established that," Dr. Walsh said. "But when you were dead, your body became property of the US Air Force. You were revived, but that did not change your status. Now do you understand?"

"I am property of the US Air Force?"

"Let's stay focused on the accident and your treatments," Dr. Walsh said.

She considered it. A person could not be property. She was certain that was illegal. But could a dead body become property? And if so, would it remain property if its life were restored? Dr. Walsh had already changed the subject, and that was definitely a sign that she should not inquire further on the matter.

Dr. Walsh continued, "The accident—you were in a plane crash—was severe. One of your arms was severed. Both of your legs were crushed. The bones were practically turned to dust. You suffered broken ribs, internal bleeding, and a skull fracture. You died."

"But I am not dead."

Dr. Walsh and Dr. Sommers exchanged a glance, one of the many odd looks people gave each other. She was sure it meant something, but she didn't know what.

"No, but only because we resuscitated you," Dr. Sommers said. "You were dead for more than twelve hours. We had to go to extreme measures in order to revive and restore you. As a result you are different from other…people."

"I am stronger, faster, and smarter."

Dr. Sommers smiled. "That's right. Do you know why you are stronger and faster?"

"No."

"Normally when a person loses a limb, they are given a prosthetic." He picked up his e-tablet and showed her a picture of a man with a prosthetic arm. "As you can see, they are quite advanced nowadays, not quite like the real thing but rather close. However, they are easily detectible."

He reverse pinched the screen and zoomed in on the prosthetic. She could see the seam where the prosthetic met the human flesh. There was a difference in skin tone and texture.

"Your replacement parts are different, better. They are indistinguishable from the rest of your body, because they are fully integrated and grown from organic and synthetic materials." Dr. Walsh nodded at his colleague. "Dr. Sommers, go ahead, please."

Dr. Sommers picked up a piece of metal that was sitting on Dr. Walsh's desk and handed it to her.

"That is titanite, a metal alloy. Try to bend it. You'll see that it's slightly flexible."

She applied pressure to the metal, and it bent easily. She nearly folded it in half.

Lieutenant Smith let out a low whistle.

She turned to look at him.

Dr. Sommers reached out and took the metal from her. "It's flexible but nearly indestructible." He stared at the folded piece of titanite. "Working it usually requires the application of a complex chemical compound."

Next he handed her a chunk of plastic. It was soft and pliable.

"And that is plystine, a bonding agent."

She squeezed it, and the material oozed through her fingers.

Dr. Walsh cleared his throat. He leaned back in his chair and smiled. "The bones you lost were replaced with a blend of compounds." He nodded at the metal and plastic. "Titanite and plystine combined with organic materials that assisted in the growth of new muscle and tissue." He leveled his eyes at her. "You must understand, this medical technology is cutting edge. It's not available to anyone else in the world."

She held up her bare arm and studied it.

"That arm wasn't damaged in the crash," Dr. Walsh said.

She looked at her other arm. There were no scars, and the skin looked the same as the rest of the skin on her body.

"Take a look at your other arm again," he said. "The one that wasn't damaged. Although it was intact, we coated the bones with titanite for extra strength, and we regrew your original muscles and tissue with stronger ones."

"If this arm was not damaged, why was it modified?" she asked.

"We wanted you to be stronger."

"This also makes me fast?"

He nodded. "The bones, muscle, and tissue—it's all

superior to regular human parts. How do you feel about this?"

"I do not feel anything."

But the truth was she wanted to know more. They weren't telling her everything. In fact, since she had woken up in that hospital room, they had told her very little. If the metals and plastics made her stronger and faster, then what made her smarter? What had made her lose her memories? Why wouldn't they tell her what her name was?

She eyed the doctors. They were watching her with great interest, and she decided not to ask any more questions. Not yet. But for the first time since she had woken up among these men, she wanted to know exactly what they had done to her and why.

- 26 -

Infiltration

City Outskirts
Swenson, Colorado

Wendy and her friends spent the morning of the mission reviewing their plans and double-checking their supplies. Eli and Jane had returned a few days earlier. Jane was relaxed, but Eli was preoccupied with his worries about the closing of the BIM project. Every day it looked more like the closure would be permanent.

Devin was in charge of the bus, making sure it was charged and stocked with food, medicine, weapons, and other supplies, most of which Wendy doubted they would need. Her plan was to get in, get what she needed, and get out unnoticed.

Eli had been tasked with installing the communications and surveillance equipment in Devin's bus. Via Blacknet he had procured a handful of microscopic recording devices that she could leave throughout the base. If she wasn't able to capture hard evidence of Kell's coup, the bugs offered a backup that wouldn't require Wendy to reenter the base. He'd also formatted a handful of blank flash drives, so she could download the contents of any computer. Wendy tucked these items into the pouches she had configured into the suit.

Jane was in charge of logistics. She mapped their route and studied blueprints of the base. Mostly she acted as Wendy's biggest supporter, secretly hoping a little reverse psychology would compel Wendy to change her mind. But Wendy remained steadfast, much to her friends' chagrin.

Devin reluctantly helped Wendy strap knives to her forearms and one of her legs, and Jane stood by while Wendy suited up. In the final moments before they were set to launch the mission, Wendy found herself sitting cross-legged in her old bedroom, breathing deeply and trying to calm herself.

Her heart had been racing on and off throughout the day. Every so often the gravity of what she was about to attempt would thrust her into a state of shock. Her mouth kept drying up. Several times she didn't hear the others when they spoke to her. During breakfast she'd spilled her orange juice, and she'd made a rapid movement while Devin was strapping one of the knives to her forearm, resulting in a tiny nick on her skin.

Jane pulled Wendy out of her meditative position, led her into her father's study, and locked the door behind them.

"You have to do something to calm your nerves, otherwise I'm going to tell them to call it off. And if you don't think the three of us can overpower you, you are sadly mistaken, sister."

"I'm fine," Wendy insisted, but even as she said it, she feared her heart would pound right out of her chest.

"Do you think we can't see how terrified and doubtful you are? Why don't you just let Devin do it?"

"You're wrong," Wendy said. "I have no doubts about this. And I can't let Devin do it because this is my fight. My father might have died trying to stop this coup."

Jane raised her brow at that. "So this is about some duty you feel to your father?"

Wendy shrugged.

"Do you think he'd want you to do this?"

"He's not here to want anything, so he doesn't get a say."

"You're angry," Jane said, studying Wendy's face.

"No, I'm not."

"Yes, you are." Jane laughed. "You're just not used to being angry. Don't you think your father would want someone like Devin to do it? He knew Devin. They trusted each other."

"It doesn't matter what my father would want. I need to do this."

Jane looked at Wendy's eyes, and that was when she realized there was more to this than any of them had imagined. Wendy wanted to prove something—to herself, about herself. Jane had seen that look on her own face before plenty of protests, especially the dangerous ones. She was torn. Part of her didn't want to lose the Wendy she knew and loved, but another part of her was curious: what would fierce Wendy be like?

She stepped aside. "It's your call, but like I said, we need to do something about those nerves, or I'm calling it off. We'll have to postpone it until you figure out how to get control of yourself. I'm not letting you go into that base while you're in klutz mode."

"What do you suggest?" Wendy asked.

Jane smiled. "I'm glad you asked."

She put her hands on Wendy's shoulders and slowly turned Wendy around. A bottle of whisky and two shot glasses were sitting on a table between two chairs.

Wendy shook her head. "That's the stupidest—"

"Half a shot. I know you're a lightweight, and that's the prescription. Take it or leave it."

Wendy turned to Jane and was about to protest, but Jane spoke first.

"Do you trust me?" she said.

"Of course," Wendy said. "You know I do, but this is not a

good idea."

"It's just enough to take the edge off." Jane folded her arms across her chest. "And it will wear off before you step foot on the base, but you'll be relaxed by then. Take the half shot or take off that suit. You can let Devin go in, or we can postpone for another week."

Wendy sighed. She hadn't done a shot of Jack Daniels since her freshman year at college. That had been the first and last time.

Jane poured half a shot for Wendy and a full shot for herself.

"Just one for you," Wendy said, taking the bottle from Jane and screwing the cap back on. "That's *my* prescription. I want you alert today."

"As if two or four would have the slightest effect on my judgment." Jane shrugged. "But anything for you."

She raised her glass and held it out. Wendy lifted hers, and they clinked.

"To breaking all the rules in the name of truth, liberty, and justice," Jane said.

They swallowed their drinks. Jane smacked her lips as Wendy's face contorted with disgust. "That's foul," she said, handing the glass back to Jane.

"You'll thank me for it later," Jane said. She reached into her pocket and pulled out a small container of mints, which she handed to Wendy. "Whisky has a strong odor," she said.

They each took a few mints and chewed on them as they headed to the garage. Wendy was pleasantly surprised to find that Jane was right. Almost immediately the whisky had taken the edge off.

"I know this is the big time," Jane said, "but I feel like we're in high school—like we're about to break into the gym or something."

"I'm guessing that's something you actually did in high

school," Wendy said.

Jane turned around and flashed Wendy a grin.

When they got to the garage, Devin and Eli were sitting in the bus. Devin was in the driver's seat, and Eli was seated in the wraparound booth behind him. He had set up the surveillance equipment on the table.

Jane opened the passenger door and climbed in as Wendy stepped into the back and slid the door closed behind her. Devin glanced at her over his shoulder.

"Seatbelts," he said.

They all buckled up, and then Devin triggered the route he had preprogrammed into the bus. The vehicle slowly backed out of the garage. Just before they pulled onto the main road, Wendy tapped her wrist and disappeared.

About half a mile from the Carter Air Force Base, Devin pulled over. He and Jane both got out of the bus. Jane was careful to leave the passenger door open, so Wendy could slip out unseen. Devin and Jane moved to the back of the bus, opened the engine door, and pretended to inspect it as Wendy unbuckled her seatbelt and eased out the open passenger door.

"I'll stay in touch," she said in a loud whisper, and then she crept off down the road toward the base.

Jane and Devin turned at the sound of her footsteps, but they couldn't see her. They closed the engine door and then climbed back into the bus.

Eli couldn't see Wendy either, but his video feed showed him whatever she saw through the goggles. He almost jumped when the viewpoint of the camera swiveled around and looked back at the van. It was just a few feet away, and he could see himself through the open window of the passenger door. He raised his hand to wave, and the camera shook as Wendy waved back.

Devin started the bus, and they drove a mile up the highway and then turned down a rocky dirt road that led to an old, abandoned, and decrepit farmhouse. Devin maneuvered the bus around a clump of trees and parked behind it. As soon as they were stopped, Jane leaped out of her seat and climbed into the booth beside Eli, so she could watch the action. Devin turned around, sitting sideways on the driver's seat, which gave him a good view of Eli's monitor.

There wasn't much to see. Wendy was walking down the side of the road, careful to keep to the far right edge of the pavement. They had learned that the suit's biggest disadvantage was that in grass and other foliage, the wearer's footsteps could be seen. She was now passing a small field of waist-high brown grasses and weeds—not something she wanted to walk through in broad daylight with the suit on.

Within a few minutes, she came to the turnoff that would take her into the base. She stopped as soon as the guardhouse came into view. This would be the first test of her stealth.

The entire base was surround by an electrical fence that was topped with barbed wire and speckled with dire warning signs. The only way in was through the front gate. Wendy's plan was to get on the ground and army-crawl underneath it. But the gate was also protected by sensors that detected movement made by anything larger than a rat. The suit's specs said it couldn't be detected by motion sensors, but if it didn't work—if she set the sensors off—she was supposed to wiggle back out and return to the bus as fast as she could.

She approached the guardhouse and peeked inside. An officer was sitting with his back straight, playing a shoot-'em-up game on his wristcom. Every few seconds, he glanced up and looked around. Wendy was suddenly tempted to tap on the glass and mess with him. She stifled a nervous giggle.

Wendy gave the guard a final glance before she got down on all fours and spread her body flat on the asphalt in front of the gate. She shimmied along the cement, feeling like a worm. The suit made a quiet sound as it brushed against the ground, so she crawled as slowly as she could until her feet were clear of the gate. It was then that she realized she had been holding her breath. She let it out with one long exhale and then folded her arms in front of her and dropped her head into them.

Just then a car pulled in and stopped behind the gate. The driver rolled down his window and chatted with the guard. Wendy angled her head and looked behind her. The gate was swinging up, and the guard was waving the car through. She hustled to her feet and scrambled out of the way just as the car passed.

If she'd waited a few minutes, she could have walked through the gate when it went up for the car.

Now that she was inside the base, she moved briskly to the main office building, where Colonel Kell's office was located. The plan was to find his office and linger there until he appeared, and then she'd shadow him until she got the evidence they needed or until he went home. Devin had scoped the base on four different occasions over the past few weeks and determined that Kell usually stayed late, and sometimes he never left the base at all.

Wendy eyed the path to the main office building. It was narrow. There was a sprawling lawn on one side of the path and a gutter of dirt and shrubs on the other side, between the path and the building. If anyone approached from the opposite direction, she'd be forced to step aside. Of course that was exactly what happened.

As Wendy was rushing down the path, two officers came out of the building and headed straight toward her. Wendy cursed under her breath. The door to the office building was only a couple of meters away. She took a gentle step off the path and into the hard dirt, but she moved hastily. As she took the step, her foot brushed against a dry shrub.

One of the officers stopped. "Did you hear that?" he said.

The other officer had already walked a few paces ahead. He

turned and looked at his friend and then glanced around. "I didn't hear anything."

"It came from those bushes," the first airman said, pointing right at Wendy. Her heart almost stopped.

The other one scanned the shrubs. "I don't see anything. Come on, are you scared of a bird or a lizard scuttling around in the bushes?"

His friend grinned and resumed walking. "No, it just caught me off guard..."

Their voices faded as they moved off into the distance. Wendy had been holding her breath again. She released it and looked up and down the path to make sure nobody else was coming before she continued on her way.

She was surprised her friends had managed to hold their tongues during the debacle. They had made an agreement: no communication unless absolutely necessary. They could transmit audio from the bus, and she would respond by nodding or shaking her head if they asked a question. She could transmit audio too, but she'd have to avoid speaking when she was in the presence of other people. Fortunately the device on her wrist allowed her to silently send text messages, but doing so was cumbersome and time consuming.

She got to the main doors of the building and was relieved to see they were set in a wide doorway on an even wider patio, complete with a bench on either side framed by potted plants that looked pretty dried out. That gave her plenty of room to maneuver.

She walked up to the massive glass window beside the main doors and saw that it was desolate inside. There was a wraparound reception desk in a lobby with a couple of couches forming a waiting area, but it was vacant. Wendy sighed. She'd have to wait for someone to go in or come out.

She milled around the patio, peeking in the window every few minutes and refraining from making contact with her friends.

After almost an hour, a horde of people, most of them in uniform and a few wearing lab coats, came swarming into the lobby. Some lingered inside the lobby in twos and threes. Others exited the building and hurried off down the path. A few paused just outside the doors, making calls, sending messages, and conferring with colleagues. Wendy peered through the window and saw a young man with slick hair taking a seat behind the reception desk. Apparently a meeting had just concluded.

Wendy waited until the crowd thinned out and lucked out when a robotic dolly stacked with boxes approached the door. The robot paused, and the double doors slid open, giving Wendy just enough time and space to slip in as the robot exited. She moved swiftly to the far side of the reception area, keeping her back to the wall and scanning the remaining loiterers.

Once she got her bearings, she turned and moved cautiously down the corridor. The first floor was mostly conference rooms and storage closets. Kell's office was on the second floor. Her next step was to wait outside the elevators. She'd thought about using the stairs. They were off the corridor, where it was unlikely anyone would see her enter the stairwell. The problem was coming out on the second floor. There was no way to know who might be walking past when she emerged. It would cause an alarm if doors started swinging open of their own accord, so the stairs had been ruled out. However, the elevator presented its own challenges. If too many people boarded while she was inside, she'd be in serious trouble. She had to wait until there were just one or two passengers going to the same floor as her.

She waited another half hour until the elevator chimed and the doors slid open. An attractive man with dark eyes and a tall woman with beady eyes and freckles stepped out, and Wendy gracefully slid in just before the doors closed behind them.

Then she was faced with a decision: hit the button for the second floor or wait until someone came along and hit it for her.

Fortunately, the decision was made for her when the elevator lurched and started to climb. It stopped at the second floor, and when the doors opened, Wendy almost gasped. Colonel Kell was standing right in front of her.

- 27 -

Underground

Carter Air Force Base
Swenson, Colorado

Wendy pressed herself against the back wall of the elevator and watched, wide-eyed, as Colonel Kell stepped inside, pressed the button for the lobby, and then stood like a statue as the elevator descended. Wendy's heart pounded against her chest, and she felt herself break out in a sweat. She glared at Kell—the man who might have murdered her parents—while she focused on keeping her breath steady and quiet. When the elevator stopped, and he stepped out, she was so distracted by his presence that she almost forgot to slip out behind him, but at the last second, she slid through the elevator doors just as they were closing.

Kell went to a conference room and propped open the door. Wendy leaned against a wall at the back of the room for almost an hour and a half, enduring a meeting on equipment and resources. Afterward most of the officers left the building, and Wendy followed Kell back to his office on the second floor. Unfortunately he shut the door behind him too quickly for her to slip inside, and she had to wait almost an hour until someone came along and knocked on his door. It was Major Nichols, the other man her father's message had mentioned. He was a big man with sandy hair cropped close to his scalp and a florid face. Wendy caught her breath when she recognized him from photos that Eli had pulled off the Internet.

He tapped the door, and when it slid open, she had plenty of time to slip in after him.

"Have a seat," Kell said to Nichols

Wendy was shocked. She was standing in the office of the commander of an air force base where they were developing top-secret projects, and it had been relatively easy getting there—too easy. Although it gave her an adrenaline rush, she found it slightly uncomfortable.

Kell and Nichols spoke briefly about the meeting Kell had just directed, and then Kell pushed a sheet of e-paper across his desk at Nichols.

"The annual budget just came in," he said.

Nichols picked up the e-paper and reviewed it. "They cut our budget again," he said.

Kell held out his hand, and Nichols passed the e-paper back to him. "The cuts aren't as severe this year, but we're taking a hit." Kell dropped the e-paper into a drawer, as if it were a smelly pair of socks. "According to my contacts in Congress, this is the last year we'll see cuts."

"Oh, so next year the budget is going to increase?" Nichols said.

"Next year it will stay the same."

"Then Project MOTH is still a go?" Nichols asked.

"Of course it's still a go," Kell said. "The only way to ensure national security is through a robust military. They have robbed the American people of the security they deserve with these reckless budget cuts. Between the right wing slashing taxes and the left wing moving funds to their ridiculous social programs, there's little left over for us, and there's almost no incentive to fund the military with no viable foreign threats and the realities of war becoming a distant memory that most voters have never lived through."

"I still think that instead of seizing the government, we should start a war," Nichols said.

Wendy blinked her eyes. Had she heard Major Nichols correctly?

Kell was frowning at Nichols. "Are you insane? Thousands of lives or more would be lost in a war. Many of them would be American lives." He shook his head. "You're just like the rest of them—too young to truly understand the horrors of war."

"I know my history," Nichols said. "I know the horrors, and I know about the spoils."

"Benefitting from war is abhorrent," Kell said.

"With all due respect, sir, I'm sure many people would say overthrowing the government to secure a larger budget for the military is abhorrent," Nichols said.

Wendy almost gasped out loud. She couldn't believe what she was hearing.

Kell's eyes were hard and cold when he responded to the major. "We are not overthrowing the government, and our objective is not to secure a larger budget. Our objective is to restore the military to ensure it can protect this nation. We will temporarily take command, only long enough to achieve our objective."

"And install a permanent military presence in DC," Nichols added.

"That's it," Jane said in Wendy's ear. "You got it, girl. That's the evidence we need."

Jane and the others chattered in her ear. Wendy couldn't make out what they were saying. She tried to keep her focus on

Kell and Nichols, but the meeting was ending. Nichols had stood and was turning toward the door.

"Wendy, you need to take the next opportunity to get out of there." That was Devin. "Mission accomplished, pull out."

Wendy shook her head. She hadn't gotten everything she'd come for.

Before Nichols reached for the door, he turned to Kell, "Underground tonight at six?" he said.

"As usual," Kell said, and Wendy's spine tingled. Either they had dinner plans at some swanky bar, or they had a meeting at the end of the day.

As soon as Nichols departed, Eli engaged the com and hissed into her ear, "Drop a bug."

"She doesn't need to drop a bug," Devin said. "We got what we need."

"We should get as much as we can," Jane said.

Wendy wanted to tell them to be quiet, but she couldn't speak in Kell's presence. She moved to a far corner of the room and typed out a message: "STAYING. BE QUIET!"

She heard her friends' voices rising for an instant before there was a quiet click, and their end of the com went mute.

Wendy took a breath and silently composed herself.

Kell was bent over his e-tablet, studying reports. Wendy reached into the pouch on her hip and removed one of the tiny bugs Eli had prepared for her. If Kell had bothered to look up, he would have seen a tiny black chip floating through the air. Wendy saw it and palmed it to conceal it within the fabric of the suit, which gloved her hand. She stepped forward and bent down slowly, trying not to make any noise, and she stuck the device to the bottom of Kell's desk. When she rose to her feet, he was still bent over his work, and Wendy had to stop herself from breathing a sigh of relief. It had been remarkably easy to bug this man's office.

She spent the rest of the afternoon standing and squatting

against the wall by the door in Kell's office. An assistant appeared with a deli sandwich shortly after Nichols left, but nobody else came in, and Kell didn't go out for the rest of the day. He worked on his com and made a few calls. Wendy found herself extremely bored.

Kell finally got up and exited his office just before six. He almost closed the door on Wendy's face. She was stunned to find herself trapped in his office. This was the moment she had dreaded—the moment when she had to take a risk—one of the many scenarios for which Devin had prepared her. However, she couldn't have known the panic that would rise up in her chest. In this scenario she had two choices: let Kell get away and try to catch up with him later or take a risk and continue pursuing him.

Wendy thought fast. She took a deep breath, and then pulled the lever that opened the door as quickly and quietly as she could. The sound of Kell's shoes tapping against the floor filled the corridor. She poked her head out and saw him walking away from her and toward the elevator. Nobody else was around. In an instant she was out of the office and quietly sliding the door closed behind her.

Wendy quickened her pace and caught up with Kell as he was entering the elevator. She had just enough time to slip in behind him. When he exited the elevator into the lobby, she followed as he disembarked. He nodded at the front desk receptionist before heading out the double doors. Wendy's heart sank. It looked like he was leaving the base for the night.

But instead of walking toward the parking lot, he walked around the building, looking around conspicuously. He stopped in front of a back door with a sign on it that said "WARNING: UNDER CONSTRUCTION. AUTHORIZED PERSONNEL ONLY." There was a security pad beside the door. Kell entered a code and used a key card to unlock the door, and then he swung it open and stepped through. Wendy had to give it the slightest push to make room for herself to squeeze through behind him, but Kell didn't notice.

Her body had tensed because she was certain something was about to go down. The hallway was riddled with construction signs. Kell came to a corridor that was sealed off with warning signs and construction tape. He looked around before he lifted a strip of tape and ducked under it. Wendy crouched and followed him. An instant later he was standing in front of a nondescript door with hazard warnings posted on it.

Kell stood before the door for about two minutes, until footsteps echoed from the corridor. Wendy turned and saw Nichols approaching.

"You're late," Kell said without turning around.

"I ran into some trouble with the new recruits," Nichols said. "You can always go ahead without me."

"The fewer trips we make up and down, the better," Kell said. He nodded at the door. "Go ahead."

Nichols frowned and opened a panel on the wall beside the door. He looked at Kell once, and then he pressed his finger against a small pad inside the panel. When he pulled his hand away, there was a tiny drop of blood on his fingertip. He was about to stick it in his mouth, but he caught Kell glaring at him and pulled out a handkerchief and used that instead.

"DNA security," Eli whispered in Wendy's ear as Kell pressed his own finger against the panel. She gave a curt nod to let him know she'd heard. She didn't know much about DNA security systems, but the fact that a machine could take blood and verify the DNA in seconds was astonishing. It was something she and Eli had discussed as a useful feature for the BIM.

A green light illuminated the panel, and then Nichols opened the door, and they stepped through, both oblivious to the fact that Wendy was on their heels.

Beyond the door was another elevator. Activating it

required a retina scan—old-school security. Wendy barely had room to slip in because Nichols stood so close to the doors. He turned his head and looked around as she passed him and scrunched up in the corner, but he didn't say anything.

The elevator had three buttons: "G" for ground floor, "B" for basement, and "S" for subbasement. Nichols hit the "S" button, and the elevator began its descent. Wendy counted off the seconds and estimated they had descended about four or five floors. They were deep underground when they exited the elevator and moved down a short corridor.

The corridor led to a door that opened onto a catwalk, which wrapped around a large, round, two-level space that was bustling with quiet activity. The catwalk on the upper floor was lined with doors. Below, about two dozen workstations were arranged in rows. A control panel wrapped halfway around the perimeter of the room and was lined with smartscreens, many of which were displaying video feeds. Beyond the control panel, there were two sets of double doors.

Wendy looked around the room, trying to capture everything on her video feed. Some of the personnel wore military uniforms while others wore lab coats. She wondered if her father had ever been down here. The atmosphere was serious, almost tense.

"Bug it," Eli whispered in her ear.

Wendy nodded. As she reached into her pouch for a bug, Kell and Nichols started to move off. She had just enough time to stick the bug to the railing on the catwalk before she scuttled after them, catching up just as they paused outside the first door on the left.

Kell turned to Nichols "Go check on the prototype," he said. "I'll be down shortly."

Wendy raised her eyebrow. *Prototype?*

Nichols walked off as Kell stepped into his office, leaving the door open and making it easy for Wendy to enter.

She noted how spartan this office was compared to his other office. The walls were bare except for a big smartscreen on one wall, with a storage console beneath it. A large, metal desk sat at the back of the room with two meager metal folding chairs facing it. The only decor was an American flag in the far corner.

Kell walked around his desk and sat down. He triggered his com and ordered two people named Lieutenants Smith and Tripp to his office.

Just as Wendy reached into her pouch for a bug, Eli whispered in her ear, "See if there's a server—a big computer—below his desk. If there is, you'll want to download its contents."

She nodded and then stepped forward and pressed the bug underneath the lip of Kell's desktop.

Someone rapped on the doorframe. Wendy turned and saw two officers standing there. She recognized the man with dark eyes and the freckled woman with beady eyes from earlier that day in the elevator.

"Come in," Kell said.

As the two officers took their seats on the rickety old folding chairs, Wendy moved around Kell's desk. She averted her eyes from his face, since every time she looked at him, she found herself filled with rage. She was tempted to give him a whip punch. He literally wouldn't know what hit him, but then alarms would be raised, and chaos would ensue. She had to remain calm and collect as much information as possible.

"Report, Smith," Kell said.

Wendy stepped behind Kell and indeed found a computer sitting on a shelf below his desktop.

The man answered, "We're almost ready to start rolling out phase two. The labs and bunkers are set up, and we've got the bodies. Walsh is the only one holding us up."

"You think the prototype is ready, then?" the colonel

asked.

"Absolutely," the man said. "The prototype's software is stabilized, but Walsh is still hung up on behavioral issues. He doesn't want to move to phase two until we resolve those problems."

"And how long will it take to resolve those issues?"

Smith shrugged. "It's tricky stuff, sir. Could take a few weeks. Could take a few months. The problem is not with the software. We don't fully understand—"

Kell held up his hand. "I'm aware of what you're dealing with."

Smith nodded. "We've been experimenting, but trial and error probably won't solve this problem. It would help if I knew what kind of hardware I was dealing with."

Kell considered this. "You don't have clearance for the hardware specs," he said. "Could we resolve these problems during phase two?"

"I don't see why they need to be resolved at all. I mean, they're just quirks."

Kell glared at Smith. "They need to be resolved, and that is final."

Smith looked at Kell thoughtfully. "Yes, of course," he said.

"Is that Walsh's only holdup?" Kell said.

"Yes, sir," Smith said. "He gave final approval on the prototype's physical performance yesterday. Today he commandeered the control box for his next round of tests, so my work on the software is on hold."

Kell nodded and then looked at the woman. "Got anything to add, Tripp?"

"We're all ready to go if this thing backfires. We tested self-destruct last night, and it worked perfectly."

"It won't affect the prototype?"

"No, sir."

Wendy listened but couldn't make heads or tails of their conversation. Whatever the prototype was, it sounded important, and Kell was eager to move forward with it. She was crouched down beside Kell's desk, so close she could have reached out and touched him. She glanced at the computer and wondered if it contained information about the prototype.

She pulled a flash drive out of her pouch and wrapped her hand around it. If they saw the thing floating around in the air, she'd be in big trouble—trapped in a corner at the back of the colonel's office. She wanted to be ready to download his computer as soon as the opportunity arose.

Wendy examined the computer, looking for a flash port. As she did, a shiver went up her spine, and she looked up to find Kell staring right at her.

The temptation to flee was all consuming, but it was quickly replaced with an urge to ram her palm into his nose. She resisted both temptations and managed to remain still.

"And how long will you need to prepare for the rollout?" Kell said, turning back toward the officers.

"I can be ready in as little as a week," the man said. Wendy eased out of her crouch and rose to her feet. Being so close to Kell suddenly seemed like a very bad idea. She could download the computer later, when he was away from his desk.

"Very well," the colonel said. "I'll take care of Walsh. You two make sure we're ready to move forward as soon as I give the order."

"Yes, sir," they said simultaneously.

"You're dismissed," the colonel said.

As the two officers rose, Wendy moved from behind the desk. Her eyes were busy darting back and forth between the colonel and his officers, so she didn't see the briefcase on the floor until she kicked it and it slid forward, knocking into the chair that the female officer had been sitting in.

The two officers both turned their heads at the sound.

"What was that?" Kell asked.

Horrified, Wendy tiptoed back to her earlier position and stood with her back flat against the wall.

"Your briefcase, sir," Smith said. He stepped over and picked it up as the colonel rose to his feet. Wendy inched across the floor, keeping her back against the wall, grateful this room had no windows or drapes that she might disturb as she worked her way around its perimeter.

Smith handed the briefcase to Colonel Kell. The woman's shoes clicked against the cement floor as she returned to the colonel's desk. She stared at the briefcase, her eyebrows pushed together.

Kell took the briefcase and gingerly turned it over in his hands. Wendy moved out of the corner and inched down the long wall toward the door.

"You must have bumped it with your foot," Smith said to the woman.

She shook her head. "I didn't. I would have felt it. It just tipped over and slid across the floor."

At that, Kell's eyes darted to hers. "It slid across the floor?"

"Yes sir. It was sitting on the floor beside your desk. I wasn't sitting close enough to have knocked it over, and even if I were, I couldn't have kicked it toward myself. When I heard the noise and turned around, it had slid about two feet, from your desk toward my chair."

"Close the door," Kell said, and the woman stepped across the room and pulled the door shut. Wendy was just a meter away from it. She closed her eyes and bit her bottom lip.

The colonel stepped out from behind his desk, and Wendy breathed a sigh of relief. She would have been in a tight spot if she hadn't moved down the wall. She continued inching toward the door.

"Show me," Kell said, handing the briefcase to the woman.

She set the briefcase on the floor, upright, with one side

pressed flush against the desk. Then she sat down in her chair.

"That's where it was while we were talking." She kicked her leg out. "It was out of my range," she said. Then she walked to the side of the desk, nodded at the colonel, and said, "Excuse me."

He stepped back, and she got behind the desk and gave the briefcase a push with her foot. It slid forward about two feet, bumped into her chair, and then toppled over onto its side.

"That's about where it was when I turned around."

Smith nodded. "Made the same sound, too."

Colonel Kell stared at the briefcase, and then his eyes moved slowly around the room.

Wendy's heart was beating faster and faster. Did he suspect there was another person in the room?

"Let's bring Jonas in here to scan the room and check my briefcase," Kell said. He tapped his com and ordered Major Jonas to his office. Smith and the woman stood, waiting, and Kell put his hands on the edge of his desk and leaned forward, keeping the briefcase within his line of sight.

The room became eerily quiet, and Wendy was certain they would hear her heart pounding. She was grateful that the invisibility suit was light, and the fabric breathed. Still, she felt a sheen of sweat on every inch of her skin. She directed all her attention to keeping her breath quiet and steady. Who knew breathing could be so difficult?

There was a knock at the door.

"Major Jonas reporting," called a voice.

"Lieutenant Tripp, the door." Kell said, nodding toward the door.

Tripp walked to the door, pulled the lever, and slid it open. A short, robust man was standing there, but there was a slight gap between him and the doorframe. Wendy decided to make a run for it. She felt trapped and cramped in that room, like she would be discovered at any moment.

She sidestepped out of the door as quickly as possible, estimating there was just enough room for her to squeeze by undetected, but as she was passing through the doorframe, Jonas stepped forward, and they collided. He was shoved back, and to the three officers who were standing in Kell's office staring at him, it appeared he'd been pushed backward by nothing at all.

Wendy was just outside the door, frozen in place, with Jonas an arm's length away. She didn't move or make a sound. She had made two fumbles within moments after hours of going undetected. Inside the office, Smith and Tripp had both dropped their jaws.

"What the hell was that?" Kell asked.

"Sorry, sir?" Jonas said.

"Why did you almost fall backward?"

"I'm not sure, sir. It felt like something pushed me."

Kell's eyes widened, and his face turned red.

"Issue an alarm. Lock down the facility!" the colonel ordered.

And then all hell broke loose.

Kell marched out of his office as Wendy moved quickly and quietly down the catwalk toward the stairs that led to the lower level.

"Lockdown!" Colonel Kell shouted.

Red lights lit up at intervals across the ceiling. Loud, deep clicks and clanks sounded throughout the facility, and a low, droning alarm sounded.

Wendy stared in horror as two guards dispatched to the elevator doors, and one moved to the bottom of the staircase. She turned and saw guards taking positions at all the intersections throughout the facility.

She was trapped.

- 28 -

Trapped

Outskirts
Swenson, Colorado

Eli watched the video feed from Wendy's goggles in horror.

"She can't get out," Jane said.

"I knew this would happen," Devin said. He pushed himself up from the driver's seat and moved to the back of the bus. It rocked under his weight. "She should have gotten out as soon as she had Kell and Nichols on video, admitting to planning a coup."

"She needed more than that," Jane said, her eyes fixed on the screen.

"What are you doing?" Eli said to Devin.

"If she can't get out of there, we're going to have to bust her out." He looked back and forth from Jane to Eli and frowned. "I'm going to have to bust her out."

"Let's just wait and see what happens. All those people have to leave at some point. She can slip out with them," Jane said.

"Besides, you can't break into that base," Eli said. "It's totally fortified."

Devin ignored them. He opened a cabinet at the back of the bus and checked his stash of weapons. Then he caught himself in the mirror that was affixed to the inside the cabinet door. He saw long dreadlocks, a hint of a beard, and tattoos covering his arms and shoulders. If things were going haywire at the base, they'd take him for a thug. Carrying an obvious weapon would be asking for trouble. He selected a mangled wooden staff that would pass for a walking stick. He already had a dagger strapped to his shin and the Swiss Army knife he always carried tucked in his pocket.

He opened a small backpack he'd packed and checked its contents: water, power bars, a hand towel, a small first-aid kit, duct tape, binoculars, and a flashlight.

He pulled a jacket out of the cabinet and put it on, and then zipped up the pack and strapped it to his back.

"Something's going down," Eli said.

Devin barreled back through the bus and slid into the booth beside Eli.

In the underground facility, lights were flashing, and people were running around frantically. Wendy was still standing right outside Kell's office. The camera swung around as Nichols came running out of a set of double doors on the lower floor. He bounded up the stairs, taking two steps at a time.

"What's going on?" His breath came fast and heavy, like he'd run a long way.

"Let's hope it's nothing, just a couple of coincidences," Smith said.

"I don't believe in coincidences," Tripp muttered under her breath.

Wendy fixed her gaze on Kell and Nichols. She didn't want to let them out of her sight. They made eye contact with each other, and Kell gave Nichols a curt nod. "Secure the prototype," he said. "At all costs."

Both men's eyes flashed with understanding. Nichols scrambled away, bounded down the stairs, and disappeared through the double doors he'd entered just a moment before.

Kell turned to the other officers. "Return to your stations, and follow emergency protocol to the letter," he said. "That's an order."

The officers looked stunned, but they saluted and said, "Yes, sir," and then they took off. Kell stepped back into his office, leaving the door wide open.

"His computer," Eli said in Wendy's ear. "You've got to do it now."

Kell went to the cabinet beside his desk and bent down to open the bottom drawer.

"Now!" Eli said.

"Get off her back," Devin said. "The mission is compromised."

"They don't know what's going on," Jane said. "She might as well collect more evidence while she's trapped down there."

Wendy wished she could tune them out, but she didn't have time to adjust the volume on the com. She hurried to Kell's desk, crouched down, and jammed the flash drive into the port on the front of his computer. Then she peeked around the desk.

Kell was turning a key in a lock on the bottom drawer of the cabinet and cursing under his breath.

"OK, it's downloading," Eli said. "That computer's hard drive is almost full. We're going to need about two minutes."

"That's too long," Devin said.

Wendy gripped her head and wished they'd shut up.

Kell finally opened the drawer.

"One and a half minutes," Eli said.

Kell removed something from the drawer and then slammed it shut. He stood up and headed for the desk with a screwdriver in his hand. As he approached, Wendy heard Eli saying, "One more minute," but Kell was coming. She snatched the flash drive from the computer, keeping it wrapped in her palm, so the colonel couldn't see it. She slipped out of the way as Kell stepped into the very spot she had just occupied. He pulled the computer off the shelf, yanking out most of the wires, and then he set it on top of his desk.

"He didn't shut it down properly!" Eli said.

"Shut up," Jane said.

"We didn't get—"

"Be quiet," Devin said.

Kell used the screwdriver to snap the back panel off the computer, and then he ripped out its hard drive. He hastily shoved the computer back on the shelf and hurried out of the office. Wendy rushed to follow him, but the door closed in her face.

"Shit," she whispered.

"Give me that," Devin said. Wendy heard the sounds of some kind of struggle in her ear.

"Wendy? This is Devin. Look, you've got to get out of there. Just open the door quickly and slip out."

"But there are a bunch of people out there," she whispered, her voice shaking. "Kell's right outside—"

"They're not going to be paying attention. There will be total chaos out there. Just open the—"

Wendy didn't bother listening to the rest. She knew Kell wasn't right outside the door. He was getting away. She pulled the lever and opened the door a crack, glancing out just in time to see Kell handing the hard drive to Jonas, who was sitting at one of the workstations on the lower floor. Then Kell disappeared through the doors that Nichols had exited through earlier. Everyone on the floor was frantic. Lights were flashing, and the alarm was still blaring. She opened the door just enough to squeeze through and then closed it behind her.

As she flew down the stairs, she stuffed the flash drive into her pouch. When she reached the double doors, she turned and scanned the room. Nobody was looking, but she didn't care. It didn't matter if they saw doors opening and closing. She opened one door just enough to slide through and found herself in a long corridor lined with doors. Kell was nowhere to be seen.

She moved quickly but cautiously. Most of the doors had windows, and she paused to peer through each one. The first two were dark. Through the third she saw a man packing items into large plastic containers and stacking them onto a robotic dolly.

She was about to peek in the fourth window when she heard voices down the hall. She skipped the next few doors and headed toward the voices.

"Give us the control box, and nobody gets hurt," someone said.

The door was not closed all the way, so Wendy could hear everything they were saying. She looked through the small window in the door and saw Nichols holding a gun on a short man with a pointy nose and frizzy gray hair. The man was shaking and clutching a black case to his chest. It was a little larger than one of Eli's old laptops and much thicker. A black woman wearing a military issue sweat suit was standing at the far end of the room, watching them with a calm look on her face. She was smallish but sturdy, with short-cropped hair, and she had a vague expression on her face, almost as if she was in a daze. Wendy angled her head and scanned the room and could barely see Kell just inside the door.

"I have not released her to you," the little man was saying.

"Dr. Walsh, you will give Major Nichols the prototype," Kell said. He stepped forward and backhanded the man. As he did, Nichols grabbed the case from the man and skittered back.

The doctor clutched his cheek and glared at Kell. "You'll

pay for that," he said. "All my work—"

"Fuck your work," Nichols said. "The prototype is not yours. You act like it's your damn pet."

"Give me the gun," Kell said, his voice eerily calm.

As Nichols handed Kell the gun, Wendy could see the little man shaking violently. He was obviously terrified.

"Now tie him up," Kell said.

Nichols rifled through the drawers and cabinets and found a roll of duct tape. He ordered the doctor to sit in the chair and started taping him to it while Kell set the black case on a counter. He snapped it open. The top half of the case held a screen and the bottom held a keyboard and a trackpad. It was already powered up. Kell tapped and swiped at it while Nichols duct taped the man in the chair to the heavy desk and then pressed a final strip of tape over the man's mouth. When they were done, Kell turned to the woman.

"Come with me," he said.

She nodded. "Yes, sir."

Wendy barely had time to back away from the door before Kell came out with the woman following him. Nichols trailed them, turning out the light and closing the door behind him.

They turned down the corridor, heading away from the central work area. Wendy remained a few steps behind as they turned down another passageway.

"We've contacted the authorities," Eli said in her ear. "FBI, CIA, NSA, Pentagon—the whole shebang. We sent them that clip of Kell and Nichols that you captured earlier."

Then Jane came on. "They've got the evidence. You planted plenty of bugs and downloaded at least half of Kell's hard drive. It's time to get out of there."

Wendy shook her head. The mission was not complete. There was one more thing she wanted from Colonel Kell.

Kell stopped at the end of the hall in front of a reinforced metal door with a sign on it that said "NO EXIT:

AUTHORIZED PERSONNEL ONLY." He pulled a ring of keys out his pocket, unlocked the door, and walked through it with Nichols and the woman right behind him. Wendy had to give the door a slight push so she'd have time to slip through. As the door slammed shut behind Wendy, the woman turned and looked right at her, causing Wendy's hair to stand on end. But the woman quickly turned and continued following Kell and Nichols. Wendy took a deep breath and then continued after them.

They descended a short stairwell and passed through another reinforced metal door at the bottom. Kell unlocked it and then stuffed the keys into his pocket as he stepped across the threshold.

They had entered some kind of tunnel system. It was cool and damp, and it smelled stale and musty. The walls were rounded, and there were support beams every thirty meters or so.

Kell and Nichols were wearing oxford shoes that thudded against the cement floor. The woman was wearing sneakers, so her steps were silent. Wendy held back and let them get about ten meters ahead before she resumed following them.

"What the hell happened?" Nichols said.

"We'll discuss it later," Kell answered. "Stay quiet, and keep walking."

Nichols answered in a loud whisper: "Yes, sir."

* * *

Back in the bus, Devin grabbed his staff, got up from the table, and pushed the side door of the bus open.

"What are you doing?" Eli said.

"Yeah, where are you going?" Jane said.

"Be quiet, or you'll distract her," Devin said, stepping out of the bus and turning to face them.

"It's muted," Eli said.

Devin grabbed the bus door. "I'm going to go help Wendy," he said, and then he slammed the door shut and disappeared.

Jane and Eli looked at each other.

"Great," Jane said. "Grieving ex-marine on the loose with a walking stick."

Eli's eyes fell on the console beside the driver's seat, and he sighed. "He didn't even take one of the com units I rigged."

Jane went to the window and pressed her face against it. "It's too late now," she said. "He's gone."

She returned to the table. Wendy was still following Kell, Nichols, and the woman through the dimly lit tunnel.

"That looks pretty scary, doesn't it?" Eli said. "Like something out of a horror movie?"

"Yeah, it looks like a place where vampires would live," Jane said. "Turn on our audio."

Eli tapped a key.

"Wendy, are you holding up OK?" Jane said.

The camera moved up and down, indicating that Wendy was nodding.

"Devin's on his way to help you."

Wendy paused briefly and gave her head a slight shake, but then she continued walking.

The tunnel extended as far as Wendy's eyes could see. Occasionally there was a service door or a hatch in the roof. She wondered where these led, but there was no time for exploring. She wanted to stay with Kell.

After standing around all day without food and water, Wendy was tired. Normally a trek of this length wouldn't faze her, but she found herself scurrying to keep up. Exhaustion had set in.

Kell and the others disappeared around a wide bend in the tunnel, and Wendy jogged a few paces to catch up. She didn't want to lose them if they slipped through one of the doors in the tunnel walls. When she came around the bend, she almost ran right into Kell.

Just as she stopped, she realized that her footsteps had been quietly echoing through the tunnel.

Kell drew the gun he had taken from Nichols.

"Who's there?" he said.

As he scanned the width of the tunnel, Wendy stepped out of the line of fire.

"I can hear someone breathing," Nichols said.

Wendy caught her breath and held it as Kell fired the gun in her direction.

- 29 -

Witnesses

Carter Air Force Base
Swenson, Colorado

Dr. Sommers was in one of the soundproofed labs, testing ocular implants. Halfway through his shift, it was time for his dinner break. When he pulled open the heavy steel door, he was overwhelmed by bleating alarms, flashing lights, and loud voices.

Several years ago, when he'd been brought into Project MOTH, he'd been trained on emergency protocol. But in a moment of panic, all training was forgotten. He ran down the corridor, across the central workroom, and through the double doors that led to the lower-level offices.

He arrived in front of Dr. Walsh's office out of breath and found the door locked. Dr. Sommers peered through the window, but the lights were out, and he couldn't see anything. Just as he was about to turn and run back down the corridor, he heard a muffled sound from beyond the door.

Dr. Sommers peered through the window again, but it was too dark to see anything. Then he heard a noise that sounded like someone was screaming into a pillow.

He backed up a few paces and ran at the door, barreling into it with his shoulder, but it didn't budge, and he was left with a throbbing ache in his shoulder. He glanced around and then kicked the handle. The door didn't budge. He kicked again and again, pushing all his muscle into it. Finally the handle snapped, and the door flew open.

He stepped inside, but the light didn't come on automatically. As he ran his finger along the wall, looking for the switch, he heard the muffled voice again.

"Just a moment," he said.

His hand found the switch, and he flicked it, blinking as his eyes adjusted to the light. When he saw Dr. Walsh duct taped to the chair, he gasped.

Dr. Walsh's face was red, and tears were streaming from his eyes. He was shaking and lurching in the chair.

"Rupert! What happened?"

Dr. Walsh responded with muffled screams.

Dr. Sommers scurried over to Dr. Walsh. "Don't worry. I'll get you out of this."

Dr. Walsh screamed louder, but Dr. Sommers couldn't make out what he was saying. He eyed the duct tape over Dr. Walsh's mouth and then reached out and peeled a bit of it away.

"You want me to do it fast or slow?" Dr. Sommers said.

Dr. Walsh muttered something, but Dr. Sommers couldn't make it out.

"Nod your head for fast. Shake it for slow."

Dr. Walsh nodded his head violently.

"OK, here goes." Dr. Sommers gripped the tape and peeled it off in one fell swoop.

Dr. Walsh let out a whooping scream.

"What happened? Who did this to you?"

"Kell's henchman. Who else would do this? Get me out of

here!"

Dr. Sommers turned and scanned the office, searching for a tool he could use to free Dr. Walsh.

"My medical kit. It's in the cabinet," Dr. Walsh said. "Hurry."

Dr. Sommers scurried over to a cabinet against the far wall. He opened it and removed the medical kit and then crossed the room and set the kit on the desk, opened it, and retrieved a scalpel.

Dr. Walsh explained what had happened as Dr. Sommers sawed at the tape with the scalpel.

"Be careful, don't cut me!" Dr. Walsh said.

Dr. Sommers paused and stared at him. "Please. I'm a trained surgeon."

"Oh Lloyd, we never should have gotten involved with these people. I'm sorry I dragged you into this."

"No regrets," Dr. Sommers said as he cut away the last bit of tape. "We're in it together, remember?"

Dr. Walsh blinked tears from his eyes and looked around, suddenly noticing the alarm and frenzy.

"The compound is in lockdown," he said. "This is bad. Very bad. What's going on out there?"

Dr. Sommers shrugged. "I ran from the lab to your office so fast, I didn't really notice. Everyone's yelling and screaming, running around."

Dr. Walsh bolted out of his chair. He opened the top drawer of his desk and scraped his fingers against the underside of the drawer. He yanked and pulled, until he finally removed a cardcom that had been taped there.

Dr. Sommers's eyes went wide. "That's not MOTH issue," he said. "You're not supposed to have that down here.

"This is my backup plan," Dr. Walsh said. He tapped and swiped the screen.

"What are you doing?" Dr. Sommers said.

"Calling the authorities. I'm done. Done with MOTH. Done with Kell. I'm turning that son of a bitch in."

Dr. Sommers snatched the com out of Dr. Walsh's hand. "Are you crazy? They'll throw us in prison!"

Dr. Walsh snatched the com back. "No they won't. We'll tell them we thought this program was sanctioned by the Air Force." He waved his arm around. "Most of the people working in this compound have no idea what Project MOTH really is."

"You don't think Kell and Nichols will tell them you were on the inside?"

"I'll cut a deal."

"Rupert, you were involved in an attempt to overthrow the US government. You were a willing participant."

"The authorities will never see those records. Didn't you get emergency protocol training? During a level-five emergency lockdown, all records self-destruct. "

Dr. Sommers paled. "All our work will be lost?"

Dr. Walsh shook his head. "Those files are backed up every day, uploaded to a secure remote node."

He paused and listened to the alarms bellowing throughout the facility. "That's definitely a level-five lockdown. They've probably already destroyed the most incriminating records."

He resumed tapping and swiping the com.

"Don't do this, Rupert," Dr. Sommers pleaded.

Dr. Walsh paused and looked at his partner. Dr. Sommers's eyes were watering. He shook his head. "I don't want you to do this. It's too dangerous. They could execute you for treason!"

Dr. Walsh looked up from the com.

"Let's just get through this," Dr. Sommers stammered, "and then we can leave. Put all this behind us."

"ROMANS will hunt me down," Dr. Walsh said. "You have no idea how powerful—"

The door burst open, and the two doctors turned toward it.

Major Jonas stood there with his gun raised, flanked by two guards. He scanned the room.

"Are you two alone in here?" he said.

"We are. Can you tell us what's going on? Why is the compound in lockdown?" Dr. Walsh said.

Jonas angled his head back and spoke to his guards. "I've got this. Clear the rest of the corridor."

The two guards slipped away, and Jonas kicked the door closed, but it didn't latch. He eyed the doctors, and then he pushed a chair in front of the door to hold it shut. He regarded the frayed tape that was still stuck to Dr. Walsh and the chair he'd been taped to.

"What happened here?" he said.

Dr. Walsh's voice shook as he spoke. "It was a misunderstanding. It's all been cleared up now."

"Is that so?" Jonas said. He raised the gun and leveled it at Dr. Walsh's head.

"What are you doing?" Dr. Sommers said. He wrapped his arms around Dr. Walsh. "Have you gone mad?"

Jonas took a broad step forward and pulled the trigger. As the sound of the gunshot blasted through the room, time slowed down for Dr. Sommers. He watched as everything moved in slow motion: Dr. Walsh's head snapped back and then bounced forward, and blood splattered all over the desk behind him.

"No!" Dr. Sommers screamed, pulling Dr. Walsh's head to his chest. Sobs filled his chest as he looked up at Jonas, who was still holding the gun. But now it was aimed at Dr. Sommers's head.

Dr. Sommers looked up at Jonas. "Why?" he said, and then he saw movement behind Jonas. Dr. Sommers wiped tears from his eyes and saw Lieutenant Smith's face appear at the little window in the door. When his eyes fell on Dr. Walsh's limp and bloody body, his eyes widened.

Jonas turned around to see what Dr. Sommers was looking at, but as he turned, Lieutenant Smith disappeared.

Then Jonas turned back toward Dr. Sommers.

"Who was it?" he said.

"I don't...I'm not sure."

"You're lying," Jonas said.

"I...I...Please."

Just then a scream blared from somewhere down the corridor followed by the sound of running footsteps. "Major Jonas!" someone yelled.

Jonas looked over his shoulder and then took a step backward, preparing to exit, but he kept the gun trained on Dr. Sommers.

"We can't have any witnesses," Jonas said. "And we don't tolerate disloyalty." And then he pulled the trigger.

- 30 -

Tunnel Vision

Carter Air Force Base
Swenson, Colorado

Wendy let her breath out as she leaped out of the way. Then she ran forward and passed Kell, stepping quickly and quietly behind one of the depressions in the wall. She didn't think she'd made a sound, but he turned and froze, facing roughly in her direction.

"Get out of there," Eli whispered.

Wendy was crouched down, trying hard to control her breath.

"It's not worth it," Jane whispered. "We've got him. The feds will be there any second."

Wendy shook her head. Kell would escape. She knew he would. A man like that would have an out. She glared at the man who had almost certainly killed her parents, and rage tore through her chest. It was all she could do to refrain from attacking him.

When she had caught her breath, she silently rose to her feet and took one step forward and then another.

"You're a murdering traitor," she said, and then she quickly stepped several paces to the side.

Kell snapped around and fired. The bullet ricocheted off the tunnel wall.

Nichols and the woman were standing several meters behind Kell. When the shot rang out, Nichols crouched to the ground. The woman didn't so much as twitch.

Wendy took a few steps back. "You think that uniform is going to protect you?" Again she sidestepped, and another bullet missed.

Her heart was pounding. She could barely control her breath. She'd heard the expression *seeing red* when a person was riddled with hatred and wrath, but she'd never thought it was meant literally. Now her vision was tinged with red. She tried to blink it away.

Kell shot again blindly. The bullet cracked against the cement wall and ricocheted, plummeting into Wendy's arm, and she cried out as pain tore through her flesh.

"Run!" It was her friends' voices in her ear, Eli and Jane both, from the sound of it. "Get the hell out of there!"

The pain was searing. Wendy grabbed at her arm instinctively, keeping her eyes on Kell.

His face changed instantaneously—from fear and caution to shock. Behind him, Wendy saw Nichols's mouth fall open. Wendy gritted her teeth against the pain. In her peripheral vision, she saw her own body. *Saw her own body.* The suit wasn't working. She was visible!

"Wha—?" Kell was clearly stunned that she had appeared out of nowhere. He lifted his arm and raised the gun, leveling it at her chest.

"That's Watson's daughter," Nichols said.

"That's right, you son of a bitch. And you're in a shit ton of trouble." Wendy stepped forward. "What's wrong?" she said. "Did you forget how to speak?"

"Where did she come from?" Nichols's eyes darted around, but Kell's remained fixed on her face.

"We're working on the suit," Eli said in her ear. "But I think you need to reboot it."

"Can't right now," she said.

"What did you say?" Kell said.

"I wasn't talking to you," she said. She took a step closer to him, still gripping the wound in her arm. She could barely feel it now, and she assumed that was due to adrenaline and shock.

"You must have come in through one of these doors," he said.

"Nope. Let's get back to you murdering my parents."

"I didn't murder your parents," he said.

"Yes you did. I have proof," she lied.

Kell glared at her through narrowed eyes. "Every war has casualties and sacrifices. It's unfortunate but necessary."

"Unfortunate?" she screamed, taking another step toward him. "There is no war, you idiot. There hasn't been a war for years. But peace just isn't good enough for men like you. If there's no war, you start one."

Kell's voice remained calm and quiet. He kept his eyes on Wendy as he said, "Major Nichols, take the prototype and go to the safe house."

"But sir—"

"That's an order," Kell hissed. He kept the gun trained on Wendy with one hand and held out the black case with other. Nichols stepped forward and took it.

Kell stepped backward until he was beside the woman. He angled his head at her. "You're to stay with Major Nichols."

"Yes sir," she said.

"Both of you are to avoid the authorities. Meet me at the safe house. I won't be long."

"Yes, sir," the woman said.

Nichols started to protest. "Are you—"

"Go!" Colonel Kell roared.

Major Nichols walked down the tunnel, looking back over his shoulder every few paces. The woman didn't so much as blink before she turned to follow him.

"Run, dammit!" Colonel Kell yelled.

Nichols paused for a beat before he took off at a steady run with the woman easily matching his pace. When their footsteps had faded, Kell and Wendy were still facing off with only a few meters between them.

"You don't understand," Kell said, holding the gun steady. "You think peace will be permanent, but there's always another war. Always. I'm not starting a war. I'm preventing one."

"By killing people?"

"By making sure our military is big enough and strong enough to win any war that comes to pass. By restoring it to what it once was."

"If there's no war, we don't need a big military. And you're not authorized to make these kinds of decisions. We live in a democracy."

"The United States is a republic, not a democracy." He squinted at her. "You could never understand."

"It's a democratic republic," she said. "And if you undermine the democracy, then there is nothing to protect. You don't have the right to decide how big or how strong the military is. You were never elected!"

"There will be a war," he said. "Maybe not today. Maybe not next year. But it will come. And America needs to be prepared."

Wendy took another step. "You're a traitor," she said.

"Don't you come any closer, or I'll shoot," he said.

Wendy stopped. She risked a quick glance at the device on her wrist. It was blinking.

"Here's what's going to happen," he said. "You're going to turn and head down the tunnel." He pointed back the way they had come. "That way."

Wendy could not remember ever feeling so angry in her life. Never—not once—had she wished harm on another human being—until today. And she hated him for that. Even now the desire to bash Kell's head in was overwhelming. She knew damn well he'd never let her walk away from this.

"Why?" she said. "So you can shoot me in the back?" She tightened her grip on her gunshot wound and breathed through her teeth. What was about to happen was going to hurt. She'd need all her strength.

She cocked her head at him and blinked her eyes wide and innocent. "This hurts like hell," she said, glancing at her wound.

"Better get yourself to a doctor, then." He nodded toward the tunnel. "That way."

Wendy scrunched up her face like she was in pain, which she was. When she thought she looked like she was in agony, she leaped forward and swung her leg around, knocking the gun clear out of Kell's grip. And then she ran for it.

He shook off the stun and went after her, but he was older and not as agile. She grabbed the weapon, danced back several meters, and then faced him, leveling it at his head.

"You're not going to shoot me," he said. "Do you have any idea how much trouble you'd get in for shooting a colonel in the United States Air Force?"

"Not as much trouble as you're going to get in for treason," she said. Then she laughed. He was so arrogant. He had no idea that his empire had fallen.

"They're already waiting for you outside," she said. "FBI, CIA, every other branch of the military." She stepped forward. "I sent them evidence of your little coup," she said. "They've got raw footage of you planning to overtake the military and overthrow the government."

He stared at her, hard. She could see panic in his eyes. He

was calculating his next move, marking his mistakes. Maybe counting his losses.

"You think one man could take over the entire military?" he said. "Young lady, you don't know what you're talking about."

He started to put his hands in his pockets.

"Keep your hands where I can see them," she said. Her hand was shaking, and the gun wobbled.

He brought his hands down to his sides. "Do you even know how to use that?" he said, nodding at the gun. "I doubt it."

"Do you want to find out the hard way?" Wendy said. She tried to keep herself steady, but her injured arm was throbbing, and the hand she was using to hold the gun was shaking.

"This is all just a misunderstanding," he said wistfully. Then, without warning, he lunged at her, his hands going for the gun.

When he lunged, the gun was pointed at his head. She tried to bring it down and out of the way. It was in that moment—a moment of shock and terror—when a powerful man was about to attack her, that she realized she didn't want to kill him. She wanted justice for her parents, but she didn't want to take this man's life.

Desperate, she pulled at the gun so he couldn't take it from her. She felt his cold hands on hers, pulling at the weapon.

Then the gun went off with a loud bang, and she felt his body lurch and go limp, falling toward her. She pushed him away, and he stumbled backward. The bullet had seared through his heart. Blood blossomed on the breast of his uniform. His hands flew to his chest, and he stared at her, his mouth gaping open. Then he coughed and gagged and dropped to his knees.

Wendy's eyes went wide as the colonel gasped, clutching his chest. She wasn't a medical doctor, but her work on the

BIM required extensive knowledge of the human body, and she knew that unless paramedics showed up within sixty seconds, he wouldn't live, and even then his chances were slim. He fell face first, his body hitting the cement with a thud an instant before his face slapped it.

"Oh my God." It was Jane's voice in her ear.

After that, it was quiet for what seemed like a long time. Wendy's mind had gone blank. There was a hard throbbing in her head, and it pushed away every thought and emotion. She couldn't process what had happened. The colonel's body lay a few meters away, but it and everything else felt distant.

"Wendy, get out of there." That was Eli, but he was far away too. Wendy stood there, feeling like she was trapped underwater.

"Wendy, you've got to get out of there. Now. Check the device. Turn the suit back on."

The device. The suit. Wendy remembered that she had been invisible. She looked around. There was nobody there to see her now.

"Try to turn the suit back on." Jane's voice was firmer, more insistent.

Wendy raised her hand and looked at the screen on her wrist. She brought her other hand around to tap it, but that hand was occupied, holding a gun. She dropped it as if it had suddenly turned scorching hot.

As she toggled the device on her wrist, she heard muffled voices in her hear.

"She can't leave it there."

"One thing at a time."

Wendy pressed her finger against the surface of the wristcom and held it until a pale light blinked. Then she tapped the directive, looked down, and watched herself disappear.

"Pick up the gun, Wendy." It was Jane. "You can't leave it there."

"I don't want it," she said.

"You can't leave it there."

It was so hard to think. Wendy gripped her temples and quickly shook her head back and forth, as if she were trying to restart her brain. Why had it been so easy to think about the suit and its functions, but she couldn't consider a simple decision like picking up a gun? She stared at it, lying there at her feet.

"Pick it up." That was Eli.

Wendy didn't want to pick it up. It was probably air force issue. Taking it would be theft, and she didn't want to be caught carrying around a service weapon.

"Pick it up!" Jane screamed.

This time Wendy responded like an obedient dog. She bent down and picked up the gun.

"Now get the hell out of there!" Jane yelled but not as loudly.

Something snapped inside Wendy. She took another look at the colonel. He had murdered her parents. He'd all but admitted it, and she had unintentionally avenged their death.

"Wendy, run!"

Wendy's mind was so clouded; she wasn't sure who was yelling into the com. She gripped her injured arm, and then she turned and fled down the tunnel.

- 31 -

Tussled

Carter Air Force Base
Swenson, Colorado

As soon as Devin reached the edge of the base, he knew he'd made a mistake in thinking he could rescue Wendy. The guard at the front gate was on alert. Devin could have easily overpowered him, but he wouldn't have gotten two steps inside before he'd be surrounded and tackled to the ground.

He walked the fence, keeping a distance of ten to twenty meters so he would stay out of range of the motion sensors. He knew alarms were going off deep within the base, but he couldn't hear them. In fact the base was quiet. A couple of officers were walking toward the parking lot, and everything seemed normal. Whatever was happening in the underground compound, it wasn't affecting the rest of the base.

Devin paced the fence, looking for a way in. He wished he had an invisibility suit. If they'd done this right, they would have waited longer, planned better, and used the other suits. The suit with the force-field shield would come in handy right now. He also didn't have the advantage of a com unit in his ear. Nor was he properly dressed. What had he been thinking? He'd just grab a stick and go running into a military base, rescue Wendy, and leave unscathed? He was off his game, and he felt like a stranger in his own skin. Muddled thoughts of Yoshi entered his mind, and he pushed them aside. This never would have happened to him when he was a marine. He had fulfilled his duties to perfection and surpassed expectations in every operation.

He finally resolved to return to the bus, hoping he could do more good from there. But then he saw a fleet of vehicles and flashing lights approaching from a distance. He peered through the dark night and then ran the length of the fence, so he could watch them approach. As they neared, he huddled down in the tall grass. He yanked off his backpack and got out his binoculars.

The first wave of four vehicles skidded up to the guardhouse as SWAT trucks arrived on the scene. Two big men got out, approached the guard, and visibly argued with him. Several men and women got out of the remaining cars and approached the guardhouse. Some wore uniforms. Some wore suits. A few were casually dressed. Within minutes they had pulled the guard out, splayed him flat on the ground, and raised the gate.

Just as they were climbing back into their vehicles, leaving two of their crew behind to watch the guard, a dozen or more vehicles showed up—mostly nondescript black sedans and SUVs plus a couple of police cars and an ambulance, even a fire truck.

It was late evening, and there were few cars in the parking lot. All the arriving vehicles pulled up to the front of the lot, near the buildings. Devin knew the building Wendy had infiltrated was at the center of the base. He wouldn't be able to see anything from his location.

He had a sudden hankering to get back to the bus and

watch the action from inside.

He shoved the binoculars back into his pack and removed the flashlight. Then he picked up his staff and ran, crouched over, through the brush. He'd gone about a quarter mile when he heard scuffling in a knot of trees nearby.

He turned off his flashlight and approached the sound with his staff at the ready and the flashlight poised on his shoulder, with his finger on the button.

There was rustling in the brush again. Devin moved stealthily, following the sound until he saw two bodies moving about—a man and a woman. It was too dark to see their faces. He issued a low, long whistle. The woman looked right at him, but she didn't react. The man turned, and Devin snapped his flashlight on, shining the light in the man's face.

"Nichols," Devin said. He didn't know the woman's name, but he noted the blank expression on her face.

Nichols shaded his eyes with his hand and glared into the light. "Who the hell are you?"

Devin quickly assessed the situation and figured that Nichols and the woman were trying to escape. In a single swift movement, he stepped forward and launched a side kick into Nichols's gut. The man went sprawling backward, dropping the black case he was carrying. His back smacked into a small tree, and he slid to the ground.

"What the hell was that for?" Nichols sputtered as he got to his feet.

Devin didn't feel like talking. He gently dropped the flashlight, and it thudded to the ground. He moved in with left-right jabs to Nichols's chest.

Nichols sidestepped just in time, and Devin's hits merely brushed him. Then Nichols got into a boxing stance, legs spread, knees bent, fists balled up in front of his chin. Nichols squinted at Devin. "I know you. You're the judo guy." He hopped around, light on his feet, but his breath was raspy. He hadn't recovered from the blow to his gut.

Devin frowned, narrowed his eyes, and assumed a fighting stance.

Nichols skipped forward, launched his left fist at Devin's face, and then brought his right fist up, coming at Devin's jaw from below. Devin deflected both attempts and nailed Nichols hard on the head with the side of his left hand and then his right.

Nichols tottered, dazed by the blows. He blinked at Devin.

"What the fuck, man? I don't even know you." He resumed his boxer dance, bouncing around on his feet. Devin lowered his head and glared at Nichols. Boxing was a primitive and inferior style of fighting.

Devin stood with his feet slightly spread apart, one foot in front of the other, his posture straight, shoulders loose but ready.

"I know you," he said. "You're a traitor."

He twirled on one foot as he raised the other and brought it crunching into Nichols's chest. Nichols gasped and grabbed at his ribs.

"Enough," Nichols pleaded through desperate breaths.

But Devin wasn't done. His next move was dangerous. He'd used it only once before, and if he did it wrong, his opponent could die.

He grabbed Nichols's arm and spun him around, and then he wrapped his own arm around Nichols's neck, so Nichols's throat was tucked into the crook of Devin's elbow. Devin squeezed gently and then pulled a little tighter. Nichols gasped for air and dug his fingers into Devin's arm, desperate for breath. Devin tightened his grip, and as soon as Nichols went limp Devin eased him to the ground and then checked his pulse.

The woman stood there, watching. She didn't move or speak. Her expression was still blank.

"He'll be fine," Devin said. "He's just unconscious. Who are you?"

She didn't answer, and Devin decided to let her be. He didn't know what her involvement was, if any. For all he knew, Nichols was taking her as a captive. He picked up his flashlight and grabbed the black case Nichols had been carrying. The woman's eyes moved to the case when he picked it up.

He tucked the case into his pack, and then he picked Nichols up under his arms and started dragging him back toward the base.

"You coming?" he said to the woman.

She blinked but didn't answer.

"Some help would be nice," he said.

But she just stood there, so he resumed dragging Nichols away, wondering if she was suffering from shock.

After a moment, she followed.

Devin headed toward the base with a mind to tie Nichols to a fence, where the authorities would find him. He'd rather personally hand the traitor over to someone in uniform, but Devin had never been arrested or interrogated, and he wasn't in the mood for it tonight. The last thing he needed was to get tangled up with the authorities. He wanted to get back to the bus and find out what was going on with Wendy. As he picked his way through the brush, he scanned the night sky. It was clear, and every star in the galaxy was visible. There was no breeze, and the night was warm.

The base came into view, and Devin picked up his pace. In the distance he saw lights flashing, vehicles and people swarming the lot, and more pulling in. He slowed and crouched. He could barely hear the woman's footsteps behind him.

Suddenly a row of flashlights appeared in the distance, spreading out into the field and heading his way. Devin froze. He had to think quickly. He turned in a full circle, scanning the terrain. There was a small clearing up ahead. Devin pulled Nichols toward it as fast as he could and dropped the man.

He looked up at the horizon. The flashlights were bobbing straight toward him, but he had plenty of time to get away. He tucked the flashlight into the crook of Nichols's arm, pointing upward, and turned it on.

"They'll find him," Devin said to the woman. "Do you need help? I can get you someplace safe."

As before, she didn't respond. For all he knew, she didn't even speak English. She gave him a blank stare and then went and stood a few feet from Nichols. She didn't look at Nichols, Devin, or the approaching flashlights.

"All right, then," Devin said. "Good luck."

As he sprinted away, it occurred to him that she could easily identify him, but his gut told him she wouldn't be a problem. Nichols could identify him too, but he was in a heap of trouble of his own. He'd be too busy trying to explain his treasonous acts to bother with some judo instructor who'd tussled him in a field. It didn't matter. There were plenty of places Devin could go, and he wasn't planning on sticking around Colorado anyway. Now that Yoshi was gone, there was nothing to keep him here and no reason to come back.

He turned and ran for the bus.

- 32 -

Making Out

Carter Air Force Base
Swenson, Colorado

After a few minutes of running through the tunnel, Wendy slowed her pace to a steady jog. Her arm was throbbing, and she was starting to feel lightheaded. She wasn't sure whether it was from shock or blood loss.

She paused under a fluorescent light and sat on the ground, leaning against the tunnel wall.

"What are you doing?" Eli said.

"Give me a minute," Wendy said.

She used the wristcom to separate a strip of the suit's fabric so she could use it as a tourniquet. She wrapped it around the wound and pulled it tight. Then she leaned her head back against the tunnel wall to catch her breath.

"Jane? Eli?"

"We're here," Jane said.

Wendy sighed and pushed herself to her feet. She tapped the wristcom and pulled up the GPS application.

"Where am I?" she said.

"You're underground, past the perimeter of the base. That tunnel is not on any map or blueprints we've seen, but it's got to come out somewhere."

Wendy walked at a brisk pace and then alternated between walking and jogging. After what felt like twenty miles but was only two, the tunnel started sloping upward. Wendy rounded a bend and saw a faint light ahead.

* * *

Eli and Jane watched the tunnel bounce and bob as Wendy made her way through it.

"How long can the thing be?" Eli wondered aloud.

Jane didn't answer. She stared at the screen with a dazed look and a frown on her face.

"What's wrong?" Eli said.

Jane focused her eyes on Eli and blinked. "Nothing," she said. "It's nothing."

She leaned back and stretched her arms up, and then she tilted her head from side to side. It was stiff from sitting in front of the laptop for hours. She needed to get up and move around. She wanted to get her blood flowing so she could think. She slid to the edge of the booth and headed for a cabinet near the back of the bus for a bottle of water, but something caught her eye: lights in the distance.

She moved to the back of the bus and peered out the rear window. Two vehicles had pulled off the road and were heading toward the bus.

"Get up," she said, heading back to Eli and pointing as his equipment. "Hide that stuff. Hurry."

Eli looked up at her and opened his mouth to protest.

"Someone's coming," she said.

Eli snapped the laptop shut. Together they quickly gathered the equipment and stuffed it into one of the cabinets above the table.

"Now what?" Eli whispered. With the laptop closed, it was eerily dark inside the van.

Jane returned to the back window. The lights were getting closer. She had to think fast. She reached into the overhead sleeping compartment and pulled out a blanket. Turning toward Eli, she pointed at the floor and said, "Lie down."

"Lie down?"

"Do it!"

Eli eased himself to the floor of the van, cringing when he thought about all the shoes that had walked over it, including his own. He felt like he was lying in filth and grime, which he was.

But all thoughts of dirt disappeared when Jane came down on top of him, wrapping them both in the blanket and grabbing his face in both hands. She kissed him long and hard.

"Just go with it," she whispered. Then she dove at his face with hers.

At first Eli was like a limp rag, and Jane thought he'd never been kissed. But after the initial shock wore off, he responded. His hand snaked around her back, and he pulled her closer. He was a surprisingly good kisser, and she liked the way he squeezed her lower back with the tips of his fingers.

They were both about to forget why they were lying on the floor of Devin's VW bus, making out like a couple of high school sweethearts, when a bright light shone through the window. It was followed by a sharp rap. Jane looked up toward the light, but she couldn't see anything. Her hair was disheveled from Eli running his hand through it.

"Come on out," a loud, authoritative voice beyond the window said.

"You know where we're going with this, right?" Jane whispered.

Eli was still so surprised, he almost didn't hear her. After a beat, he nodded and whispered back, "Yeah."

Jane got up and smoothed her clothing. As Eli pushed himself up, she moved to the door. "This way," she whispered, and she climbed out with Eli on her heels.

A policeman was standing there with one hand holding a flashlight propped on his shoulder and the other resting on the gun at his hip. Another officer stood behind him.

"Check the area," the first officer said, and the other one wandered off.

"What's going on here?" the first officer said.

"Oh, nothing. We're on a road trip," Jane said. "We pulled over to eat dinner, and…" She giggled. "And that led to dessert." She reached out and grabbed Eli's hand. "Right babe?"

"What?" Eli said, stunned. "Oh yeah, right. Dessert."

The officer shook his head. "You two look a little old for parking and necking."

Jane blinked at him. "We're not parking and necking. We were on a road—"

"A road trip. Right." He craned his neck as the other officer returned. "See anything?"

"It's clear," the other officer said.

"All right," the first officer said. "You two, back in the van. Get out of here."

"We're not quite—"

"Or we can take you in," he added.

"Right. OK." Jane nodded and tugged on Eli's hand. "Come on, hon. Let's get out of here."

They climbed back into the bus, and Jane flashed a smile at the officers before she yanked the door shut.

Eli was still stunned as he started to slide into the booth.

"Passenger seat," Jane hissed as she climbed into the driver's seat.

She pressed the driverless power button. "Start engine,"

she said, but the vehicle didn't respond.

"Shit," she whispered.

"Engage motor," Eli said, and the old engine rumbled to life.

Jane stared at him.

"It's an older system. The early models had specific commands," he said.

Jane sighed. "Get us out of here," she said.

"Navigate to…" Eli paused and considered the command. "Where should we go?"

"Just head into town," Jane said.

"Navigate to downtown Swenson," he said.

The bus lurched as it shifted gears, and then it backed out and turned toward the road.

Jane waved at the officers as the bus bumbled past them.

* * *

Devin came around the back of the dilapidated farmhouse just in time to see the bus pulling away. He started to run forward and was about to call for them to stop, but he halted when he caught sight of the two police officers walking back to their patrol car. He watched as they climbed in and drove off, but by then the bus was gone.

* * *

"Wendy? Are you there?" It was Eli. He sounded frantic. The bus was passing the base, and it was swarming with cars, flashing lights, and people.

"I'm here," she whispered.

"We had to shut down the systems, but I'm booting everything back up. Where are you?"

"I'm out of the tunnel and heading for the bus." She

glanced at the GPS app on her wristcom. "Wait a minute, you guys are moving."

"We ran into some trouble. There are cops everywhere," he said. "They found us—"

"They found you?"

"Yeah, but we're OK. They thought we were..." Eli cleared his throat and glanced at Jane. "They let us go. They don't know anything."

As Wendy breathed a sigh of relief, Jane spoke up. "Wendy, how's your arm?"

"There's a hole in it," Wendy said. "And it hurts. Where's Devin?"

"He's still out there somewhere," Jane said.

"When can you come back for us?" Wendy said.

"I don't think we can, Wen," Jane said. "There are too many cops."

"OK," Wendy said. She pressed her fingers into her temples and tried to think. Her mouth was dry, and her stomach felt like a hollow pit. She was tempted to lie down in the weeds and let the exhaustion have its way with her.

Wendy heard the muffled sound of Eli and Jane exchanging words.

"Hey, we think Devin will go back to where the bus was parked," Eli said. "I just marked the spot where we were parked on the map. Can you see it?"

Wendy glanced at her com again. A green dot that designated the bus was behind her and moving away, and there was a yellow dot where it had been sitting while she was in the base. "Yeah, I see it," she said. "I'm close."

"That's the best place to look for him, but we don't know where he went or long he'll be gone."

"OK, I'll find Devin, and we'll meet up with you later."

"Later?" Eli said. "When? Where?"

"Go into town. Get to the dojo. Do you know where it is?"

"We can find it," Jane said.

"Go there and wait," Wendy said.

"What are you going to do? You're injured. You can't walk all the way—"

"I need to get off the com," Wendy said. "Someone might hear me." There was nobody around, but she didn't want to talk anymore. "Over and out," she said, and then she turned off her com.

* * *

Devin didn't know whether Wendy had made it back to the bus before it had driven off. He didn't know whether they were coming back. He squatted with his back against a tree, balancing himself with his staff.

Why had he left his com behind? What a stupid thing to do. And then he'd had the foolish notion that he could breach an air force base, alone and with no equipment. He wiped the sweat off his face with the sleeve of his jacket. The whole mission had gone to hell, and it was all his fault. What had he been thinking?

Devin hung his head in shame. Yoshi would be disappointed. He'd barely had time to grieve for his mentor, the man who had been a father to him. And now he was squatting in the shrubs, Wendy was in grave danger, and Eli and Jane were gone.

"You should have stayed on the bus."

Devin jumped to his feet and turned toward the voice. Recognition came slowly.

"Wendy?"

There was a scuffling sound in the nearby grass, and then she appeared. Her face was damp with sweat, and she looked pale. A swatch of the suit's strange fabric was tied around her upper arm.

"Are you hurt?" he said, stepping forward.

"I'll be OK," she said. "But we need to get out of here. We're going to have to walk back to town."

"Hold on," Devin said. He slipped off his backpack and opened it, and then he handed her a bottle of water.

She eagerly took the bottle and started to twist the cap but winced with pain when she tried to use her arm.

"Here," Devin said. "Give it to me." He eyed her as he twisted off the cap and handed the bottle back to her.

As she gulped the water, he removed a power bar and another bottled water from his bag. When she had downed the entire bottle, he handed her the power bar.

"Sit down," he said. "And eat this."

They settled down in the dirt, and Wendy munched on the power bar while Devin told her about his scuffle with Major Nichols. He opened the black case and showed her the computer inside, but neither of them could figure out how to turn it on.

"It's the prototype," Wendy said. She leaned her head back against the tree. "I'm glad you got it."

Devin nodded and closed the case. "Now it's your turn. I left the bus right after you followed Kell and his people into the tunnel. What happened?"

Devin sipped his water as Wendy told him what had happened. When she got to the part where the gun had gone off, her voice trailed off.

"He's dead, isn't he?" Devin said.

Wendy nodded. "I didn't mean to. It just happened."

"He killed your parents," Devin said.

Wendy shook her head. "I know. Part of me is glad he's dead. Part of me thinks he deserved it. But another part of me..." She shook her head and looked away.

"Taking a life is a big deal," Devin said. "It's not an easy thing to live with."

Wendy turned her head and looked at him. "Have you…Did you ever…"

Devin didn't look at her. He stared straight ahead and nodded.

"When you were in the marines?"

"Yeah," he said.

Her voice was quiet and trembling. "How do you live with it?"

"You just do," he said. "The same way you live with everything else that's happened to you and all the other mistakes you've made. You get up every day, you live your life. Sometimes you think about it. Sometimes you don't. Sometimes you regret it. Sometimes you know there was no other way."

Wendy nodded.

"It doesn't get any easier," he said. "You'll think about it less as time goes on, but it never gets any easier."

They sat quietly for a few minutes. Devin checked Wendy's wound. He removed the first-aid kit from his pack and wiped the wound with an alcohol cloth, and then he smeared ointment on it and topped it off with a numbing agent before wrapping it in gauze. It took every ounce of Wendy's focus to refrain from screaming at the pain.

"It'll stay numb for a few hours, but we'll have to take out the bullet and sew it up as soon as possible," he said.

Wendy nodded, her lips tight as the pain melted away. "We'd better get going," she said. "We have a long walk ahead of us."

- 33 -

On the Run

Carter Air Force Base
Swenson, Colorado

She watched as the big man with dreadlocks who had fought Major Nichols—and won—ran off with the black box.

Until today she had seen the black box mostly in Lieutenant Smith's possession. For an instant she considered running after him and taking back the box, but something stopped her—Colonel Kell.

Colonel Kell's orders had been clear: stay with Major Nichols, and keep away from the authorities. For reasons unknown to her, she was compelled to follow his orders, no matter what.

She angled her head and looked down at the major. He was lying on his back in the grass, battered, bruised, and unconscious. She looked up and glanced toward the base. People were coming. She saw their silhouettes and lights bobbing on the horizon. They would reach her position in minutes. She squinted her eyes and everything illuminated. It was dark outside, but she could see the approaching people as if it were broad daylight. Almost all of them wore uniforms; the authorities were coming.

She kneeled beside the major. "Major Nichols?" she said. "Major Nichols, you must wake up. The authorities are coming."

He didn't respond.

She lightly slapped his cheeks, and then she gripped him by the shoulders and gave him a good shake, but he didn't rouse. She pushed herself to her feet, grabbed the flashlight that was tucked into his armpit, and stuck it in her waistband. Then she gripped him under his arms and started dragging him away from the base. But then she noticed the drag marks his unconscious body was leaving in the ground. Easy for the authorities to track.

She dropped Nichols and looked toward the base again. She had maybe two minutes. The people approaching were fanned out, crossing back and forth as they moved over the field. They were searching for something, and it occurred to her that they were looking for her or Major Nichols. Or perhaps they were looking for both of them.

She bent down and heaved Major Nichols over her shoulder. He wasn't heavy, but it was awkward carrying him in this manner. Then she took off, running. As she ran, she counted to forty-five seconds, and then she eased the major to the ground, ran back, and covered her tracks.

She repeated this several times, moving and working quickly. Once or twice, she thought she might have gotten too close to the approaching searchers. Finally she made a long dash through the farm fields that stretched across the land for over a mile, and then she found herself entering the foothills that marked the edge of the county. She had just crested the first small hill when Major Nichols began to stir.

She found a small, relatively flat clearing and heaved him off her shoulder. He thudded to the ground.

Major Nichols blinked his eyes open and groaned. "What the hell?" he muttered.

She stood nearby, looking over her shoulder to see if the authorities were coming. She saw the lights of the base in the distance. In the surrounding fields, she saw the little bobbing pins of light. They were still searching the fields, but they were a long way off now.

She turned back to Major Nichols. He was sitting up, cradling one of his arms and wincing in pain.

"Who was that guy?" he said.

"I do not know what guy you are referring to."

He stared at her. "How many guys were there?"

She glanced over her shoulder again. "There are many men and women searching the fields."

Nichols struggled to his feet and looked at the landscape below. "Probably looking for us," he said.

"Colonel Kell said to avoid the authorities." She pointed at the tiny lights down below. "Those are the authorities. I saw their uniforms."

Major Nichols pointed at himself. "I'm the authorities."

"I am to remain with you and avoid all other authorities until Colonel Kell rejoins us."

Nichols looked down at his uniform. It was filthy, torn in several spots. He dusted himself off as best he could. "We should have gone straight to the parking lot and grabbed a vehicle. Now we'll have to make the whole trek on foot."

"That is not a problem," she said.

He frowned at her. "Maybe not for you." He eyed the distance from where they were standing to the base below. "How did we get way up here?"

"I carried you."

"You carried me?"

"That is what I said."

He looked around. "Where's the control box?"

She didn't respond.

"The black box," he said, his voice rising. "I had it before that thug jumped me. Where is it?"

"Are you referring to Lieutenant Smith's black case?"

"It's not Smith's case, but yeah, that's the one I'm referring to. Where is it?"

"The man took it."

"The man who attacked me?"

"Yes."

"Motherfucker!" Major Nichols slammed his fist into a tree trunk. "Ow! Son of a bitch!"

She didn't respond, but she understood that he was experiencing anger.

Nichols walked toward her and didn't stop until his face was inches from hers. She didn't flinch.

"Why didn't you stop him?"

"I was not ordered to stop him."

"You dumb bitch!" he spat. "Do you have any idea what you've done? The MOTH compound has been seized. That control box is our only way to...Oh, hell!" He started pacing. "Kell's going to skin me alive."

She visualized Colonel Kell skinning Major Nichols alive and thought it unlikely but didn't say so.

Nichols continued pacing. "Who was that punk who jumped me? Where did he come from?"

"I do not know."

He suddenly stopped. "Watson's daughter," he said. "She was in the tunnel. The two of them must have been in on it together. But how? Why?"

"I do not know."

"Will you stop saying that? Damn, you're useless!" He walked past her, bumping her with his shoulder as he passed. She turned and kept her gaze fixed on him as he raised his arm and stared at his wristcom.

He swiped the com, but nothing happened. Then he swiped it again. It didn't respond. He swiped it several more times as she surveyed the horizon and saw that the searchers were returning to the base.

"The authorities are retreating," she said. "We can go to the safe house now."

When she turned back around, she saw that the color had drained from Major Nichols's face. He was still staring at the surface of his wristcom. "All data deleted," he said. His eyes met hers, and she saw an unfamiliar emotion there. Was it fear?

"This isn't supposed to happen," he said. "I should be able to access the remote node in case of emergency…"

He staggered back a few feet and braced himself against a tree. "The backups are down," he said, looking at her.

She didn't respond.

"It means the dead man's switch was triggered," Nichols said. "Colonel Kell is dead."

She tilted her head to one side. Colonel Kell was dead? Her job was to follow Colonel Kell's orders, and his last orders had been to stay with Major Nichols, avoid the authorities, and meet Colonel Kell at the safe house.

"Then he will not be meeting us at the safe house," she said.

- 34 -

Spotted

Swenson, Colorado

Wendy and Devin crept out of the clump of trees where they had been resting, passed the decrepit farmhouse, and headed down the dirt road that led to the highway. In the distance they saw the base surrounded by flashing lights as vehicles sped up and down the highway.

"I'm going to turn on my suit," Wendy said. "But we need to make sure nobody sees you."

"Let's cross the highway and get off-road on the other side," Devin said. "It's not much, but we'll be farther from the base and less likely to be seen."

Wendy looked around. "We could hide or head in the opposite direction until Eli and Jane can come get us."

But Devin shook his head. "We need to keep moving. That bullet needs to come out of your arm ASAP."

"OK," Wendy said. "Give me the black case."

"What are you going to do with it?"

"If I carry it, nobody will be able to see it," she said.

Devin nodded. "You mean if I'm captured, they won't be

able to confiscate it."

Wendy was about to respond, but Devin held up his hand. "You're right. It's smart thinking."

Wendy turned her back as she reconfigured the suit, and the top part of the suit fell away. She stretched her good arm out behind her, and he handed her the case. She almost dropped it.

"Do you want me to help you?" Devin said quietly.

Wendy looked at him over her shoulder and sighed. "I guess this is no time for modesty. Yeah, I could use your help. I want to wear it like a backpack."

She eased herself to the ground, and Devin helped her position the case against her back. Wendy tapped the device on her wrist and configured the suit to stretch itself back over her upper body.

"That can't be comfortable," Devin said.

"It's fine," Wendy said.

Devin glanced up and down the highway. "It's going to take an hour or two to get back to town. You should let your friends know we're on the way."

"Good thinking," Wendy said. She turned on her com and sent a message to Jane and Eli, and then Devin and Wendy started their long trek to town.

They spent the first hour walking through the tall, wild grass along the side of the highway, which slowed them down but kept them off the road and out of sight. Then they passed several farms, some of which were fenced, which meant Devin had to walk on the road where he was exposed. He fell into a pattern of crouching and hiding until the coast was clear of cars, and then he'd run the length of a fence. They'd been walking and sprinting for over an hour when they finally saw the lights of downtown Swenson.

As they neared the edge of town, they saw two police cars and an army truck.

"A checkpoint," Devin said.

"They're probably just looking for drunk drivers," Wendy said. "It's Friday night."

But Devin shook his head. "Not with an army vehicle." He pulled Wendy into the shadows, away from a nearby streetlight. "We need to stay out of sight," he said.

They backtracked and turned onto a private country road. There were only a few houses, and they were all set back far from the street. After about a quarter of a mile, they crossed one of the private properties and cut through a small grove that ended at a suburban neighborhood fence.

They scouted the fence until they found a section that backed a darkened house. Devin whistled and made some noise, trying to rouse any dogs that might be inside, but all remained quiet. Devin hopped the fence with ease, but Wendy couldn't pull herself up due to her injury, so Devin hopped back and got on all fours so she could step onto his back. She put her good arm over the fence and dangled there as Devin helped her hoist her body up until she was straddling the fence. Then he hopped over to the other side, reached up, and caught her as she let go and fell into his arms.

Wendy felt winded as Devin set her on her feet. She tried to take a step but faltered and stumbled, regaining her balance just in time to avoid crumpling to the ground.

Devin gripped her arm to steady her. "Are you all right?" he said.

"I'll be fine. I just got dizzy for a second," Wendy said. "Give me a minute to get my bearings."

Devin eyed her and then looked around. They were in a nondescript backyard.

"Stay here," Devin said, and then he disappeared around the side of the house. Wendy heard the quiet sound of a latch clicking followed by a low squeak. Devin returned a moment later.

"It's a quiet neighborhood," he said. "Nobody's around."

"OK, let's go," she said.

"You sure you can walk?"

Wendy nodded. "My legs are fine."

"All right. Follow me," he said.

Devin led her across the backyard to the side of the house and through an open gate. And then they were on the street.

"We're just a few blocks from downtown," Devin whispered.

"You better not talk to me," Wendy said. "People will think you're crazy, talking to some imaginary friend."

They walked quietly for a few blocks. Then Devin covered his mouth with his hand and spoke, keeping his voice low. "It's almost midnight," he said. "Downtown is going to be crawling with bar hoppers and law enforcement."

"Just try to blend in," she said.

"I'm not worried about me," he said. "You're tired and wounded. The last thing we need is for you to bump into some cop."

"I'm fine," Wendy said. "Let's keep walking."

A moment later they entered the downtown area of Swenson, which stretched for six city blocks on a main drag and a secondary street that were connected by a series of smaller streets and walkways.

They turned onto one of the smaller streets, which wasn't very busy. Most of the businesses were closed except for one dive bar. Wendy and Devin easily avoided the clump of people outside the bar by crossing the street. They took an alley that led to the main downtown street.

Devin's eyes went wide as they exited the alley and Swenson's main intersection came into view. On each of three corners, there were large groups of people. One group stood in a line outside a club with loud, thumping music. Young adults were loitering around, smoking and talking, and one couple was making out. On another corner there was a similar group standing outside a small theater where a live band was playing. There was a police car pulled over at the third corner with its lights on, and two officers were questioning someone.

Wendy gripped Devin's arm and pulled him into a dark doorway several buildings away from the commotion. "They're all focused on the police. I'm going to go in the street and walk on the other side of the parked cars, so I can avoid the crowd."

Devin glanced at the street. The traffic was sparse but steady. He shook his head. "There are too many cars. They won't detect you while you're wearing the suit, so you need to stay out of the street. It's better to risk moving through the crowd." He leaned back and examined the group outside the dance club. "They're all drunk anyway. You could probably roll right through them, and they wouldn't even notice."

Wendy leaned out, looked at the groups of people and the street, and then nodded. "I agree," she said. "But listen, don't try to stay with me. There's a coffee shop about three doors down from the dance club. It'll be closed, so we'll meet there, just outside the front door. If something goes wrong, or if there are too many people around, we'll meet at the dojo. It's only five or six blocks away."

Devin didn't like the idea of splitting up, but if Wendy was worried about staying with him, she'd be less focused, and she would put herself in greater danger.

"You go first," Wendy said.

"No, you go first," Devin said. "I don't want you to worry about staying with me. Just get through that intersection, and we'll meet at that coffee shop."

"OK," she said. "See you there." And then she stepped out of the doorway and headed toward the intersection. She walked slowly, keeping her body as close to the buildings as possible. When a group of three bar hoppers approached, she had to press her body flat against the facade to let them pass. By the time she neared the dance club, the line had thinned, and there were fewer people blocking the way.

She estimated there were about a dozen people in front of the club. Half of them were gathered on the far side of the sidewalk beneath a streetlight, smoking and talking. The others were on the building side of the sidewalk and spread out, mostly in pairs—two girls talking quietly under the eaves, a couple arguing quietly, plus the bouncer and his sidekick. Wendy scoped the situation and decided her best bet was to walk down the center of the sidewalk.

She moved slowly at first, planning to quicken her pace as she passed the entrance. That was the most congested area. There would be plenty of room for her to walk, but the two bouncers would be on her left, and the smokers under the streetlight would be on her right. She would be surrounded but only for a couple of seconds.

As she passed the entrance, there was a loud noise to her left, and a horde of people came swarming out of the door. The bouncers were pushed back against the building amid shouting and screaming.

Wendy would have made it if she'd stayed her course and continued walking by the din, but instinct took over, and without thought, she paused, only momentarily, to turn and see what the commotion was all about.

At the center of the mess there were two women clawing the crowd, trying to tackle each other. As Wendy stopped to turn her head, one of them barreled into her, and she went flying backward into the group of smokers under the streetlight.

She smashed into a woman and saw a lit cigarette flying through the air. The woman screamed as she fell into the street, and Wendy toppled down on top of her. The woman's purse fell into the gutter, and its contents scattered into the street and on the sidewalk.

"What the hell?" the woman yelled. She pushed and clawed at Wendy. "Something's on me!" she screamed.

Wendy scrambled to her feet and launched into a sprint, but she hadn't paused to take in her surroundings, and she smacked her forehead into the lamppost.

"Ow!" she cried, grabbing her head.

Meanwhile the crowd outside the bar had thickened. The bouncers had moved in and were holding the two screaming women back from each other. Drunken patrons surrounded them, yelling and pushing against the crowd.

Wendy was dazed. She shook her head and blinked her eyes, trying to clear her mind.

As she swiveled her head, she saw the woman she had knocked over on her hands and knees, grabbing her things and stuffing them back into her purse. The woman was cursing under her breath.

"Hey, where did she come from?" someone said behind her.

Someone else laughed. "What kind of getup is that? Are those goggles?"

Wendy glanced around but couldn't tell who had spoken. She turned back to the woman, who had crawled into the street on her hands and knees to gather her things. Her eyes were droopy and her movements were sloppy. She was wasted.

"Whoa, did you see that?"

"Yeah, that woman just disappeared!"

Wendy ignored the voices and stared at the woman in the street, still dazed. Then something moved in her peripheral vision. A motorcycle was approaching, and its rider was looking at the brouhaha outside the club instead of watching the road. Wendy turned her gaze back to the woman. Now she was sitting on her knees in the street, shoving items into her purse, and the motorcycle was heading straight for her.

Wendy darted into the street, grabbed the woman's arms,

and dragged her to the curb. Wendy heard gasps behind her as the woman kicked and screamed, "What the hell? Something's got me! Let go of me!" The motorcycle braked and skidded, and then revved up and sped off.

The woman kicked and clawed, and Wendy gasped as the woman's foot made contact with her gunshot wound.

"There she is again!"

Wendy gripped her wound and stepped back a few paces. She leaned against the lamppost, closing her eyes and squeezing the injury until the sting subsided.

When she opened her eyes, the woman was staring at her.

"It was you. You saved my life," she slurred. "Thank you."

"You're welco—" Wendy broke off when she realized the woman was looking right at her. *Looking right at her.* Then Wendy looked down and saw her own body. "Dammit, not again!" she said.

Wendy turned, ready to flee, but found about twenty people blocking her way. About half were turned toward her, and they were all staring at her.

A tall, skinny guy pointed at her. "I saw her appear out of nowhere!"

"Who are you?" someone else said.

"How did you do that?"

"Leave her alone. She saved my life!"

Wendy started shaking. Her head was still throbbing, and the wound in her arm was stinging despite the numbing agent that Devin had applied. She scanned the crowd. Some of them looked confused. Some looked angry. They were closing in on her.

Wendy glanced over her shoulder. Drawn by the commotion, the cops were approaching, and they were already halfway across the intersection. They'd arrive in a matter of seconds.

She took a step back as she swiped at the device on her

wrist, and then she took a deep breath and waited for the suit to reboot.

"Where did she go?"

"See! I told you she disappeared!"

Wendy looked around one last time and then pushed her way through the crowd and ran toward the coffee shop.

- 35 -

The Hacker

Swenson, Colorado

Devin gave Wendy plenty of time to get a head start. He was about to start walking to the coffee shop, where he was supposed to meet her, when pandemonium broke outside the club door. He ran to the club and found madness and hysteria. About two dozen people were clustered in a circle, and at its center Devin could barely make out a head of red hair. It was Wendy. He was about to make a dash for her when she disappeared. He held back and watched as the crowd parted, with people getting pushed back by an invisible force. He almost called out Wendy's name but caught himself just in time. The last thing they needed was for anyone to hear her name. He pushed through the crowd and paused outside the coffee shop a few doors down.

"Wendy," he whispered loudly. "Are you here?" Then he called her name louder. "Wendy!"

There was no reply, so he turned and sprinted for the dojo.

* * *

Jane and Eli were huddled around the VW's table, waiting for Wendy to show up or contact them. Eli had immersed himself in monitoring the feeds coming out of the MOTH compound, which was now swarming with cops, agents, and Pentagon officials. Jane sat beside him with her feet on the seat and her knees tucked under her chin, lost in thought. They hadn't heard from Wendy in a couple of hours, and their nerves were frazzled.

Eli looked up from the monitor he'd been watching. "It's confirmed," he said. "The MOTH project was not sanctioned by the air force."

Jane didn't respond. She was lost in thought.

"Did you hear me?" Eli said.

"Huh? What?" Jane said, snapping to attention.

"I'm monitoring the bugs that Wendy dropped. The air force just confirmed that the MOTH project was a rogue operation," Eli said.

"Oh," Jane said.

Eli glanced at the time on his wristcom and then looked out the bus window. The streets were deserted.

"They should have been here by now," he said.

Jane nodded but didn't say anything.

"What's up?" Eli said.

"Nothing," she said.

"You've been acting weird ever since Wendy got out of the tunnel."

"Well, this is a pretty weird situation," Jane said. She straightened her legs and stretched them beneath the table.

Eli shook his head. "Something's bothering you. Something you're not telling me."

She swiveled her head around and looked at him. "What are you, psychic?"

Eli looked away. "Fine, if you don't want to—"

"DNA," Jane said.

Eli looked confused. "DNA?"

"Yep, DNA."

"What about it?"

Jane sighed and got up from the table. She stepped to a cabinet near the back of the bus and rifled through the shelves. "All we have is water," she said, pulling out a bottle. "I could use something stronger."

"This is hardly the time for drinking," Eli said.

Jane twisted the cap off the water bottle and eased back into the seat. "Wendy was shot in the tunnel. She bled in the tunnel. She left her DNA in the tunnel."

Eli's mouth fell open.

Jane continued. "I didn't say anything earlier because Wendy's tired and injured, and there's nothing she could have done."

"She could have gone back and cleaned it up!" Eli sputtered.

"Yeah, with that mop and the bucket of bleach she has in her back pocket," Jane said.

"We're screwed," Eli said, forgetting all about the situation he was monitoring inside the base. "We're all going to go to prison."

"I doubt it," Jane said. "At least I hope not." She took a long draw from the water bottle.

Eli ran a hand through his hair, causing it to stick up. "What are you thinking?"

"Worst-case scenario is they find the blood, match it, and pick her up. I think—and I'm not sure about this—but I think they'd go easy on us, since we did stop a potential coup d'etat."

"And you can think of a better scenario than that?" Eli said. "I mean, they're going to find the blood. They're going to match it eventually. Unless we all go into hiding—"

"They need something to match it to," Jane said.

"You don't think Wendy's DNA is on file?"

"Doesn't matter," Jane said. "Even if her blood isn't on file, the air force will most definitely have her father's blood on file. They'll be able to tell the blood came from someone related to him, and Wendy and her aunt would top the list of suspects."

Eli got up from the table, pulled his yo-yo out of his pocket, and started pacing. "This is bad. This is very, very bad."

"Settle down," Jane said. "I have a plan."

Eli stared at her.

"I'm not sure if it's possible," she said. "Most of it will depend on you."

"Me?"

"Yeah. And whether you can find a way to hack into the authorities' databases. If you can do that, you can either delete or modify the records so there's nothing to match it to."

Eli almost dropped his yo-yo. "You expect me to hack into a military database? Do you have any idea how dangerous that is?"

"Oh, come off it. You're not fooling me."

"What's that supposed to mean?"

Jane got to her feet and set her water bottle down on the table. "You're a hacker. Maybe not good enough to hack into the air force database. But you, my friend, are definitely a hacker."

"Wait a minute—"

Jane held up her hand. "You hacked into the post office like you were tying your shoes. I don't know how deep into it you are, but you're definitely into it."

Eli's shoulders drooped as he sighed. Then he slid back into the booth. "Is it that obvious?"

"Probably not," Jane said, sliding into the booth next to him. "But I've had my eye on you, and I know a hacker when I see one. Remember how I was supposed to go to Mexico to

285

train activists?"

"Yeah, so?"

"I was going to train hackers. Hacktivists."

Eli's eyes lit up. "So you're a hacker too?"

"Are you kidding? No, I'm not a hacker. I teach them to think strategically. Back when hacktivism started, they knocked out websites, took over their opponents' social media accounts, and reported events that mainstream media wasn't reporting. It wasn't very effective, not on a large scale. You know what hacktivists do now?"

"I might," Eli said.

Jane rolled her eyes. "Whatever," she said. "Now they hack into the mainstream media. They break into the most popular entertainment websites and get their message out to tens of millions of viewers."

Eli shrugged. "It's a good way to reach huge portions of the population."

Jane nodded. "I agree. They've also been known to steal money from their opponents and reroute it to the causes they support."

"Hackers do a lot of things," Eli said.

"And they rarely get caught," Jane pointed out.

They were both quiet for a few seconds.

"I got caught when I was sixteen," Eli said.

"Caught hacking?"

He nodded. "It wasn't that bad, but at the time I was terrified. They threatened me with prison. Can you imagine me in prison?"

Jane grinned. "No, I don't see that going over too well, although they do have computers in there."

"I was hacking into school records," Eli said. "Changing grades, getting people accepted into college, that kind of thing."

"You got caught doing that?"

"I was only sixteen," Eli said. "Most successful hackers work in security. I worked at an online game shop. Tech support."

"What happened?"

"I was banned from gadgets and devices for one year. I could use a computer for anything related to work and school; that was it."

"Damn," Jane said.

"Yeah, it was like I was living at the turn of the twenty-first century. They also made me go through this training program about values and ethics, responsible computer usage, that kind of stuff."

"But it didn't take?" Jane said.

"Oh it took. I got my values and ethics in order."

"But you didn't stop hacking?"

Eli shook his head. "I did for a while, but after college I started doing freelance cybersecurity."

"That often leads to hacking," Jane said, nodding like she'd heard this story a hundred times before.

"Jobs in cybersecurity are the gateway to hacking," Eli agreed. "I still do it on the side. Cybersecurity, I mean."

"So," Jane said. "That's how you earn the bucks. When I saw your apartment, I figured either you came from a big-money family, or you had something going on the side. What's the deal? You just hack for fun?"

"I do it only occasionally."

"The question is whether you'll do it now. Can you get into the database?"

"What if I can't?"

"Then I have some other contacts I could ask. I'd rather you do it, so we don't have to involve anyone else." Jane glanced at the monitor. "We've got to act fast. They're going to get into that tunnel any minute, and once they find that blood…"

Eli looked around. "I can't do it from here."

"You need your equipment back at Wendy's?"

"No, I have what I need, but I need a LAN line. A direct connection."

"I'm sure there's one in the dojo," Jane said. She glanced out the window. "We'll have to wait until Devin gets here."

"Does Wendy know?" Eli said quietly.

"That you're a hacker?"

Eli nodded, and Jane shrugged. "She hasn't said anything to me about it."

"Promise you won't tell her?"

Jane studied Eli for a long moment. "If that's what you want, I won't tell her. But I also won't lie to her. If she figures it out and asks me about it—"

"She wouldn't ask you. She would ask me," Eli said.

"Maybe," Jane said. "But if you want my advice, and I'm sure you do, I think you should tell her. Secrets between friends are a bad idea, especially considering what we've all done here tonight."

"So you're going to tell her about the DNA?"

"Yeah, she has a right to know about that. And that's another reason you should tell her. Once I tell her about the DNA—"

"All right, all right. I see where you're going with this. Once you tell her about the DNA, you'll have to tell her that I hacked into the records so they couldn't match it to her." Eli sighed. "Don't worry, I won't put you in a position to lie to her." Eli shoved the yo-yo back in his pocket and slid into the booth. "We'll tell her everything."

"She'll probably be surprised, but she won't be mad at you," Jane said, resting a hand on Eli's arm. It startled him, and he almost jumped out of the seat, so Jane pulled her arm back.

"Geez," she said. "A few hours ago, you had your tongue down my throat. Now I can't touch your arm?"

"Sorry," he said, feeling his face flush. "You startled me. I'm just on edge."

"Yeah, aren't we all?" Jane said, staring at him. Then she caught movement in her peripheral vision.

She got up and looked out the window.

"Someone's coming," she said.

- 36 -

Flicker

Swenson, Colorado

"It's Devin," Jane said. Then she pulled the side door of the bus open.

Eli arched his head and saw Devin hurtling down the street toward the van.

"Come on, get in," Jane said when Devin stopped just outside the bus door.

"Where's Wendy?" Devin said, and then he suddenly hurled forward, pushed by an invisible force.

A voice cried out, and then Wendy appeared behind Devin. He turned around and caught her just as she passed out.

The hours that followed were a blur. Wendy faded in and out of consciousness as someone carried her inside and up some stairs. "What happened?" she muttered. "Did we get them?" Then they were shoving something in her mouth—a pill.

Devin was hovering over her, and Jane was at his side. They were talking, and then they were running around, and then they were hovering over her again.

"This is going to hurt," Devin said. "You need to try to keep still." He looked at Jane. "Hold her down while I remove the bullet."

Then came the blinding pain in her arm. It consumed her whole body until the world went black, and she drifted into nothingness. After that, strange dreams interspersed with moments of clarity—Jane scooping scrambled eggs into her mouth and wiping her face and hands with a damp cloth, Eli reading to her, and Devin holding her jaw and telling her to swallow a pill.

Finally she opened her eyes, and the world seemed steady again.

"There's our girl." It was Jane, sitting on the bed beside Wendy. "How's your arm?"

Wendy blinked and gripped her injured arm. "It hurts," she said. "But it's just a dull ache."

"You were on heavy painkillers," Jane said. "But we're weaning you off of them now. It's going to hurt, but the only other option is addiction. We figured you'd prefer to put up with a little soreness over becoming a junkie."

Wendy pushed herself up with her good arm and looked around. She was in her old bedroom at her parents' house.

"What happened?" she said. "Did they—are we—"

"We'll fill you in on everything," Jane said. "But first you need to eat, and you need a bath. She crinkled up her nose. "You're getting pretty ripe. Sponging your face and limbs only does so much good."

"How long have I been out of it?" Wendy asked.

"Two and a half days," Jane said. "It's Monday morning. We caught an infection just in time. And you can thank Devin's field training for that."

Jane called Devin to tell him Wendy was awake, and then she wrapped Wendy's wound in plastic and taped it tight, so it wouldn't get wet. She filled the bath and helped Wendy into it.

Once Wendy was scrubbed, rinsed, and dried, Jane led her downstairs and made her sit while Jane fixed breakfast: eggs, fruit, and toast.

Wendy was famished. But halfway through the meal, her mind had filled with questions. She set her fork down. "I want to know what happened. Do the authorities know about Kell—what he was planning, what he did to my parents? And what happened with Nichols? He saw Devin and me—"

"Major Nichols was not apprehended. We don't know how he did it, but he got away. He's a fugitive, and there's a massive manhunt for him."

Wendy rubbed her temples. "I want Nichols brought to justice, but if they find him…"

"If they find him, he'll probably tell them about you and Devin, and then you two will become fugitives."

Wendy stared at her plate.

"Close call, huh?" Jane said.

Wendy nodded in a daze.

"Finish your breakfast."

* * *

Devin arrived just as Wendy was swallowing the last of her orange juice, and Jane was clearing the dishes.

"Perfect timing," Jane said. "We're just about to go down to the basement to see Eli and fill Wendy in on everything."

Jane helped Wendy down the basement stairs with Devin following. They found Eli slumped over the table, sound asleep, with his hand resting on the black case that Devin had taken from Major Nichols.

Jane helped Wendy into a chair and then went to Eli and tickled the back of his neck. "Wake up, Captain Computer, our hero has risen."

Eli roused and then sat straight up in his chair when he

realized everyone was sitting around the table, looking at him.

"I must have dozed off," he said, rubbing his eyes and blushing.

Jane turned to Wendy. "He's been doing that a lot over the past few days." She turned to Eli. "Wendy's ready to be debriefed."

"OK," Eli said, wiping his mouth to make sure he wasn't drooling. He situated a laptop in front of himself. "Um, there's a lot to cover. Let's start with what went down at the base." He rubbed his eyes. "We've got two bugs in there: We did have one in each of Kell's offices plus the one you stuck to the railing, but the one on the railing is dead. I've still got hours and hours of audio and video to go through. What we know so far is that the authorities did uncover evidence of a coup that was underway. Kell, Nichols, and some doctor named Walsh were involved for sure. They were running a secret operation—"

"Project," Devin said.

Eli stared at him with a questioning look.

"It's a project, not an operation."

"Oh right," Eli said. "Project MOTH: Military Optimized Techno-Hybrids. It was a rogue project, not sanctioned by the air force. We don't know what they were working on, but it sounds like some kind of biotech, and we do know they developed a fully functional prototype." He pointed at the black case. "I think this is the prototype."

Wendy nodded. "That's what I figured too. What is it?"

Eli shrugged. "I have no idea." He opened the case, revealing what looked like a laptop computer inside. "I can't even power it up. I've tried everything. There are billions of possible key combinations. We're not getting into that thing anytime soon. And I think it's nuclear powered."

Wendy pushed her chair back.

Eli shook his head. "It's perfectly safe. It's emitting

293

radiation but not enough to be dangerous."

"And you have no idea what this prototype does?"

Eli shook his head. "No, but we think it's probably a weapon."

"It's got to be a pretty powerful weapon if Kell thought he could use it to overtake the entire military," Devin said.

Wendy stared at the black box. "Shouldn't we turn it over to the authorities? I don't think we should be in possession of something like that."

"We probably should, but it would be very difficult, if not impossible, to get that to them safely without them being able to trace it back to us," Jane said. "For now we hold on to it."

"They think Nichols has it," Eli said.

Wendy chewed on her bottom lip. "OK," she finally said. "What else do we know?"

Eli exchanged a questioning look with Devin and Jane. Jane nodded at him, and he continued. "Several people in the compound were murdered."

"Murdered?" Wendy said.

"Yeah, seven of them. Kell and Nichols didn't do it. They were long gone when the bodies started piling up. But we only know that because we were able to compare the time stamps on your audio feed and the feeds coming from the compound. The authorities still think Kell or Nichols took them out."

"Most of the people the authorities found in that compound—the ones who were left alive—claim they didn't know the project was not sanctioned by the Air Force.

"How could they not know?" Wendy said.

"They follow orders," Devin said. "They're doing top-secret work that they can't discuss with anyone. Unless Kell and Nichols told them about the purpose of the project, a better question is: How could they know?"

"Oh," Wendy said, nodding. "That makes sense. But how do we know some of them aren't lying?"

"We don't," Devin said. "They've all been taken in for questioning. The Pentagon will work it out. They have ways of getting people to tell the truth."

"Tell her your theory," Jane said to Devin.

"I think the people who were killed were the ones who knew what Kell and Nichols were really up to. They knew about the coup. Or maybe they only suspected, like your father," Devin said. "Which means there's still someone out there who was involved."

"The person who killed them all," Wendy said.

"Right," Devin said.

"And Nichols," Wendy said. "Nichols is still out there."

"And he knows about us," Devin said.

"So does that chick he was with," Jane added.

"Plus you were seen by the drunkards downtown outside the club," Devin said.

"Oh, that's right," Wendy said, sinking her face into her hands. "Those people saw me."

When she lifted her head, Eli was shifting uncomfortably in his chair, and Devin's eyes had wandered off and were staring at the floor. But Jane was looking right at Wendy.

"What?" Wendy said. "Why are you all acting funny?"

Jane turned to Eli. "You'd better show her."

Eli slid the laptop toward himself and opened a bunch of tabs and windows. "Come on over," he said to Wendy.

She got up from the chair she'd been sitting in and walked around the table, positioning herself behind Eli and Devin. There was a photograph on the screen.

"Is that me?" she said.

"Yep, that's you," Eli said.

The photographer had been standing behind Wendy and slightly to the left. The outline of her cheekbone was visible, as were her hair, the goggles, and her shoulders.

She leaned forward to get a better view.

"Fortunately this is the best shot they got," Eli said.

"You can't be identified from it," Jane said. "Eli already checked it against facial recognition software."

Eli showed her two more pictures. One was from the front, but it was severely blurred, which was pure luck. Another was a lower body shot, showing her legs in the suit. "That's it for still images," Eli said.

Then he showed her two videos. The first one was blurry, and the camera was bouncing around, jostled by the crowd, and nothing could be made out clearly. It mostly panned across the back of her suit, capturing a few wisps of her hair.

"This one would have been a real problem if the photographer had aimed it at your face even once," Devin said.

"Because they can freeze the frames?" Wendy said.

"Right," Devin said.

The last video was the most incriminating. It jostled around as much as the first, but it was focused on Wendy's legs when she vanished. The entire scene was blurry.

"Some people are saying this one's a trick, or the camera malfunctioned," Eli said.

"Some people?"

"Yeah. You made the news."

Then he showed her the worst of the lot—an article in the local paper: "Mysterious redheaded woman flickers and disappears."

"Flickers?" Wendy said.

The others were silent.

"Can I read that?" she said.

Eli vacated his seat so Wendy could take it. There were several quotes from witnesses who said she'd been flickering, and then she had disappeared.

"I don't remember flickering," Wendy said.

"The suit was malfunctioning. We—Devin and I—tested it, and it's definitely…um…flickering," Eli said. "If it's struck with force in certain spots, it malfunctions."

"Just show her the website," Jane said.

"What website?" Wendy asked.

Eli cleared his throat and jammed his hands into his pockets.

"I'll show her," Devin said. He slid the laptop toward himself and typed in a domain name, pecking at the keys one finger at a time.

Wendy leaned over and looked at the screen. "Whoisflicker-dot-com?" she said. Then she gasped. It was a site dedicated to finding out who the mysterious invisible woman was, and they were calling her Flicker.

"It's not so bad," Eli said, "You're like a superhero now."

Wendy scrolled through the site with her mouth hanging open and her heart rate increasing.

"They think I'm an alien?" she said.

"It's just one of many theories," Eli said. "The most popular one is that you work for the government."

"Yeah, you're a spy," Devin said.

Jane stood up. "I think it's pretty cool."

Wendy glared at her.

"Well, as long as they never figure out who Flicker really is, it's cool."

Wendy leaned in and read a few of the posts on the website. "It says here that 'witnesses at the scene were questioned by military police officers.'"

"The military still doesn't know who sent them the evidence," Devin said. He nodded at the screen. "That was one of the two leads they had."

Wendy pushed the laptop away. "And what was the other lead?" she said.

"Your DNA," Jane said.

Wendy stared at Jane for a moment, her face blank. Then it dawned on her. "My blood."

Jane nodded. "Right, but Eli took care of it." She patted Eli on the back and smiled at Wendy.

"What did you do, Eli?" Wendy said, frowning.

Eli shuffled his feet and stared at the floor. "Your blood wasn't in any databases, but your father's was. I was going to delete the record of his DNA, but then I had another idea. I hacked into the mainframe that processes new samples, and when the samples they took from the tunnel went in for processing, I altered them." He shrugged. "So there's no match."

"No match in the database?" Wendy said.

"Right."

"But they still have the physical sample?"

"It was a close call, Wendy. Eli took a big risk hacking into that database," Jane said.

"I'm sorry," Wendy said. "Eli, thank you."

"There is a chance they could retest the physical sample," Jane said. "It happens sometimes. I've seen it." She looked at Eli. "We're working on it."

"The samples are stored in a refrigerated section of a warehouse," Eli said. "We think there's a way to push through a work order to destroy it."

"We hope to eliminate it by tomorrow night," Jane said. She stepped forward and squeezed Wendy's shoulder. "So everything's fine. We're all in the clear or just about."

Wendy pushed the laptop away. "I set off an alarm. I left blood at the crime scene. I let people see me. I really blew it," she said.

"No," Devin said. "You didn't."

They all looked at him as if he was crazy.

"I killed a man," she whispered.

"It didn't go exactly as planned," he said. "But we're all here, and we're OK." He nodded at her bullet wound. "You're going to be fine. We not only confirmed that Kell was organizing a coup; we stopped it. It seems like things went haywire, but we accomplished the mission."

"He's right," Jane said.

"Yeah," Eli added.

"Maybe," Wendy said. "Except Nichols is still out there."

"With that strange woman," Jane added.

"Wendy and I are going to have to lay low for a while," Devin said.

- 37 -

California

Wendy was tugging her suitcase down the stairs, favoring her injured arm, when Jane appeared in the foyer.

"Let me help you with that," Jane said. She bounded up the stairs and took Wendy's suitcase, carrying it down the rest of the way.

"Thanks," Wendy said, rubbing her sore arm as they moved through the house.

"Everything's locked up," Jane said. "Your aunt's coming over next week?"

"Yeah, she's going to move in here and rent her house out," Wendy said. "I'm just glad I don't have to sell it." She paused outside the kitchen door and looked around one last time. Then she locked the door behind her and followed Jane out to the garage.

Devin and Eli had just finished reinstalling the backseats in the car that had belonged to Wendy's mom. They had all agreed it would be best to stay off airplanes with the equipment they would be carrying, so Wendy, Eli, and Jane were driving back to Massachusetts.

Devin came around the back of the car as Jane hefted Wendy's suitcase into the trunk.

"Are you guys finished?" Jane said.

"We sure are." Eli grinned as he opened the back door and stepped aside.

"Let's have a look," Jane said.

Wendy leaned in one of the windows and watched as Jane ran her hand underneath the backseat. She found a hidden lever and gave it a tug. The seat popped up, revealing a storage space beneath. The silver case that Wendy had found in her treehouse was sitting there. She still didn't know where her father had gotten it, and she wasn't sure whether she'd ever unravel that particular mystery.

"The black case is underneath the other seat," Eli said, pointing to the other side of the car.

Jane closed the seat and then slid in and bounced on it. "Feels normal," she said.

She climbed out of the car and gave Eli a high five. "Good work, boys." She walked around the car to Devin.

"It's been a real adventure," she said. "Don't be a stranger." She gave him a high five before she walked back to the other side of the car and climbed into the driver's seat.

Eli came around next and held out his hand. Devin raised one eyebrow as they shook. "It was an honor," Eli said. "And thanks for your service."

"Anytime," Devin said.

Eli nodded and climbed into the backseat as Wendy came around to Devin.

"I don't know how to thank you," she said. "And I'm sorry. I should have listened to you—"

"No more apologies." Devin said, bending down to look in her eyes. "It didn't go down perfectly, but you did great. Mission accomplished, remember?"

"Yeah, except Nichols is still out there, and we're about to drive halfway across the country with a bunch of stolen military equipment."

"You're going to be fine," he said. "Just hide it in a safe place, and don't mess with it until you decide what you're going to do next."

"When do you leave for Japan?" she asked.

"Tomorrow," he said.

"How long do you think you'll be out of the country?"

Devin shrugged. "Until I feel like coming back."

Wendy nodded.

"You need to lay low," he said. "In case Nichols resurfaces. I've been thinking about it, and I don't think he'd tell them about us. If they find us, they'll get the prototype, and I bet that's the last thing he wants."

"Unless he thinks he can use it as a bargaining chip."

"He was involved in a coup to overthrow the US government. There are no bargaining chips for him. I'm more worried about him coming around looking for it."

Wendy glanced back at the car. The windows were rolled up, and Jane and Eli were talking. She turned back to Devin.

"I'm going to close the lab and move out of Cambridge." She looked over her shoulder again. "I haven't told them yet."

"You should move out of the state. And cover your tracks. Just for a while."

She nodded and laughed nervously. "I don't even know how to do that. Cover my tracks."

"They can help you," Devin said, eyeing Jane and Eli. "They're good friends."

"The best," Wendy said.

She reached up and wrapped her arms around Devin, and they exchanged a long, warm hug. "Keep in touch," she whispered, and then she got in the car.

Devin walked alongside the car as it backed out, and

Wendy turned and watched through the back window as the garage door closed behind them. Devin waved one last time before heading to his bus. Then she turned around for the long drive ahead.

* * *

They'd been on the road for almost an hour before anyone spoke.

"That was crazy," Eli said suddenly.

"You just realized that?" Jane said, watching him in the rearview mirror.

"Well, yeah. I mean, no. You know what sucks? We can never tell anyone. Nobody will ever know what we did."

"Oh, you never know," Jane said. "In twenty or thirty years, maybe we'll be able to talk about it. Or one of us could fictionalize it in a novel."

"Or a video game," Eli said.

Jane gave Wendy a sideways glance. Wendy was staring out the window. Jane gave her a gentle nudge with her elbow.

"What's on your mind?" Jane said.

Wendy sighed and gave Jane a weak smile. "Oh, just thinking about what's next."

"Got any ideas?"

Wendy turned and looked at each of them. "Well, for starters, I'm going to have to close the lab."

"That's not necessary," Eli said.

"Yes," Wendy said, turning around in her seat to face him. "It is necessary. There's no grant money, and even if there were..." She shook her head and bit her bottom lip.

"Nichols," Jane said.

"Right," Wendy said. "Nichols is out there. He saw me. I need to get to someplace where he won't be able to find me."

Eli stared at her. "Does that mean you're moving? Leaving

303

Cambridge?"

"I have no choice." Wendy turned and faced forward.

They drove for a few minutes, and then Jane spoke quietly. "What will you do?"

Wendy shrugged. "I was thinking about finishing my mom's book for her. It's all written. It just needs a little fact-checking, some editing."

"Let me know if you want any help. I'd love—"

"What's next is we're going to finish the BIM," Eli said from the backseat.

Wendy frowned and turned around in her seat to look at him. "Eli, I already told you—"

"I've got the money," he said.

Wendy shook her head. "I don't think you understand how much the BIM program costs—"

"Unless it costs more than a quarter of a billion dollars, we're good to go."

"That's not funny, Eli," Wendy said, turning back toward the road.

"I'm not kidding," he said. "I've got two hundred and fifty million dollars, and I already invested a bunch of it, so pretty soon I'll have a lot more than that."

Jane scrutinized him in the rearview mirror. "What did you do, win the lottery?"

"You guys think I'm joking," Eli said, shaking his head. He pulled out his yo-yo and held it up. "Do you know how many yo-yos I could buy with a quarter of a billion dollars?"

Wendy turned around again and studied Eli's face. "OK, I'll play along," she said. "Where did you get it?"

"Does it matter?" he said.

Wendy rolled her eyes. "Of course it matters. If you really do have a quarter of a billion dollars, then where did it come from?"

"Technically it's not my money. It's ours."

"Where did you get it, Eli?"

Eli stared out the window for a few seconds. "Kell," he said.

Jane almost slammed on the brakes.

"Kell?" Wendy said. "What are you talking about?"

"The files you downloaded from his computer," Eli said. "Everything was there: bank account numbers, passwords."

"Kell had two hundred and fifty million bucks?" Jane said.

But Wendy shook her head. "That wasn't his money. That belonged to the military. If you're serious, Eli, we have to give it back. Taking a few trinkets is one thing; we can't run with a quarter of a billion taxpayer dollars!"

Eli snorted. "Trinkets? Is that what we're calling them now? Besides, the money didn't belong to the military," Eli said. "It was Kell's personal stash, earmarked for Project MOTH. I don't know where he got it. I tried to trace it, but it led nowhere. I looked into the military budget for Carter Air Force Base, and I can assure you Kell's funds came from another source."

"Where the hell did he get that kind money?" Jane said.

"Why didn't you mention this before?" Wendy said, eyeing Eli suspiciously. "Why didn't you tell us about this back at the house?"

Eli shrugged. "I figured it was just between the three of us."

Wendy frowned. "You didn't want Devin to know?"

"It's not that. I think as few people as possible should know about this. We could get in a lot of trouble—especially me. Only the three of us need to know, and I'm only telling Jane because she's going to be our lawyer."

"I'm a civil lawyer, not a business lawyer," Jane said.

"You can't do both?" Eli asked.

"I can't ask the two of you to leave Massachusetts," Wendy said. "And I can't stay there."

"If you close the lab and move away, I'm not staying there anyway," Eli said. "My job's all that keeps me there."

Jane looked at Eli in the rearview mirror. "And where would you go?" she asked.

He fiddled with his yo-yo. "I was thinking California," he said.

Wendy stared out the window.

"California," Jane said.

"We'll build a new lab," Eli said. "We'll finish the BIM."

"And what about that stuff we've got stashed under the backseat?" Jane asked. "What are you going to do with that?"

"Well, I guess that's up to Wendy," Eli said.

Jane looked over at Wendy. "What do you think, Wendy Bird?"

Wendy turned toward Eli again. "California?"

He nodded.

"A quarter of a billion dollars?" she said.

He nodded again.

"Well then," she said. "I guess this adventure isn't over."

Metamorphosis Book 2 is Coming Soon—Get a Free Review Copy

Thank you for reading *Engineered Underground*, the first book in the Metamorphosis series. If you'd like to be notified when new books in the series are released, sign up for my newsletter at www.melissadonovan.com. As a subscriber, you'll also get exclusive offers, news, and other goodies.

To receive a free, advanced review copy (ARC) of the next book in the series, leave a review on any major bookseller's website or on Goodreads. Then send me a link to your review (melissa@melissadonovan.com), and you'll receive a copy of the next book before it comes out.

Leaving a review only takes a few minutes. It's a fast and easy way to help fellow readers find more books they'll love and help authors write more books you'll love.

Keep reading!

Best,
Melissa

Acknowledgements

I'd like to thank my beta readers for providing critical feedback on this book. Their input was invaluable: Scott Wolman, David Higgins, Zena Wolman-Silber, Melek Gursoy, and Scott Grother.

I'd especially like to thank my dad for helping me develop ideas for this story and for rooting out several technical problems during development.

I don't come from a military family, but some of my family members have served in the military dating as far back as the Civil War, in which one of my ancestors fought for the North. Both of my grandfathers served during World War II. My dad was in the Army Reserves, and my young cousin recently joined the Navy. I'm proud of all of them. I thank the men and women who bravely serve our country in the name of liberty and democracy.

This book was initially inspired by articles that were published during the summer of 2013—articles that asked why there weren't any superhero movies with female leads. I too was bothered by the absence of women in prominent roles in superhero films, because I love superhero films, and I'm a girl. So I decided to write my own superhero story, and Wendy Watson was born. But without the amazing characters and stories that DC and Marvel have created, this book would not exist. So I'd like to thank the creators of all the fantastic superheroes that I and legions of other fans adore.

About the Author

Born and raised in California, Melissa Donovan inherited a love of literature from her mom, who taught her to read by age four. At thirteen, she started penning poetry and song lyrics. Shortly thereafter, journaling became a daily habit, and a writer was born.

Melissa earned a BA in English with a concentration in creative writing from Sonoma State University. Since then, she has worked as a business writer, blogger, copywriter, and writing coach.

Melissa's poetry has appeared in *convergence: an online poetry of journal and art*. Her Adventures in Writing series features creative writing exercises and prompts, plus best practices to help writers master the craft. Learn more about her books on the craft of writing by visiting her blog, Writing Forward (www.writingforward.com).

Melissa's debut novel, *Engineered Underground*, is the first book in the Metamorphosis Series. It's a science fiction series with elements of military, superheroes, mystery, and adventure.

Visit www.melissadonovan.com to learn more about her work and to get updates on new releases.

Other Books by Melissa Donovan

ADVENTURES IN WRITING (SERIES)

101 Creative Writing Exercises
10 Core Practices for Better Writing
1200 Creative Writing Prompts

Adventures in Writing: The Complete Collection